D0464729

Once Upon a Seaside Murder

Also available by Maggie Blackburn

Beach Reads Mysteries

Little Bookshop of Murder

Victoria Town Mysteries
(writing as Mollie Cox Bryan)

Merry Scary Victorian Christmas

Masquerade Murder

Killer Spring Fling

Cumberland Creek Mysteries
(writing as Mollie Cox Bryan)

Scrapbook of the Dead

Scrappily Ever After

Scrappy Summer

A Crafty Christmas

Death of an Irish Diva

Scrapped

Scrapbook of Secrets

Cora Craft Mysteries
(writing as Mollie Cox Bryan)

Assault and Beadery

Macrame Murder

No Charm Intended

Death Among the Doilies

Hollywood Biography Mysteries
(writing as Mollie Cox Bryan)

The Jean Harlow Bombshell

Buttermilk Creek Mysteries
(writing as Mollie Cox Bryan)

Goodnight Moo

Christmas Cow Bells

Once Upon a Seaside Murder

A BEACH READS MYSTERY

Maggie Blackburn

NEW YORK

This is a work of fiction. All of the names, characters, organizations, places and events portrayed in this novel are either products of the author's imagination or are used fictitiously. Any resemblance to real or actual events, locales, or persons, living or dead, is entirely coincidental.

PUBLISHER'S NOTE: The recipes contained in this book are to be followed exactly as written. The publisher is not responsible for your specific health or allergy needs that may require medical supervision. The publisher is not responsible for any adverse reaction to the recipes contained in this book.

Published in the United States by Crooked Lane Books, an imprint of The Quick Brown Fox & Company LLC.

Crooked Lane Books and its logo are trademarks of The Quick Brown Fox & Company LLC.

Library of Congress Catalog-in-Publication data available upon request.

ISBN (hardcover): 978-1-64385-832-6
ISBN (ePub): 978-1-64385-833-3

Cover design by Mary Ann Lasher

Printed in the United States.

www.crookedlanebooks.com

Crooked Lane Books
34 West 27th St., 10th Floor
New York, NY 10001

First Edition: October 2021

10 9 8 7 6 5 4 3 2 1

For Bob, with love and gratitude.

Chapter One

Even though Hildy Merriweather's heart was pagan, she loved Christmas.

It thrilled her to tell anybody who asked why it didn't conflict with her Goddess-loving pagan ways. "As we practice Christmas today, it has very little to do with the birth of Christ. In fact, the Christmas tree, the holly, all of it, has pagan roots in the solstice. As far as historians can tell, Christ was born in April and his birthday was tacked on the solstice celebration as a sneaky way of getting pagans to convert," she'd say, and then she'd offer you the best vegan brownie you'd ever eaten. Disarming? Yes. But that was Hildy—Summer's mother—and she was all peace, love, and stardust. But she was gone.

Summer drew in a breath as she walked in the sand. The sound of the ocean had always soothed her, ever since she was a child. Christmas without her mother . . . she didn't know how she'd get through it. But get through it she must.

It was one of the busiest times of the year for Beach Reads, the bookstore her mom had left to her. Still on sabbatical and considering her options for now, she was back home running the bookstore she'd always despised as a child and young woman.

She didn't quite hate the store anymore. Life was full of surprises—and she'd had plenty since she'd been back on Brigid's Island. She now knew who her biological father was; she also now knew her half brother and half sister, though they'd been out of the country for many months. She was expecting them to return to the island any day now.

Summer lifted her face to the rising sun and turned back to her home, the one she'd grown up in, a pink beach cottage with turquoise shutters, its rickety porch swing swaying in the breeze. Early-morning calm and peace filled her. This time of day was the only time Summer had to herself. How had her mom run a bookstore, raised her, and made sure everything was taken care of around the house? Hildy wasn't an organized person. But she got it all done.

Summer walked up the path. Her mom's parrot, Mr. Darcy, was in the window watching for her. The African gray provided interesting company. Summer's cousin Piper was back at work, her Aunt Agatha was busy with her volunteer work, and her niece Mia was in school—until tomorrow; then she planned to help Summer with the Christmas shoppers. People were living their lives, without Hildy. Which was as it should be. Life went on. But Hildy's death had changed Summer forever. Sorting out the emotional debris might take the rest of her life.

When she entered the house, Darcy waddled over to her. He liked to exercise in the morning, so she'd let him out of his cage earlier. "Good morning, Mr. Darcy."

He flapped his wings and turned around a few times.

"Silly bird," she said. "Time to go back in your cage. I'm off to Beach Reads."

She bent over and held up her arm, and he stepped onto it. "Good boy."

"Treat!" he squawked.

"Of course." She placed him in the cage and offered him a treat, which he accepted.

She found her bag and readied herself to drive to the store, as the forecast was calling for rain. She didn't mind a summer rain, but a winter beach rain could be unpleasant.

Her keys were next to the box. *The* box. Her half brother, Sam, had given her a box of letters, cards, and photos of his father and Summer's mom. She'd yet to open it. It seemed so personal . . . Was she ready to see her mom as a young, crazy-in-love woman? Maybe soon. Not this morning.

Twenty-minutes later, Summer opened the door to Beach Reads. The scent of patchouli greeted her as it always did, no matter how much anyone cleaned or how much time had passed. It was as if her mom's favorite smell permeated the walls, creaky wooden floors, bookcases, and overstuffed chairs. But as she walked deeper into the store, the smell of brewed coffee replaced the patchouli, along with cinnamon and peppermint. Poppy, Hildy's trusted assistant, now Summer's, must be here.

"Yoo-hoo!" Summer called, walking into her office and finding an empty room. "Yoo-hoo!"

"We're in the back!"

We?

Why were people gathered in the storage room?

"Hey." Marilyn bounded into the office. One of Summer's mom's best friends, spiky-haired Marilyn sported wildflower tattoos and often said she wouldn't rest until every part of her body was a flower.

"What are you doing here?"

"Good morning to you too," Marilyn said, as Poppy came along.

"I'm sorry. Good morning. What's going on?"

"We were back there searching for a banner, and man, we found this very interesting stuff," Marilyn said, placing a box on Summer's desk, her tattoos peeking out as her shirt sleeve slid up her wrist. Marilyn was an active Mermaid Pie Book Club member. She also was a librarian.

Summer could only imagine the space in the back. She refused to enter it, certain there must be spiders lurking in the cracks and crevices. No matter how much therapy and medication she tried, arachnophobia ruled her life. "Did you find what you were searching for?"

"No." Poppy glanced at her watch. "We were looking for a banner that says, 'Have a Cozy Christmas.' It's for the cozy mystery event. Maybe we can search more tomorrow. It's almost time to open."

"Okay," Marilyn said. "Same place and time?" She turned to go, then back to Summer. "When you get a chance, you should look through that box. There's a scrapbook full of newspaper clippings. If you don't want them, I'll take them to the library to archive."

Summer placed her purse on the chair. "Why would I want them?"

"Because they were Hildy's," Poppy chimed in, her blue eyes wide as saucers. Poppy reminded Summer of a young Goldie Hawn—not just physically but also personality-wise.

"Mom had a scrapbook with clippings?" Summer opened the flap of the box. Her skin tingled. It wasn't like her mom to clip newspaper articles and paste them in a book unless the articles were about her daughter.

"Evidently. I gotta run. Should I turn the OPEN sign on when I'm leaving?" Marilyn reached for her bag and jingled her keys, a habit she seemed to enjoy.

"You may as well," Poppy said. "The register is ready."

After Marilyn left, Poppy turned to Summer. "You might not want to read that stuff."

"Why not?"

Poppy hesitated. "A lot of what's in there is about an unsolved murder that happened a long time ago. I don't know why Marilyn finds it interesting. There's nothing interesting about murder. Not to me. Not anymore." She blinked several times as if holding back tears.

Summer's stomach clenched. Murder wasn't her favorite subject either. She'd stopped watching any crime shows. She hadn't read any true-crime or murder mysteries lately. She didn't listen to the news or read newspapers anymore. When your mom had been murdered, the subject lost all its appeal.

Chapter Two

Summer set the box aside.

After turning on the computer, she updated Beach Read's blog. They'd gotten in several new books that customers had suggested. Deep in concentration, she jumped when someone said her name.

"Sorry, love, didn't mean to scare you." Aunt Agatha reached over and embraced her with her long arms. "I thought I'd stop by to check on you."

"And the store, right?"

Agatha wasn't fooling her. Summer knew how concerned her mom's sister was about the Beach Reads legacy continuing.

Agatha's pageboy haircut moved when she nodded. "Things look great. Very Christmasy. I love the tree made of books. And I'm so glad you're continuing the book drive for kids. I saw the article in the paper."

Summer's mind flashed to the reporter who'd interviewed her. Yvonne Smith had gotten several details wrong in the article. It didn't surprise Summer at all. She was in her grade at school and she was always a bit strange. Not only that, but she tried to break her and Cash up at one point, making up some wild story about Summer and a football player. She was an attention-seeking goofball.

She turned her attention back to Aunt Agatha. "Thanks. Are you coming to the cozy Christmas event?"

"Maybe." Agatha eyeballed the box.

"Marilyn and Poppy found it in the storage room."

A white-gray eyebrow lifted. "The storage room? I'd forgotten about that place."

Something about the hush in her voice sparked Summer's curiosity. "Did you all have secret sex club meetings back there or something?"

Agatha guffawed. "Right. Honestly, Summer, I have to wonder about you sometimes." She fiddled with her scarf. "Our sex club meetings were always held at your house." She laughed and elbowed her niece.

"That's hilarious," Summer said. "Sit down. Can I get you coffee or tea?"

Her aunt took a seat. "No. I can't stay long." She reached for the box and pulled it to her lap, losing control of it in the process. It fell over, its contents spilling all over the floor. "Damn!"

She leaped to her feet and crouched over to gather what had fallen.

Summer made her way toward her aunt. As they picked up various scraps and papers, Agatha paled. "What is all this? Why would Hildy keep these?"

Summer sighed. "I don't know. Poppy said it's clippings and such about an unsolved murder."

Aunt Agatha's long, manicured fingers ran over an old scrapbook. "What's this?"

Summer shrugged. "Your guess is as good as mine. But you know Mom. She was a woman who could keep secrets."

"Humph. Ain't that right." Agatha cracked open the scrapbook and scanned the pages. She lifted her face. "I remember now. I remember your mom's fascination with this case."

Summer frowned. "My mom's fascination with a murder case?"

"I know. It doesn't sound like Hildy at all, does it?"

"No." Hildy hadn't talked of negative things. She eschewed bad energy.

"But now that I know who your biological father is, it makes sense."

Summer leaned toward her. "What do you mean?"

"The murder victim worked for the Bellamy family," Agatha said. "Your father's mother, I believe. Or maybe it was his grandmother?"

Summer's interest was suddenly piqued. She hungered for more information about her dad's family. Sam and Fatima, her half brother and half sister, had introduced themselves, then left the island. They had business in the Middle East. They had been here on the island for years and she didn't know it. Of course, they went to private schools and ran in completely different circles than she and her family. She couldn't wait to get to know them.

And yet she was also nervous. She had no idea what these people were like. All she knew was that her mom had loved Omar, their father. And in true Summer Merriweather fashion, she'd set aside all the emotions she could be feeling. She'd also set aside any notion of research into her new family. She needed to unpack this slowly.

"I know you must want to know more about them. I do too," Aunt Agatha said. "I remember bits and pieces about them over the years. But your mom . . . well, she never opened up to me about any of it." She looked off into her own distance.

Poppy stuck her head into the office. "I could use help."

"Oh!" Summer stood. "I'll be right there." She turned back to Agatha. "We'll have to talk about all this later. Duty calls."

"I really need to get going anyway. I've got things to do for the Christmas charity ball. Are you sure you're not interested in attending?"

Summer would rather stick needles in her eyes. Nor was she excited about the events she'd been hooked into—the cozy mystery event and the Mermaid Pie Book Club's annual Christmas Secret Goddess party. "I'm happy to buy a ticket. But you'll never catch me in a ball gown."

Agatha laughed as they walked out of the office into the bookstore proper. She wrapped her scarf around her neck. "It's getting colder by the minute. Don't like the winter at all. Neither did Hildy."

Hence Summer's name. She'd always hated her name, just like she'd always hated the bookstore. But these days she didn't have the energy to hate anything.

Now that I have you, I get Summer all year long, Hildy used to say.

"Well, I'll see you later." Aunt Agatha turned and hugged her.

Summer sank into the embrace. It was the next best thing to Hildy's.

When her aunt had gone, she headed toward the register to give Poppy a break, walking by the books stacked into a Christmas tree shape. And she almost smashed into a man who was turning to face her.

Her heart jumped into her mouth. *Cash.* The man she'd left at the altar fourteen years ago stood like a sturdy oak in front of her. She hadn't seen him since. Her face heated. She'd run off like a coward.

And he looked good. Very good. He'd stayed here on the island, married six months after she left.

He nodded. "Summer."

"Cash. Can I help you?" The room stood still, as if the books and walls, wreaths, and people stopped in their tracks and watched them. Watched the years tumble away. Summer concentrated on breathing, keeping her cool, as her heart pounded against her rib cage.

His lips moved. Still thick and full. "I have a list." He pulled out a piece of paper. "My daughter is quite a reader. She's thirteen, and all she wants for Christmas is books." He shifted his weight. "Guess I could've ordered online, but I like to support this place. Always have." His eyes took in the space. "Not quite the same without her."

Summer blinked back a tear. She'd not cry here in front of Cash. "No." She swallowed. "Can I see the list? We'll get your daughter—"

"Bess."

"We'll get Bess all taken care of for Christmas." Summer glanced over the list. One typical YA book, a very popular one, and then there were several mysteries along with *Romeo and Juliet* and *Hamlet*. She clutched her chest. "Shakespeare?"

He grinned, shook his head. "Yeah. I don't know what we're going to do with her."

"Follow me," Summer said. One thing she'd given herself and the people of Brigid's Island in the past few months was a Shakespeare section. Yes, off in a corner. More like a nook. In fact, a sign hung above it: *Bard's Nook*.

It was a bookcase full of Shakespeare titles, next to an overstuffed chair, with a print of Shakespeare on the wall. Her eyes met Cash's. He grinned, aware of her own passion for Shakespeare. How it had all but consumed her as a teenager. How she'd railed against the romances her mom adored. "How about that?" he said.

How about it, indeed.

Chapter Three

Summer left Cash to browse the Shakespeare section. Hovering wouldn't be cool. No customer liked it, especially not Cash Singer.

She'd imagined running into him many times over the years. And the incident had turned out to be undramatic. No yelling, no sobbing, and no running into each other's arms and embracing. Her stomach tightened. She was in the wrong. She should've told him all those years ago how she was feeling instead of running off. She'd never regretted her decision to not marry him, but she'd often regretted the way she'd managed it. *Coward. Summer Merriweather. Mom was so right about me.*

But Summer was unlike her mom, and her cousin Piper, for that matter. It took her a while to process things, and sometimes she needed to run away to do it. That had always bothered Hildy. How had her mom gotten to be so brave? Why were they so different in this way?

"Holly Jolly Christmas" played in the background as Summer marched to the register. She refrained from rolling her eyes. She was so tired of Christmas music.

"I need a bathroom break," Poppy said.

"Well, I'm here." Summer straightened the mermaid-Santa pins on display at the register. A local woman made them, and sales were brisk. Summer wouldn't wear one if it were the last available piece of jewelry on the planet. But customers loved them.

A customer approached with an armful of books. "Where can I find the newest J. D. Robb?"

"The mysteries are upstairs, and it's all alphabetized by author last name."

"Thanks." She headed toward the stairs.

The upstairs of the bookstore had always been Summer's favorite space. She remembered when her mom had had it built. How proud and happy Hildy had been the day it opened. More books, overstuffed chairs, and mermaid paintings than any young girl in love with Shakespeare needed. But the balcony? The balcony was another matter indeed. She'd loved to sit at one of the café tables beneath the umbrella, reading, while the sound of the waves surrounded her. She'd always wondered where her mom had gotten the money for expansion—heck, she'd always wondered where she'd gotten the money for the bookstore.

A line was forming—more customers. Summer struggled to concentrate while checking them out. Her mind wasn't what it used to be before her mom died. Small tasks like this were harder than they should be. And yet, as much as Summer wanted to retreat to bed, she wouldn't allow herself. *Must keep moving. Mustn't stop and dwell on loss. On anger. On regrets.*

Her psychiatrist had offered her a prescription, which she'd refused. Along with what she was taking for her arachnophobia, she'd be a medicated zombie mess. No. These were hard feelings, but she needed to manage them head on. She wanted to find a way to live with her grief. But she had a long way to go. It had only been six months since Hildy's death.

"Maybe you shouldn't be here." A male voice brought her back to earth.

Cash stood on the other side of the cash register.

"Pardon?"

He smiled. "You look, um, kind of far away." He placed his books on the table.

Was she that easily read?

"I'm sorry. I didn't realize," she said, and slid the books to the scanner. Her face heated.

He shrugged. "No worries."

"Great choice of books." She needed to fill any pause in the conversation. At one point in time, she'd planned to marry this man. He'd known her very well. And she him. Yet here they were, acting like polite acquaintances.

He took the bag from her. "I'm surprised you're here. Are you sure you should be?"

"What do you mean?" She wondered what he was getting at and wished he'd spit it out.

He leaned closer to her. "I mean, I'm sure you're reminded of her every day here. How will you get over her if you're here, in the place she built and loved?"

Summer swallowed a burning sensation creeping up her throat. She took a breath and met his gaze. "I don't run away anymore, Cash."

His face fell, and his mouth dropped open. "I, ah—"

Summer craned her neck to signal to him that there was another customer behind him. "Can I help you?"

The customer stepped forward, and they proceeded with the checkout. When they were finished, Cash was gone.

Would it be easier to heal from her mother's death if she moved back to Staunton and continued teaching at the university? A part of her screamed yes. Go back to the world of the mind, where she could feed herself with Shakespeare's words and cocoon herself in the academic world.

But some force held her here at this very bookstore. Even as she warmed to romances and mysteries—still not a superfan—she suspected it wasn't the books that kept her here.

It was the opposite of running away to get over her mom's death. The bookstore was the one place she could still sense her. Hildy was in the creaking floorboards, each comfy chair and book nook, and in the bookshelves holding hundreds of books. Hildy's presence was in the authors' autographs on the walls and floors and the plain but free coffee available for customers all day long. She breathed life into this space. Now that she was physically gone, this bookstore embodied her.

Summer wasn't sure she could ever leave.

A crowd of women gathered at the front window, laughing and pointing.

"What's going on over there?" Summer asked as Poppy came over to relieve her of her register duties.

"He's gone!" someone said.

"Our infamous masked streaker is at it again." Poppy's face reddened.

"Streaker?" Summer thought maybe she'd heard wrong. A streaker on Brigid's Island?

Poppy frowned. "Yes, he only comes out around the holidays. Starts with Hanukkah."

Poppy was matter-of-fact about it, which made Summer curious. "Have you seen him?"

"Oh yes." Poppy waved her hand. "I think everybody has. He's been doing it for years, never been caught." She sighed, watching the women disperse from the window. "If you've seen him once, why bother again? Bless his heart." She frowned dramatically.

Chapter Four

After the shop closed, Summer and Poppy cleaned and readied themselves for the next day.

Poppy walked into Summer's office. "I'll close. Why don't you just go home? I'll see you in the morning."

Summer grabbed the box on her desk, the one holding the scrapbook of clippings. "Okay." She started gathering her things. "Do you think we ordered enough books for the event?"

Poppy shrugged. "I think so. So you're taking the box home?"

Summer tucked it under her arm. "Yes. Aunt Agatha said the case had something to do with my father's family. I might look over some of this stuff." Given that the Bellamy clan was in Egypt right now and her curiosity was killing her, she might swallow her fear and check it out.

"Honestly." Poppy followed Summer out through the front end of the store. "Your brother comes in here and lays the news on you, then leaves the country. Who does that?"

Summer pushed the door open with her hip. "There was some kind of family business he had to attend to."

"For months? Well, have a good night, Summer. Be on the watch for Jack the streaker!" She laughed as the door shut and disappeared into the back.

Nobody was more disappointed than Summer that her half brother and sister had left the island shortly after they'd met her. She walked through the chilly misty rain to her car and placed the box on the passenger seat. Tonight she'd crack open a bottle of wine and get to know her family, or at least a part of her family.

* * *

After feeding Mr. Darcy and grabbing a bowl of soup, Summer did as she'd planned. Opening the box, she slid out the scrapbook first.

She cracked it open, and a mildew smell wafted toward her. The yellowed pages cracked as she turned them.

> **Bellamy Housemaid Found Murdered**
> *Jamila Bastana, maid of Arwa Gibran, fiancée to Omar Bellamy of Bellamy Shipping, was found in a rowboat with a bullet through her heart, washed up on shore at Mermaid Point.*

Shipping? Summer wondered if her family was still in shipping.

Oh Summer, you are losing your edge. It's been months since you found out about your family, and you've yet to even Google these people. It was as if she had been in a form of stasis these past few months, barely able to move to take care of absolute necessities.

Mermaid Point was on the other side of Brigid's Island, more remote and sprawling than the area where Summer had grown up. Beach Reads sat at the corner of the town's boardwalk, and the rest of the town seemed to spring from there. The farther away you were from the boardwalk and the tiny neighborhoods built around it, the more wild and secluded things became. For a seventy-mile-long island with a population of 2,200, the differences were vast.

Summer continued reading the article.

> She had been reported missing the day before.

It had happened about a year before Summer was born. Had her mom known Arwa? Was she dating her dad secretly at the time? Just how long and how far back did their relationship go?

She glanced at the box Sam had given her. She should open it. Maybe it held the answers she wanted. Why was it so hard?

She went back to reading about Arwa.

> A Fulbright scholar and activist for women's rights, Gibran reports that her relationship with her maid was personal. According to the grieving woman, their relationship was more friendly than employer-employee.

Summer read on.

> Jamila's family is in Egypt, where she will be laid to rest.

She couldn't take her eyes off the photo of Jamila. The young woman had been just twenty-two.

Was Arwa Sam's mom? All he'd ever said about her was that she died several years ago.

Maybe Sam could shed light on this for her. He must know something more about the incident.

Summer flipped the scrapbook page over to a photo cut out from a magazine. The woman startled her. Rima Bellamy, Omar's mother, stared out from the page. Summer could've been looking at a photo of herself. The full lips, high cheekbones, almond-shaped eyes . . . yes, but there was something more. Her expression. A chill ran up Summer's spine. She shivered and shut the scrapbook. It was enough for today. More than enough. Her head swam with ideas and possibilities.

As she was closing the scrapbook, a clipping fell out. This one was dated 1996. Hildy had been following the case all those years?

It was an article about cold cases on the island. There were three. One was "the maid of Arwa Bellamy."

The gist of the article was that maybe these cases could be solved with new technology. But only one victim's family had been interested in exploring possibilities offered by the new technology. The Bellamys, as a representative of Jamila's family, hadn't appeared to be interested either.

Why not? Why wouldn't you want to know who'd killed your loved one so that there could be justice?

The plot thickened.

Summer knew that revenge didn't help. Though it gave her some sense of satisfaction to know that her mom's killer was in prison, it didn't take away the grief. Maybe someone in the Bellamy clan didn't care to pursue further investigation because they knew it wouldn't bring Jamila back, nor would it be good to unearth painful memories.

Maybe.

But something pricked at Summer. There was more to this story. And the biggest part of that "more" was why Hildy would keep all this. What was her fascination with it? It didn't seem like something she'd dwell on.

Summer set the scrapbook aside. At least for tonight. She needed to get to bed. Morning came way too soon these days.

As she lay in bed reading, her phone rang. She answered.

"Hi, Summer, it's Glads." Gladys, better known as Glads, was another of Hildy's best friends. Summer imagined her pacing as she talked, as she never sat still; wearing one of her many T-shirts; messing with her ill-fitting glasses.

"What's up?"

"I just wanted you to know that one author might not make it. Mimi Sinclair?"

"Why? What's wrong?"

"She lives in Pittsburgh, and they're getting a snowstorm. She's going to leave tomorrow, but if it gets rough, she's turning back. She's also trying to talk her husband into bringing her, apparently."

"So that would leave two mystery authors on our panel." Summer pulled her comforter closer around her. "We'll be okay."

"But this is the one I really love. She's the one whose book is based on a local murder."

How many murders could there have been on the small island? Summer sat up in bed. "What murder is that?"

"The name of the book is *Mermaid Point Murder*," Glads said.

Chapter Five

Glads and Marilyn, two original members of the Mermaid Pie Book Club, had approached Summer to have this cozy mystery author event and said they'd take care of all the details. Summer had barely been paying attention. She hadn't read any of the books. She'd been way too busy with the bookstore. The event was just one less thing she had to worry about—it was in expert hands.

But to discover that one author had written about the murder at Mermaid Point, probably the very murder she'd been reading about, made Summer feel like a lazy heel. Where had her head been?

She pulled her spider-fighting bedtime nylon mask over her face. One of the ways her arachnophobia gripped her was in her obsession over spiders getting into any of the orifices of her head while she slept; hence the mask. She flipped on the radio. The sound of voices helped her to sleep. The volume was so low, she barely understood a word. But it didn't matter. What mattered was the lulling and comfort of other human voices.

Mermaid Point Murder. Summer needed to learn more. She couldn't write this off as another strange coincidence in her life. There's been so many since her mom died that she'd lost track. But this took the vegan cupcake. She got the feeling there was something she needed to pay attention to here.

"I got it, Ma. I'll read the book tomorrow," she muttered, and then dozed off. But not before considering that she might have lost her mind.

* * *

Just as Summer poured her first cup of coffee, the doorbell rang. Who could be here so early?

She opened it to her Aunt Agatha, cousin Piper, and fifteen-year-old niece Mia, all with their arms full of food.

"Surprise," Aunt Agatha said. "We brought breakfast. To celebrate Mia's first official day of working at Beach Reads."

Summer attempted a smile. "Thank you."

Piper laughed. "I told Mom this wasn't a good idea."

"Witness to that." Mia walked into the kitchen. "But let's eat anyway."

Summer glanced at her watch. "I have a bit of time, I suppose."

Aunt Agatha slid a casserole out of the carrier, its cheesy scent wafting through the kitchen.

"You can be late. You're the owner," Mia said.

"That's not how it works." Piper poked her.

"Right," Summer said as they gathered around the table and began passing around the breakfast casserole.

"I had the weirdest dream last night," Piper said. "I dreamed I was onstage and forgot my lines."

"That's not weird. That's a standard stress dream," Aunt Agatha said.

Summer recalled her own dream. She laughed.

"What's so funny? My stress?" Piper's eyes were puffy and red.

"What? No. I just remembered my dream. About mermaids."

The women quieted.

"Your mom dreamed of them often," Agatha said. "Do you remember?"

"I kinda do. But I don't remember much about the dream, just that there were mermaids, and I didn't seem surprised to see them at all." Summer sliced into her casserole.

"I've often thought if they were real, they'd be scary, not friendly," Piper said.

"Right." Summer shoved eggs into her mouth.

"Why do you have that box?" Aunt Agatha said, pointing to it on the kitchen counter.

"I brought it home to sort. There's so much junk at the store. I wanted to look through it, try to make sense of why Mom kept it."

"What is it?" Mia asked.

"It's full of clippings about a murder that happened on Mermaid Point in the 1980s."

"Why would Aunt Hildy have it?"

"Good question," Piper said.

"The woman who was killed was the maid of Arwa Bellamy—before she was a Bellamy," Summer replied.

"They never found the killer," Piper said.

"What do you know about it?"

"Not much. In fact, not much at all, but I read an article about cold cases. Maybe it was a blog post or a newspaper article. And they listed it."

Aunt Agatha dropped her fork onto her plate. "Don't we have better things to talk about?"

Piper reached over and patted her mom's hand. "You're right. Let's not talk about this."

If Summer were a dog, her ears would have pricked up. Aunt Agatha knew something. But Summer didn't want to upset her.

She'd broach the subject at another time. Agatha and Hildy had been close their whole lives. Agatha must know more. In the meantime, Summer was going to read that book. The incident had captured her mom's attention for so long that it had ignited Summer's curiosity.

"Have you heard from Sam?" Mia asked.

"Not recently," Summer said. "The last I heard, he and Fatima were on their way back from the Middle East. God only knows when they'll be back. Travel is a nightmare these days."

"I can't wait to get to know them," Mia said. "How cool that you're part Egyptian."

Summer smiled. "It is, right?" Growing up, she'd longed to be thin, blue eyed, and blond like the rest of her family, but later she had grown into being comfortable with herself—olive skinned, shorter, and rounder. But it was good to know the reason she looked so different from the rest of her family.

The sound of sirens blared while they ate their breakfast.

"Wonder what's going on?" Agatha said. She rose and walked over to the other side of the room and gazed out the window. "Fire trucks. Ambulances. Cops."

"Must be an accident." Piper stood up from the table and rinsed her dish off in the sink.

But fear struck Summer's heart, and she witnessed how the sound bothered the women around her as well. They knew it meant that someone's life might be plunged into loss.

As she left her house later, she glanced at the box her brother had given her months ago, still sitting on the hall table, untouched.

Chapter Six

When Summer and Mia entered the bookstore, the potent scent of coffee perked up their brain cells. Poppy was already up and at it. Summer got Mia situated and made her way to the cozy mystery section of the store.

Summer ran her fingers over the mysteries, with their bright, colorful spines, until she found *Mermaid Point Murder*. She slipped it out. Its vibrant, almost cartoonlike cover spoke nothing of murder, except in spelling out the word itself. A mermaid and a cat sat on a rocky hill. Oh, brother. Had this writer ever been to Mermaid Point? Maybe that was unfair. Maybe she'd had nothing to do with the cover. From what Summer had learned from various authors, some of them had cover control and some didn't.

If she remembered correctly, Mermaid Point was a pointy sandbar jutting out into the ocean, but it was not a part of the island she'd spent a lot of time exploring.

"What are you doing?" Mia asked as she came around the corner.

"Studying this book. The writer is one of our cozy mystery panelists. If she can make it through the snowstorm, that is," Summer said. "This section is kind of a mess. Do you mind straightening it and walking through the whole upstairs here?"

Mia reached for the book. "Sure. *Mermaid Point Murder*?" Her blond hair was pulled back into a long ponytail, and for a moment she reminded Summer so much of Piper at that age that her heart ached.

Summer nodded. "I'm just curious. It's loosely based on the murder we talked about this morning."

Mia shrugged. "It's kinda weird. Aunt Hildy never even read murder mystery books. Why would she keep all that stuff about a murder that happened so long ago?"

"That's a good question. I aim to find out." Summer hadn't realize her intention until just now. But yes, she needed to know what had pulled her mom into this mystery. Was it just that the victim was a Bellamy employee? Or was it something else?

Mia's face fell. "Should you? I mean, we're all still grieving. It might not be a good thing for you to do."

Out of the mouths of babes who'd been in therapy for months.

"You may be right. I don't know. I'll proceed with caution. It happened such a long time ago. I doubt most people remember it."

Summer recalled something her therapist had told her: families of murder victims were never the same again. You often got young people lashing out, becoming violent themselves. Sometimes family members wanted nothing to do with anything murder related. Other times, people became obsessed with it. Sometimes having a murder victim in the family created an interest so deep that survivors became cops or detectives.

Aunt Agatha was the type who didn't want to hear or see anything murder related. Summer agreed with her. Or at least she had until they'd found the box yesterday. Until she'd learned of the book. She'd always trusted her instincts, but even she had to admit that this was a strange coincidence. One her mom would have paid attention to, as would her mom's friends.

Yet before Hildy died, Summer wouldn't have given any credence to coincidences. She'd pooh-poohed her mom when she talked about them. She now was uncertain of her opinion. Coincidences were entirely illogical. But then again, so much of life and death was.

Summer made her way to the coffeepot and poured herself a cup. She took the book and coffee and went into her office.

"Good morning," Poppy said as she passed her by. "We've got online orders this morning."

"Hooray. That's working out." It was a new service Beach Reads was offering for people who couldn't make it to the store. They could get signed copies of certain books by purchasing them online.

"Your mom never would've gone for it. But yeah, it's working out," Poppy said. "I loved Hildy. But she was the most stubborn person I ever met."

Summer laughed. "True."

Summer still wasn't certain she'd be running the bookstore forever, but while she was on sabbatical for a year, she was in charge. Hildy had wanted her to have the place, but Summer had mixed feelings. While she was here, though, why not make a few changes? Bring the store into the new century?

Glads and Marilyn came bounding into the office. Glads, short and wiry, and Marilyn, tall and lanky with a long, pointy nose, were quite the duo.

"You'll never believe this," Glads said. "I talked with Mimi Sinclair, the cozy mystery author last night, and she's on her way."

"Good." Why wouldn't Summer believe that?

"But listen to this." Marilyn's eyes lit.

Summer gestured for her to go on.

"When I talked to Mimi last night, she told me she'd been warned to stay away from the island."

Summer blinked. "Come again?"

"Yeah. Her book has stirred things up with someone."

"That's crazy," Summer said. She'd been paying only half attention to this event. That was the deal: she provided the books, they organized. But now they had her full attention.

"Right?" Glads said.

"Evidently, there are still people around who remember it and don't want it talked about." Marilyn placed her hands on her hips, and a tattooed daisy peeked out from under her sweater on one side and a rose on the other.

"But why? It happened such a long time ago. What would it matter now?" Summer asked.

"It wasn't much more than thirty years ago. That's not ancient history. I'm sure a lot of older people remember it," Glads said.

Summer considered the way murder's slimy tendrils had wrapped around her heart and would forevermore. "I suppose you're right. It might matter even more to me if she were my relative."

"Or even friend," Glads said.

"Yes, even though it happened all those years ago, it might be fresh for her people," Marilyn said, frowning.

The three of them stood silent for a moment.

"But still," Summer said. "Threatening an author is not cool. No matter the circumstances. We can't have that."

"I'm afraid for her. She's upset, but she's still coming. She said she wouldn't let some fool tell her what to do. Though it might be foolish for her to come," Glads said.

"We have her booked at the B and B with the others, but I wonder if she should stay somewhere else. Just to be on the safe side," Marilyn said.

"I have a houseful right now, or I'd have her stay with me."

Summer straightened in her chair. "She'll stay with me. I have extra room. It's no problem. I'll bring her along with me later."

"Are you sure?" Marilyn said, tapping Summer's shoulder. "You may not want to welcome any more drama into your life."

Kindness emanated from Marilyn, as it did from all of her mom's friends. It comforted and shamed Summer all at once. She wanted to be kinder herself. "Thank you, Marilyn. I don't mind at all."

Chapter Seven

Since losing her mom, Summer had taken a long, hard look at herself. Kindness wasn't her finest attribute—even though she'd had superb role models and many opportunities to show kindness. It was important to her to demonstrate how smart she was, how she knew the best way to handle everything because of her education. But when it came right down to it these days, she reflected, her education hadn't prepared her much for life's challenges. Being bright and articulate couldn't heal broken hearts, couldn't bring people back to you, and did very little to comfort you. Oh, she cocooned herself in the mirage that she didn't need people, not even the students she was trying to educate. But that was another story.

Summer's phone dinged, alerting her to a text message—from Sam.

I'm back. I have a surprise for you. When can we get together?

When? She needed to go home and prepare for her guest, Mimi, and then she'd be entertaining her for a couple of days. It would have to be Monday at the very earliest. Her heart sank. She'd been looking forward to seeing Sam and Fatima. She had so many questions.

So good to know you're back, she texted. *We have a cozy mystery author event tomorrow and I'm tied up with it until Monday.*

Where and what time? Maybe we can attend. We can at least see you—even for just a minute.

She hadn't expected that enthusiasm. Turned out he'd been wanting to see her as much as she'd wanted to see him and his sister. She texted him the details. She'd welcome laying eyes on them again.

She walked out into the store, which wasn't teeming with customers, just a steady stream. So she knew Poppy and Mia could manage. Mia knew the store well and was up to the challenge.

"Poppy, do you think it would be okay if I went home for a while? You can text me if you need help."

"Sure. Mia's here now. I think we'll be okay." She paused. "Is everything okay?"

"Yes, Mimi is going to stay with me while she's here, and I need to clean up and maybe get groceries in the house."

"I thought we booked her at the B and B." She leaned on the cash register counter and clasped her hands together.

"She was. Until she was threatened. Her book is loosely based on the Mermaid Point murder, and someone doesn't like that she's written it. Which is so odd, right? It all happened such a long time ago."

Poppy's color drained. "Do you want to get involved with this? It could be dangerous for you."

Summer shrugged. Poppy could be dramatic. "What can happen? Nobody will even know where she is."

"Still, I think you should let the police know so they can keep an eye on your place."

Summer laughed. "Don't be ridiculous. If Chief Ben Singer knew about this, he'd not care at all."

Poppy's blue eyes widened. "Look, from what I've read about that case, it's one of his few unsolved cases. He might have a professional interest."

Summer's stomach twisted. Chief Ben Singer held grudges. And Summer wasn't his favorite person. Even though she'd helped crack her mom's murder case, he held it against her because she'd stuck her nose in places it didn't belong. And then she'd stood his only son up at the altar.

Cash had gotten over it a long time ago, but the same couldn't be said for the chief.

"I think you should at least let him know."

"I will not." Summer had enough on her plate without having to deal with an aging, bitter cop who had a list of grievances against her.

Poppy stood. "Then I will."

"Do what you want," Summer said. "I'd rather not deal with him. I'm leaving and will be back later this afternoon."

Poppy reddened. "Fine."

Summer left the store. Reaching out to Ben was the last thing she wanted to do. Even though he'd apologized to her over the complete debacle of an investigation he'd run concerning her mom's death, it was backhanded. "You never should have put yourself and your family at risk, Summer," he'd said. "Promise me you won't do anything like this again."

And why would she? Hildy was her mom. Of course Summer had wanted to know how she'd died. She hadn't thought twice about putting her own life at risk in doing so; she'd had no choice at the time. She shivered, recalling how she'd been attacked. She couldn't imagine involving herself in another murder investigation. No thank you. Not for her.

Summer walked briskly down the boardwalk. The air nipped at her face. The salty sea smelled stronger this time of year without any of the other scents fighting it. No hot dogs or candy apples. The boardwalk was closed for the season. Even the noise from the arcade had died down. Summer loved the quiet and the fresh sea breeze. Like every beach community, Brigid's Island had to make peace with the tourist season. Many had a love-hate relationship with it—including Summer, who used to love the tourist season as a teenager, but now, not so much.

She opened her front door and placed her bag on the entryway table, next to the box her half brother had entrusted her with before he left the country. She walked down the short hall and into the living room, straightened magazines on the table, grabbed some cups and glasses off of it. All the while her mom's goddess statues looked on. Isis. Brigid. Kali. Diana.

"Summer! Summer!" Mr. Darcy squawked as she left the room to place the cups and glasses in the sink. "Summer home!"

The bird had gotten used to her routines. But he'd never get over losing Hildy. He still called for her almost every night.

Chapter Eight

As Summer was finishing putting fresh sheets on the bed for Mimi, her phone alerted her to a text message. She ignored it as she spread the quilt over the top of the bed and smoothed it. She placed the pillows in their spots and plumped them just as her phone alerted her again. She slipped it out of her pocket.

It was Piper, her cousin and almost sister. *Where are you? I just stopped by the bookstore, and Poppy said you'd left. How could you leave Mia there without you?*

Summer froze. *Is she okay?*

No response. If anything had happened to her niece, she'd never forgive herself. She'd never considered that Mia might need her to be there. She'd grown up hanging out at the bookstore and had helped there over the summer and the holidays.

But Mia had taken Hildy's death harder than any of them.

Piper! She sent the text.

Her phone rang.

"Piper? I'm sorry I—"

"A few months ago, my daughter was in the hospital because she was suicidal. And you left her there to deal with the Christmas madness on her own?" Piper sobbed.

"Poppy is there." Summer's face heated. Her throat throbbed. She'd never intentionally do anything to put her niece in danger. "I'm on my way back to the store. I needed to get ready for Mimi. She's staying here, and I had no clean sheets on the bed, and I needed to—"

"Did you check on her before you left? Honestly."

Summer drew in a breath. "I thought the idea was to keep her busy."

"Yes, while someone who loved her was nearby!"

"I'm sorry. I wasn't thinking. It's just that—"

"That what? You had to rush home and clean for Mimi, so it's okay to leave Mia?"

Summer's head spun as she struggled to ground herself. But her brain clicked into gear. "Is she okay?"

"She's fine. Lucky for you."

"Piper." Summer softened her voice. "Are you okay? You've been so focused on everybody else's grief and healing . . ."

"Oh, for god's sake, Summer!" She clicked off. No good-bye. No see you later. Nothing.

Was Piper overreacting? Or was Summer being insensitive? Whatever. Summer's chest tightened. Evidently, her niece needed her at the bookstore.

Mia's countenance had seemed so much better this past week. The circles under her eyes were gone, and she'd started to gain weight. Her doctor must have finally found the right medicine. A pang of guilt stabbed Summer. She should've at least checked in with Mia before she left. The best thing now was to get back to the store. Pronto.

She loved Mia madly and remembered the day she was born as if it were yesterday. Summer had never wanted children, never even entertained the idea of having them, until she'd met Mia. She had assumed she'd never have a family of her own. She'd been so busy with her career as a Shakespeare professor and didn't have much time for relationships—and when she did, they were disastrous. Better to be alone.

Hildy had wanted to become a grandmother, of course.

"I just don't have the intense craving to be a mom," Summer had told her. "I doubt I'd be any good at it."

"Summer, you have an enormous heart. You'd be a great Mom," Hildy replied.

Ruminations of motherhood and aunthood tugged at Summer as she hurried to leave her now-tidy beach cottage. She glanced at her watch. Mia's shift would be over soon, and Summer needed to get to Beach Reads before she left. She needed to make this right with her niece.

Mimi arrived, suitcase in hand, just as she was heading out the door—which was a good thing, because Summer had almost forgotten she was coming. Summer welcomed the author and told her to make herself at home.

"I think I will rest up a bit, if that's okay with you," Mimi said. "I'll be along shortly. I know where the store is."

Summer felt a twinge of guilt for leaving her behind, but Mimi did look as if she could use a rest. "If you're sure?"

Mimi nodded, and Summer took her leave.

She walked along the beach, then the boardwalk, and arrived at Beach Reads. When she opened the door, she found Poppy behind the register, finishing up an order. Poppy smiled up at her in acknowledgment.

The customer took his package and walked off.

"Where's Mia?" Summer asked.

Poppy knit her brows. "I'm not sure, but I think she's helping Marilyn load books into the van. Why? Piper stopped in and seemed upset. Is everything okay?'

"I think so. I just need to talk with her."

"Okay. Then can you come back and give me a break?"

"Absolutely." Summer walked away into the back, past boxes of books and supplies, and out the back door to find her niece, Marilyn, and Glads laughing as they stacked boxes of books in a van.

"Mia?" Summer said.

"Yeah?" She lifted a box and headed for the van.

"How's everything going?"

"Great, why?"

"She's worried about our evil influence." Glads slid the last box in and grinned.

"Must be." Marilyn slapped her hands together, and flowers peeked out from under her sleeves.

"Yes, that's it all right," Summer said, rolling her eyes. She turned to Mia. "Why don't you go inside and give Poppy a break?"

She glanced at the women. "Am I in trouble?"

"Not at all. Poppy just needs a break. You can manage the register, right?"

"No problem." She wiped her hands on her apron and disappeared through the back door.

Glads and Marilyn drew closer to Summer. "What's up?" Glads said.

"Piper came by and found I wasn't here. She acted like Mia needed me to be here and was having a rough time."

"That's odd. Mia's been a big help. She's such a joy these days," Marilyn said.

"Yeah, I'd say it's Piper that has the problem, not Mia." Glads shut the van door.

Summer's stomach dropped. "I wondered about that."

"Who takes care of the caregiver?" Glads said.

Summer folded her arms. "Who will she let take care of her? That's the question."

"What about her husband?"

Summer shrugged. "He's always working. Never around." After this cozy Christmas event, she vowed, she would make Piper a priority. Maybe she'd treat her to a spa day. Yes, that would be her Christmas gift to Piper.

Right now, though, she wasn't sure Piper would even take it from her.

Chapter Nine

After the last customer left, Summer locked the shop. The cozy mystery authors, including Mimi, had arrived. They gathered in the stock room, which was just outside Summer's office. The caterers, buzzing around setting plates and silverware, had brought tables, chairs, linens, and food. Hildy had always said it was important to treat guest authors right. Many of them traveled at their own expense just to meet readers and perhaps sell a book or two. They were the backbone of the industry.

"Unsung heroes," Hildy often called them. "Where would we be without stories?"

Summer went into the back, where everybody had gathered to have drinks before dinner. The three authors huddled together, and Glads, Marilyn, and Poppy stood off by themselves in a clutch. Summer made a mental note to make sure they sat scrambled at the table.

"Dinner is ready," Summer said. "We're eating upstairs."

"How lovely. I've not been up there in a while," said Peg Andrews, one of the guest authors. She stood tall and thin and had a long nose and white hair swept into a bun. "Hildy was so proud of that addition."

Her words warmed Summer's heart. "That she was."

They sat at the table, surrounded by full bookshelves and lit candles with a view of the sea waves rolling in the distance, as the sky melted into a bright-orange sunset.

"To Hildy," Peg said, holding up a glass.

"To Hildy!" Everybody cheered.

As Summer lifted her glass, she beamed. Everybody here had known Hildy, had loved Hildy. She drew in the ambience with a sudden sharp clarity. The white tablecloths, the pine-and-poinsettia centerpieces, the candlelight, the scent of bayberry—all of it added up to an elegant Christmas tableau for these hardworking writers. Hildy would have been proud.

It was always surprising and sometimes jarring to meet authors. Summer found herself needing to adjust her expectations. For a group of people who wrote about murder, they seemed like pretty normal folks.

The evening flew by with conversation about books, Hildy, and agents. Not one mention was made of the murder at Mermaid Point. Summer was grateful for that. Later, she and Mimi went back to the house.

"I'd love to stay up and chat with you," Mimi said. "But I'm afraid I'm exhausted. Such a long drive. The roads weren't too bad. Well, not as bad as they could've been. I'm thankful my husband drove me here. He's staying a few days in Raleigh to go antiquing, staying at Bluebeard's Roost. Such a name. I'm catching a plane home."

Mimi looked tired and disheveled. She was heavier than her author picture suggested and grayer too. She'd not updated that picture in a while. And she didn't wear any makeup, which, Summer hated to admit, would've helped with her washed-out, maybe even haggard countenance.

"I'll show you to your room," Summer said.

"Thanks so much for having me. I do feel a bit safer here." She followed Summer up the stairs. "It's crazy. I've never been threatened like this before."

Summer wanted to ask about the specifics of the threat, but she deemed it best to wait until the morning to probe. Mimi yawned, prompting Summer to do the same.

Summer opened the door, clicked on the light, and Mimi walked through. She stopped and dropped her bag, gasping. "That's not funny!"

"What are you talking about?" A form beneath the covers took shape in front of Summer's eyes. It was clearly meant to resemble a body. Summer's mouth dropped.

Mimi squinted. "You didn't do that?"

"No," Summer said. "How would anybody get in here? The house was locked."

"Pshaw. Locks are easy enough to pick. I suggest we call the police."

"The police? What will we tell them, that someone broke in and made it look like there was a body in your bed?" Summer said.

Mimi leveled a glared at her. "That's exactly what we're going to do."

"Maybe it's just a joke," Summer said.

Mimi's eyebrows drew together. "Seriously? Call the cops or I will."

"Okay," Summer said.

"Why the reluctance?"

"Our chief of police is a pain."

"They all are a pain. But that's their job." She picked up her bag.

"That's not what I mean." Summer following her back down the stairs. She didn't want to tell Mimi the whole story about Ben

Singer. And she didn't want to call him. And yet someone had been in her house. She scanned the living room. Everything looked like it was still there.

"Who even knew you were staying here?" Summer asked.

"The other authors and myself. My husband. That's it. Who did you tell?"

"Just the staff and my cousin." Summer picked up the phone. "They were all with us tonight."

"Maybe whoever sent the threat knows I'm here. Maybe they've been watching."

Summer felt a chill go through her. She needed to ask Mimi more, but for now, she needed to call the police.

* * *

Chief Singer stood with his hand on his hips, surveying the bedroom. "Jesus, we used to do that when we were kids."

Summer glanced at Mimi. "I didn't."

Mimi shrugged.

He walked over to the window and opened it, gazed down. "I suppose someone could've come in through here. See?"

The room was above the patio. An intruder could've jumped up on its shorter roof and gotten into the room. Well. Summer remembered now. This had been her room, and Cash had sneaked in here a few times.

"The window wasn't locked," the chief said, locking it. "Now the only way someone can get in is if they break the window. And that's not likely."

"Well, none of it's bloody likely." Mimi's voice held a weary edge.

"Yes, ma'am." He was behaving himself. Acting like a pro. It surprised Summer.

"Do you think this could be the same person who threatened her?" Summer asked.

"Poppy told me about that." He walked around the bed toward them. His face darkened. "I suppose anything is possible."

Mimi knit her brows. "You worked the Bellamy case, didn't you?"

"Yes, it was my first murder case." He frowned at Summer. "There's only been five during my whole career."

"I remember talking with you."

"Yeah, I remember too."

She blinked. "You were very helpful."

"I aim to please."

That was a first. Summer wanted to scream. "Hello. What should we do about this?" she asked.

"I'll get a tech over here tomorrow to see if there's any prints. We'll ask around and keep an eye on the place. As much as we can." He turned and grinned at Mimi. "I promise we'll do our best to keep you safe while you're here."

Summer's ears burned with indignation. This was not the Ben Singer she knew.

Chapter Ten

Chief Singer left the house. Summer locked the door behind him.

"Well, he completely underplayed that," Mimi said, crossing her arms. "I mean, someone broke in here and formed a pillow body in the bed. It's kind of creepy."

"I agree. He didn't want to scare you. I can't think of another reason someone would do that—unless it's the same person who threatened you."

She tilted her head. "Can you believe that? A case that's thirty-five years old would warrant such interest from the locals?"

"I think it's strange as well. But you never know about people, do you?"

"Ain't that the truth?"

Summer yawned, tired but wired. "I'm sure I won't fall asleep soon. Would you like a cup of chamomile tea?"

"Yes, please, I'm with you. It's going to take me a while to shake this off. Especially after the note I got." She sat down at the kitchen table.

"What did the note say?" Summer asked as she filled the electric teakettle with water and shut the faucet off.

"It said to stop butting my nose in where it didn't belong and to stay away from Brigid's Island or I'd end up like Jamila."

Summer reached into the cupboard and retrieved two mugs. She sat them next to the kettle. "So why are you here? Most people wouldn't show."

"I thought about it." Mimi tapped her fingers on the table and looked off to the side. "I thought hard about it. But it made me so angry. I thought, who do they think they are, trying to bully me? The best way to deal with a bully is to face them. So here I am."

Summer admired that. She wasn't so sure she'd have the guts. But it would depend on the circumstances. "Well, good for you." She leaned on the counter, waiting for the water to heat. "Do you have a theory about who threatened you?"

"No clue. But I aim to find out while I'm here. I'm booked in over at the B and B a few more days next week."

Summer's heart sped up. "Why would you do that?"

Mimi's chin lifted, her double chin jiggling. "As I said, I won't be bullied."

Summer quieted. The teakettle whistled, and she poured the steaming water. "What's your interest in this case?"

"I have a thing about mermaids. Just like your mom did."

"You knew Mom?" Summer beamed.

"Of course. Not well. Like, we weren't best buds or anything like that. But I knew her well enough to know how much she loved mermaids."

Summer set Mimi's cup in front of her. "Sugar or cream?"

"Neither. Thank you."

Summer sat down at the Formica table at the center of the small kitchen, which was jammed with dishes, vegan cookbooks, and herbs and spices. "But the murder had nothing to do with mermaids."

Mimi laughed. "No. But the name Mermaid Point drew me in last time I was here. I remembered it. And wow, finding out there was a murder there was just icing on the cake."

"I confess I've not had time to read your book. It's in my bag. I planned to start reading it tonight." Summer sighed. "I had little to do with the event. With Mom's death, it's all I can do to manage the everyday tasks." Summer wondered why she was telling a complete stranger this. She quieted herself.

"I was so sorry to hear about her death. It must be very difficult for you. I can't imagine." Mimi drank her tea.

Summer wanted to change the subject, but she was getting tired and her normally sharp brain was foggy. "Thank you." She paused. "How accurate is your retelling of the case?"

"As accurate as I could make it," she said. "Cold cases aren't easy. Files get lost. People go away or die, so you can't talk with them. And cozy readers don't care about the murder too much. I used just enough of the real-life murder details to make it interesting to them."

Summer drank her tea, feeling the warmth of the brew travel down her throat. "Cozy mystery readers don't care about the murder?"

"I mean, they do, but not in a graphic sense. No blood or gore. They like the puzzle aspect. They like the characters, setting, and so on."

Summer had yet to read a cozy. The name turned her off. Perhaps she'd been harsh in her judgment once again, like she had been with romances. "So you just used the real case as a jumping point. For inspiration?'

"Yes."

"But why would that offend someone enough to threaten you? And to break into my house and make a fake body out of pillows?"

Mimi squinted her eyes. "I've been thinking about this. Maybe it's just the attention on Mermaid Point, and they just want me to leave it alone. The case was never solved and they want to keep it like that."

Summer recalled the article about cold cases—how the loved ones of another victim were interested in solving their case but the Bellamys were not interested in getting to the bottom of this one. That seemed suspicious in and of itself. She damn sure had wanted to see her mother's killer put behind bars.

The murder at Mermaid Point was a tangled web of mystery waiting to be solved. But she mentally drooped as she mulled over her mother's interest. It was as if every time Summer turned around, her mom's hand was guiding her in a direction she hadn't planned. Sitting here and talking with Mimi, a cozy mystery writer, was just another one of those surprises. She drew in a breath and hoped for Mimi's safety.

Mimi stood. "Thanks for the tea. I'm ready to hit the sack."

"Me too."

Summer followed Mimi to her room and helped her dismantle the pillow body.

"Are you going to be okay in here?" Summer wasn't sure she would be able to sleep in that bed herself knowing that some stranger had been there.

Mimi reached into her bag and set something on the side table. A small pistol. "I'll be fine now."

Chapter Eleven

What could Summer do? But her chest burned. A gun in the house. Hildy would be turning over in her grave—if she'd had one. According to her wishes, she'd been cremated. As it was, Summer turned and tossed enough for both her and Hildy.

It seemed as if she'd just fallen asleep when a pounding at the front door awakened her. She pulled off her face mask and dragged herself downstairs, head swimming in sleep.

She peeped through the keyhole. Glads and Marilyn stood there with the other two cozy mystery authors, all fresh and ready for the day. What time was it anyway? She opened the door.

"Did we wake you?" Marilyn said, grinning.

"Uh, yeah. Come in, ladies. What's up?"

"We brought breakfast," Marilyn said. "Where's Mimi?"

"Probably still in bed—"

"No, here I am, dear." She came out of the living room. "I was just chatting with the bird. He's delightful."

"Oh, that's Mr. Darcy," Glads said. "He'll talk your ear off."

"How did you sleep?" Lucy, one of the authors, asked Mimi.

"Fine, after the shenanigans." Mimi explained what had happened. The others sat and listened, offering very little comment.

Was Summer the only one freaked out by the pillow body from last night? And the gun in her house?

And was she the only one dying for coffee?

Marilyn set a carafe of the brew on the table. "Coffee."

"This is a nice surprise," Summer said, with a tone that belied her words.

"Surprise? It's on the schedule," Mimi said.

Summer had not seen a schedule.

"Didn't you get the email?" Glads said.

Summer took her in, noting that her new pink hair looked even pinker this morning. "No." She watched as the group tucked into their breakfast.

"Looks like we've gotten good press coverage." Glads pulled out a newspaper from her bag and handed it to Summer.

Summer read the headline: *Cozy Mystery Author Revisits Murder at Mermaid Point.* The article was by Yvonne Smith.

She gasped. "Oh no!"

"What's the big deal?" Glads asked. "It's great publicity. We'll have a huge crowd at the library today."

"Yes, but it may be the wrong kind of crowd," said Lucy. "I'm all for meeting readers and signing books but not dealing with psychos."

Summer's head spun as she skimmed the rest of the article. Then she glanced at Mimi, who seemed to be calmer than the rest. "You knew about this."

"I was interviewed for it. But that's before I was threatened. And before last night." She paused. "Do you think we can have protection?"

Summer refrained from rolling her eyes.

"By whom?" Marilyn asked. "We've got a police force of two, and one is past retirement age."

"Maybe we can hire a private security firm," Glads said.

"At this late juncture?" Summer sipped her coffee. "That article is going to bring all the kooks."

"I'm so sorry. I didn't mean to cause such a stir on your little island," Mimi said.

Summer suddenly disliked her. It was the way she said *little island*. It was the way she presumed it was okay to have a gun in her home. And it was the way she had publicized the event. It was all about Mimi. Nothing in the article mentioned the other two cozy mystery writers. Summer couldn't wait for tomorrow when the woman would leave this house.

"Oh, Mimi," Lucy said. "You're a pro at causing a stir."

The other writer, Peg, laughed nervously.

"Thank you, Lucy," Mimi said. "But my life has been threatened, so . . ."

"Are you sure it's not just another publicity stunt? I mean, let's not scare everybody here if it is," she said.

Summer's ears pricked up. She liked Lucy. Yes, she did.

"Jesus, Lucy, someone broke in here last night. How would I have set that up? I was the last person to arrive, and I certainly didn't know where this place was." Mimi reached for a muffin and took a bite.

"True. The police said it was clear that someone broke in through the window," Summer said. "I didn't have it locked. I never think about locking my windows. You're damn straight I do now."

Silence passed over the table. Mimi and Lucy glared at each other. Summer awkwardly tapped her fingers on the table. Turned out these cozy mystery authors weren't so cozy.

"Let's go over the schedule." Glads handed out sheets of paper. Thank goodness for Glads, who broke through the awkwardness with her lovely pink-haired self.

A couple of months ago, Glads and Marilyn had stepped right in with the cozy mystery Christmas panel. Summer was in awe. Grief had dulled her normally sharp self. Maybe her shrink was right; perhaps she was depressed and needed medication. But damn. Wasn't it okay to be set back by the death of your mom? How fast were you supposed to come back from such a thing?

"Summer?" Glads patted her hand. "What do you think? Dinner tonight? Should I make reservations at the Beach Shack?"

"Huh? Oh yes, that would be fabulous. Thank you."

Polite conversation buzzed around her. But Summer pondered her mom, her interest in the case at Mermaid Point, the pillow body, and Mimi, who seemed to set things swirling, even among other authors. She vowed to read a few chapters of her book this morning before she headed out to the store. She crossed her arms and hugged herself to keep from shivering.

Chapter Twelve

"I'll catch up with you ladies later." Summer stood at the door and waved them off. She needed a few moments to herself before heading to Beach Reads. She wanted to read the book—just a few chapters in and then the ending. She wanted to know what the big deal was.

But first, she needed to check in with Poppy to see how things were shaping up at the store on the Saturday before Christmas.

"Hello," said a breathless Poppy when she called.

"How's it going?"

"It's packed, and we need help. It's just Mia and me here. Piper just left, almost unwillingly. I think the event has brought a lot of people to the store today."

Summer glanced at the book in her hand. Oh well. "I'll be right over."

Okay, no reading for her today. But as soon as she could, she would read *Mermaid Point Murder*. Either someone was upset just because of the attention it was causing, or someone was upset by the actual content. In either case, Summer wanted to know why. After all, it concerned her new family—and her mother. A fact she hadn't divulged to the authors. She was glad she hadn't. After listening to the other writers' interactions with Mimi, Summer had gathered that Mimi could be a bit unscrupulous. Once again, she found herself not wanting her to stay at her house with Mimi. But she could manage for the sake of Beach Reads.

* * *

Poppy hadn't been kidding when she said the place was packed. By the time Summer arrived, the shop was almost completely sold out of Mimi's books. All of them, not just *Mermaid Point Murder*. A few of the other panelists' books had sold as well.

"We have more books at the library." Poppy placed one woman's purchases in a bag.

"Great. I can't wait to see the panel." The customer's excitement was palpable.

Summer felt an odd mix of fear and anticipation. Mimi's article had helped promote the event. But something about it was frightening. Why were so many people curious about this murder? Was that it? Or was it just the local angle?

She rushed into her office to text Glads to alert her to the crowd. She slipped her purse off and set it on the chair. She pressed send on the text message, then slipped her phone back into her purse. Movement caught her eye, and she turned her head to find herself face-to-face with a huge, hairy spider. A wave of electricity seemed to shoot through her as a blood-curdling shriek shot from deep in her chest. The room spun as she attempted to remember her calming words, her deep breaths—and she hit the floor.

She awakened to Poppy patting her face. "Summer?" The word came out as if in slow motion. "Summer." The sound was getting clearer.

"Spider," Summer said, wheezing.

"This?" Mia picked it up. "Look, Aunt Summer, it's fake."

Summer didn't care. "Get it out of here!"

Mia took the fake spider out of the room, then came back as Poppy tried to help Summer sit up.

"There's something else," Mia said, lifting a sheet of paper. Her eyes widened as she read it.

"What is it?" Summer asked, forcing the words past her pounding head.

Poppy reached over and took the sheet from her. *Bookstore Owner Dies From Hosting Cozy Mystery Event* had been typed in headline format and pasted on the paper.

"What the h—"

A customer knocked on the door. "Can we get some help out here? Please?"

Summer's head was spinning.

"I'll call Mom and Gram. They will come. In the meantime, Poppy, you take care of her, and I've got the register." Mia said.

"Okay," Summer said. "I'll be right there." She started to stand and became dizzy.

"You took quite a fall," Poppy said, helping her up and over to her chair. "Don't move. I'll get you some water."

Water, yes. It sounded like just what she needed. What the hell was going on here? A fake spider on her desk. A strange note. She'd just fainted over a fake spider. Score zero for her months of intensive therapy.

Poppy came back and handed her a bottle of water. "Drink up." She pulled her phone out of her apron.

"I'm calling Ben, whether you like it or not. He needs to see this, and he needs to have someone at the library."

"Please don't," Summer said, knowing Poppy wouldn't listen.

* * *

Message received. Someone didn't want any attention on the cold case. Summer was half inclined to agree. It had happened ages ago. Let it rest.

But the other half of her mind sparked with curiosity, especially because of Hildy's interest, along with the involvement of the Bellamy family. Summer was eager to get home and check through Hildy's old box.

Soon, Piper and Agatha were both there—Piper in the front of the store, helping Mia, and Agatha and Poppy with Summer.

"You've got a nasty goose egg on your head," Agatha said. "Do you have ice?"

"I think so," Poppy said, off to find the ice.

Aunt Agatha's jaw clenched. "I think you should cancel this event."

"What? Why?"

"It's not worth the drama. You've already sold a lot of books. Do you need to have it?"

Poppy brought a small ice pack over to them, and Agatha pressed it to Summer's head.

"The event is not about selling books," Poppy said. "It's about the book community. We like to get authors and readers together every chance we get. It's good for business, yes, but that's not the only reason we do it."

"I know about all that. I'm Hildy's sister, don't forget. But I'm not sure she'd have an event like this if she thought she was jeopardizing the lives of people."

"That's a little dramatic," Chief Singer said, walking into the room. "But I'm not surprised."

Chapter Thirteen

"Maybe this is a little dramatic too," Summer said, shoving the note in his direction.

As he read it, his eyebrows lifted. "Okay, what do you want to do?"

Summer wasn't prepared for that question. She had steeled herself to be humiliated, not taken seriously. "I don't know what to do. We've got people attending the event. I'd hate to disappoint."

"But it sounds like this person means business." Agatha stepped forward. "Better disappointed than dead."

Singer shook his head as he read over the note. "I'd not take this so seriously if Mimi hadn't already been threatened and then the incident at your house last night."

"What incident?" Agatha's eyes widened.

Summer explained to her aunt, whose mouth dropped.

This was getting ridiculous. Summer determined to get to the root. "Can I ask you something, Ben?"

"Sure."

"What's this all about? Is this about a cold case that happened thirty-five years ago?"

He placed his hands on his hips. "It looks like it."

"Who'd care so much?" Summer asked.

"That's a brilliant question, and I've been thinking about it and haven't come up with one person." He scratched his chin.

"It was a crazy time, I remember," Agatha said. "The whole island was in an uproar about the murder. But her family was in the Middle East, right?"

"Yes, but her employer was here, and this is where she lived."

Her employer was the Bellamy family. Once again, Summer wished she could talk with her half brother sooner. The young woman had been far from home, working for a family, and then she'd been killed, never to lay eyes on her home again. What a tragedy.

"Did she have any friends on the island?" Summer asked.

"That's a good question. We never found any. She mostly stayed on the grounds of the Bellamy property. They kept her busy."

A picture was forming in Summer's mind. *Young. Naive. Hard worker. Explores the beach one day and boom, someone kills her.* As ironic as Romeo and Juliet. Her stomach clenched.

"I hate to interrupt, but we need to decide," Poppy said.

Summer turned to Ben. "Can you be there or have someone else there?" She hated asking anybody for a favor, him especially. But what if something crazy happened? Wouldn't it be a deterrent to have him there?

"Sure," he said. "We'll be there."

"That makes me feel better," Agatha said.

"Thanks, Ben."

"Hildy would turn over in her grave, if she had one." Agatha crossed her arms. "A police presence at a book event."

Summer smiled. "Right? It's crazy. But it's the safest thing to do. It can't hurt."

"Excuse me, ladies," Ben said. "I'm going to make a few calls, and we'll see you over at the library in about an hour, right?"

Summer sat back down, took a swig of water.

"How did this note and the spider get in here?" Agatha said.

"Who knows?"

"I thought you were getting security cameras."

"It's on the list of things to do." Summer took another long pull of her water. She'd been dealing with her fear of spiders since she was a child. She and Piper thought it traced back to a book she'd seen as a girl, but the discovery of the seed of her illness hadn't seemed to make a difference in her healing yet. She and her therapist were still working on it.

Summer glanced at her watch. Poppy would be shutting the store down in a few minutes to make the trek to the library.

"It's been so packed today. I doubt it would be difficult to slip back here with nobody seeing," Summer said.

"Someone had to have seen something," Agatha said. "What's most troubling is that whoever did it is familiar enough to know about the spider thing."

"Either that or they have a sick sense of humor and just did it for attention, not knowing. I hate to mention it, but remember there was a viral video of me shrieking over some spiders loose in my classroom? It could be anybody who saw that."

"You're white as a sheet," Agatha said. "Please drink more water."

Summer did as she was told. Which didn't happen very often. "What do you know about this case? I think you need to tell me."

Aunt Agatha sighed. "Not a thing. I told you that. But I remember your mom's obsession with the case. I sort of tuned it out because I was busy with other things. I'd just gotten married and was so happy in my little world." She paused, her expression turning reflective. "I wish I'd paid more attention. She drove me crazy with all of it. I was so glad when she dropped it; after you were born, I never heard another word. She must've been seeing him then, don't you think?"

Summer saw the hurt on Aunt Agatha's face. Her sister had kept this huge secret for years. Secrets between sisters rarely led to good feelings. "It adds up. But there must be a reason she kept my father a secret all these years. Even from you." She frowned in thought. "It has to be more than her stubbornness."

Agatha cracked a smile, which was rare these days. "You must be right. Sometimes I wanted to throttle her." She laughed at the thought. "I've never throttled anything in my life. Maybe I should have."

Summer stood and wrapped her arm around her aunt. "There's still time for throttling."

Aunt Agatha laughed again. "Sure there is."

"Do you have any aspirin?"

"Of course."

"My head is pounding."

"You fainted and smacked your head." Agatha dug in her purse and handed her a bottle. "Here you are."

Summer downed the aspirin just as Poppy's voice came over the store speaker. "Shoppers, please make your selections. We are closing in fifteen minutes."

A chill traveled up Summer's spine. "I guess that's it, then. I need to head to the library." She grabbed her purse.

"I'll go with you. In fact, let me drive. You still look wobbly to me," Agatha said.

Summer acquiesced. "Wobbly" didn't even begin to express how she felt. She gripped the back of the chair with one hand and took one more swallow of water, trying to ignore her sick stomach.

Chapter Fourteen

The parking lot of the Brigid's Island Public Library was full. Summer, Agatha, Mia, and Piper parked two blocks away. The drive over had been silent, the tension thick among them.

Summer's head still throbbed, and Piper wouldn't even make eye contact with her. Mia stared out the window, and Aunt Agatha hummed as she drove.

Getting out of the car was a tremendous relief. Summer welcomed the two-block walk to the library—and the fresh air. She glanced at Piper, hoping to resolve her problem after this fiasco of an event.

The four of them entered through the back of the library and snaked through the offices to the event room.

Marilyn, buzzing around like a honeybee on steroids, found her way to them. "What do you think of the setup? Do you think the flowers are too much? You know how I am about flowers."

"I've never seen a book event look so festive," Aunt Agatha said.

"Roses on the panelist table, poinsettias on the checkout table, sparkling pinecones on the bookshelves. I'd say Marilyn was here," Piper said, smiling. "It's lovely."

"Do you need more chairs?" A man came up to Marilyn. He wore a polo shirt bearing the library logo and khakis.

"We might," Marilyn said.

"Can I help?" Mia asked.

"Sure," the man said. "Follow me."

Summer wondered how they'd get another row of chairs in the room.

The authors and their moderator, Glads, huddled in the corner. They were giggling about something just as Poppy came up to Summer. "We've got a hit here. Who knew cozy mystery authors would bring in hordes of people?"

"I wonder if it's because of the controversy," Summer said. "Have you seen Ben?"

"Not yet."

Someone touched Summer's shoulder, and she jumped and gasped. She turned to find her half brother. "Sam!" She hugged him.

"I'm sorry, I didn't mean to startle you." He pulled away from her, regarding her. "Are you okay?"

"I passed out earlier. I'm fine now. Just a tiny bit nervous. The event has taken on a life of its own."

His jaw twitched. "I read the paper." He was a Bellamy. Summer was certain he knew more about the cold case than most. "You passed out? Are you okay?"

"I'm fine. I was just startled." Petrified, more like. "Let's talk about what was in the paper."

He stiffened. "It happened a long time ago."

She patted his hand. "My mom saved a box full of clippings and stuff. She followed the case for years. I had no idea."

His face fell.

"Summer, we need to get this show on the road," Marilyn said, coming up to them. "Places, everyone." She smiled.

"We'll talk later?"

Sam nodded. "Fatima is coming with a surprise for you."

Summer's heart sped up. She had a brother and sister, and they were here, supporting her bookstore.

She grinned. "It's not more baklava, is it? I love it, but I'm not sure how much more my hips can take!"

He laughed, waved, and moved toward the chairs. Summer took up her place behind one of the book tables. She, Poppy, and Mia each had a tableful of one author's books. Hers was Mimi's. Of course. She couldn't get away from the woman if she tried, could she? Summer couldn't wait for Mimi to leave.

The crowd filed into the room. Some stopped and bought a few books, which was the smart thing to do, since Summer imagined there'd be long lines after the event.

A well-dressed man stopped at her table. It amazed Summer that there were so many people she didn't know on her tiny island. This man was one of them. He carried himself with a certain elegance. His hair was so dark it was almost blue. He slipped his sunglasses off as he approached the table. "Hello," he said, smiling, showing off a beautiful mouthful of teeth.

"Hi. Can I help you?"

"Yes, I want to buy the books," he said with a British accent.

"Sure." Summer stood, handing him a book and taking his credit card.

He looked confused.

"Is there a problem?"

"I want to buy all of your books," he said.

Summer didn't think she'd heard him correctly. His accent must be throwing her off—though she'd spent loads of time in England. "I'm sorry?"

"Yes, I'd like to purchase all of these books. I'm buying them for my employees as gifts this year."

Summer didn't believe a word of it. His eyes and tone told her his explanation was a complete fabrication.

"Just these books?" Summer gestured to *Mermaid Point Murder.*

He nodded.

It would be a good sale. Good for business. But what about the others who had come, some traveling quite a distance, to buy this book and get it signed by the author?

"I'm sorry. I can't do that," Summer said, immediately regretting it when it was clear he wasn't happy with her. "We have a two-book limit. It's our policy at events like this."

"Excuse me?" he said in a loud voice. "Are you refusing my business?" People turned to watch.

Summer's face heated. What was going on here? Who was this man, and why did he want all the books? He must not want other people to read it.

"I'm happy to put in an order for you, sir, but I can't let you buy all of these books. It wouldn't be fair to the other people here." Summer's eyes met his. She would not be bullied, even though his stance gave her prickles.

"Fair? You won't take my money, and you have the audacity to throw around words like *fair*?" Still loud. So loud the crowd hushed.

"Is there a problem here?" Ben said as he stalked up through the crowd.

The man shoved his credit card back in his wallet. "No sale," he said, and walked out.

Ben stood with his hands on his hips.

"He wanted to buy all of Mimi's books. I couldn't allow it because other people are here who are planning to buy them."

"Is that so?" He squinted his eyes. "I'll see what I can do." He was through the door before Summer could say no. *Don't go. There is a "weird vibe" here, as my mom used to say. I'd like a bodyguard, please.*

Two women walked by her, giggling. "A *real* streaker. Right outside the library."

Make that two bodyguards.

Chapter Fifteen

Even though Summer's instincts had told her this event was going to tank, it didn't. It rolled along smoothly, and Mimi even allowed the others on the panel to talk, much to the delight of very talented moderators Marilyn and Glads, who didn't put up with grandstanding—or a panel hog.

Summer found herself enjoying the discussion. Her mouth dropped when Peg talked about her background. Peg had been a Shakespeare professor at Harvard before she started writing cozy mysteries and romances. She'd made more money writing than teaching, so she'd quit. One of her older series had incorporated a Shakespeare theme. Summer made a note to check it out. A Shakespeare-themed cozy. Intriguing.

During a break, Fatima stood in line at Summer's table. She had an older woman with her.

"Good to see you." Summer reached for her sister's hands.

Fatima smiled. "We've just gotten here. Missed the whole first part. Anyway, I want you to meet our grandmother."

"Our?"

She nodded. "Yes. She's our father's mother."

"Does she know?" Summer lowered her voice.

Fatima nodded, just as the old woman reached across the table and hugged Summer. "Of course she knows," she said in a British accent. "She's no dummy." She winked. Her voice had a rich timbre and not a hint of an Egyptian accent. "My name is Rima. You can call me that or Grandma. Whatever you're comfortable with."

The woman appeared as grandmotherly as Ben Singer. She didn't look a day over fifty, but she had to be in her eighties. Her olive skin bore few wrinkles. She was the woman from the newspaper, the one who bore a striking resemblance to Summer.

Summer smiled. It was all she could do. She had a grandmother. A brother. A sister. A year ago, she'd never have believed any of this. Summer placed her hand over the top book in her stack—*Mermaid Point Murder*. Maybe Rima shouldn't see this book.

Rima's face fell. "What is this?" She grabbed it and held it up to Fatima.

"It's just a book," Fatima said. "What's wrong, Grandma?"

She opened her mouth, but nothing came out. Her hand went to her mouth and her eyes rolled back in her hand. She swayed.

Fatima squealed as Summer ran out from behind the table. The old woman was going down. Summer tried to reach her before it happened. But she didn't. The woman passed out on the floor, with Fatima softening her fall, gently patting her face. "Grandma!" she said repeatedly.

Summer's eyes searched for Ben as a crowd gathered around.

"Please stay back and give her air!" Summer yelled.

Sam broke through the crowd. "Fatima? Grandma?"

"I'll call 911," Summer said.

"No," Sam said. "She wouldn't want that. I'll take care of this."

He scooped the older woman into his arms as if she were a fragile bird.

He exited the room with Fatima following, leaving Summer to handle the crowd.

"Sorry, everybody, she just passed out," Summer said. "It's okay. Her grandson is taking care of her."

But was it okay? Summer went back behind the table. Rima had suffered a shock—the shock being the book. She must remember the murder; seeing it in print must have stunned her.

Summer's heart raced. She wished that Mimi had never written this book and had never been invited here.

She still didn't quite get her mom's interest in it, other than the family connection. Maybe that was enough.

* * *

Who was that? Mia mouthed to her.

Summer walked over to Mia's table, since the break was almost over and nobody was at her own table. "That was my grandmother."

Mia frowned. "Is she okay?"

"I hope so. It seemed as if she fainted from the shock of seeing the book."

Mia's eyes widened. "I've never known anybody to faint from shock before. I thought that only happened in books."

"It must've been quite a shock. She may have known the young woman who was killed. It had happened all those years ago, but the murder might still be fresh for her. Or maybe she'd filed it away and the book was an unpleasant reminder."

Mia grinned. "But then again, you passed out from shock earlier. It must be a family trait."

Summer hadn't considered that.

"Everybody, please take your seat. We're getting ready to start," Marilyn said into the microphone.

Glads walked through with fresh water for everybody as they took their places.

"I have one more question, and then we'll take questions from the audience," Marilyn said.

The crowd quieted as she asked each of the authors in turn what their next project was. Then she opened the floor to the audience for questions.

"I'd like to know how you skirted the line between fact and fiction." A woman stood and addressed her question to Mimi. "It seems a fine balance. How much did you make up? How much was real?"

Mimi smiled. "Thank you for your question." She paused. "I took the very bones from the case. A young woman was murdered, and her body was found at a place called Mermaid Point, located on a small island. I made the rest up. The romance. The family drama. That's all mine. It's been a cold case for over thirty years, and there's not much else to know about it. I tried to reach out to the family, but they have been noncommunicative."

Of course they had been. *A cozy mystery writer calls and wants information about the murder of a family member long gone cold?* Summer got it. She wouldn't want to talk either.

Another question for Mimi. Summer refrained from rolling her eyes.

"Yvonne Smith from the *Brigid Herald*. I'd like to know about the ethics of what you just talked about. Is it considered ethical to use an unsolved cold-case murder in a novel? Because personally, I'd think you'd do better just making it up."

"I didn't mean to offend anybody," Mimi said. "I loved the name Mermaid Point, and so I researched it. And as for your question about ethics. It's ethical, as long as you let people know what you're doing. And I did."

"Any more questions?" Marilyn asked. "Could we have some for the other authors?"

Chapter Sixteen

After the panel, people stood in lines to buy books and get them signed. Beach Reads was making money, the authors were pleased that people were interested in their books, and the customers were thrilled. The mood was jovial. Summer tried to catch the spirit, but her mind was too busy trying to process everything that had happened, from the rude man offering to buy all the books to a grandmother she hadn't even known about passing out in front of her.

Yvonne Smith, the reporter, walked up to Summer. "Congrats on a very successful event."

Summer's skin prickled. "Thank you."

"Did you know it would cause such a fuss?" she asked.

"What?"

"Mimi's book. Did you have any idea it would cause such a fuss?"

Summer squinted her eyes. "Go away, please. You're not interviewing me. I don't give you permission to use any of what I said."

"But—"

Summer walked away, and Yvonne followed.

"If I could just have a few minutes of your time, Summer."

She was like a pesky gnat. Summer kept walking. "Get lost."

And Yvonne stopped following her. Thank goodness. Summer despised reporters. Not all reporters, just today's reporters. They used to report the facts. These days, nobody seemed to care.

With the books sold and the customers gone, the crew cleaned the room and then gathered in a corner to discuss the event.

"Huge success," Poppy said.

Marilyn beamed. "It really was."

"Great moderating," Glads said.

Glads rolled her eyes. "That Mimi."

"You handled her well," Summer said, and meant it.

"So, tell us about the guy who wanted to buy us out of stock," Glads said.

"Nothing to tell. I've never seen him before. He had very black hair and a British accent."

"Good for you for not selling to him," Marilyn said. "Who does he think he is?"

"He's someone who doesn't want that book read," Mia spoke up.

"Why not?" Poppy said. But Summer followed Mia's thinking.

"People broke into Aunt Summer's house. Mimi was threatened. Now this. It makes sense. There's something in that book." Mia held her arms out.

"You and your imagination," Piper said.

"I think she's right," Glads said. "There's something in the book that someone finds threatening. It's the only thing that makes sense."

"In any case, it's over. Maybe we can go back to our normal lives," Summer stated.

"Normal? Who wants that?" Marilyn said and laughed.

Summer gathered her belongings. Aunt Agatha signaled that she wanted to go. "I'll see you all at the dinner tonight."

"Looking forward to it," Glads said.

Agatha grabbed Summer's arm as she, Piper, and Mia clutched together and left the building. "I researched Rima," she said.

Summer had to think a minute. "Oh? My grandmother?'

"I was curious about her when she passed out, so I looked her up on my phone."

"Geez, Mom, you're turning into Nancy Drew," Piper said.

"I'm ignoring that remark," she said, and turned back to Summer as they walked toward the car.

Piper glanced at Summer and shrugged.

"What did you find out, Gram?" Mia asked.

"She was here during the murder thirty-five years ago. She found the body."

Summer stopped walking; her heart lurched. No wonder she'd passed out when she saw the book. "How awful."

Aunt Agatha nodded, her pageboy haircut bobbing. "Right? The only other things I could find about her were news items from overseas."

"Could it be that she's not been back to the island since then?" Summer asked.

"If I found the body of my maid on the beach here, I might never come back," Piper said.

"Indeed," Summer said. "Poor thing."

"Way to make an impression, Aunt Summer," Mia said, and smiled. "You know, long-lost granddaughter hands her gram a murder mystery that's a terrible memory."

Summer pinched her playfully. "Thanks for pointing that out, Mia."

"Anytime, Aunt Summer."

After they situated themselves in the car, Summer texted Sam. *How is she?*

The text came back right away. *She is fine, albeit embarrassed.*

"I'm sorry. I didn't know the book would upset her."

It took a few beats for him to respond.

"I didn't either."

"Rima is fine," Summer announced in the car. "Sam didn't know she'd get so upset about the book."

"Have you read it?" Agatha asked.

"No."

"I have, and I can see why the family would be upset. Sometimes it's best to let sleeping dogs lie."

"But Mimi has every right to write about what she wants," Piper said.

"Of course she does. But I wonder if she even talked with the family."

"She said she tried. They wouldn't talk to her."

Agatha braked at a red light. "That should have told her something. There's plenty of other stories out there. Hell, she could have used the title and made the murder victim a man. The story is too close to what we know happened, and the rest of it? Well, I don't know anything about the case, really, but it rang true to me."

Summer's ear pricked up.

"I didn't think so at all," Piper said. "It felt very contrived to me. But then again, all of Mimi's books do. I stopped reading them years ago."

Summer believed it, for Mimi herself was contrived.

"It'd be the same for us if someone wrote about Hildy. We wouldn't like it. No matter how many years had passed. No matter how close to the truth it was. There are plenty of other stories out there. Mimi is supposed to be a fiction author. How about she makes something up? Isn't that what fiction writers do?" Agatha's voice was almost shrill as she pulled up to Summer's house.

They sat in silence a few moments, each in their own contemplations. Summer drew in air.

"Does anybody want to come in?"

Silence.

"Okay. See you soon." She opened the door, and a wave of weariness overtook her. Maybe there was time for a nap. She leaned back into the car. "Thank you all for helping today. I love you all." She blew them a kiss.

"Love you too," she heard Agatha say as she turned to walk toward her house.

What a day. And it wasn't over yet.

Chapter Seventeen

Summer paused to take in her decorated front porch. Lights were strung across the roof and outlining the windows, and Santa sat on the porch swing. She didn't know why her mom had a fake Santa, but what the heck. He looked good sitting on the swing.

She walked forward and opened the door. Mr. Darcy squawked from the living room.

"Sorry, boy, I know it's been a long day. Are you hungry?" Summer walked up to his cage.

"Hungry!" the bird repeated.

Summer scooped food into his feeder, then made her way upstairs to lie down. She slipped into bed and stared at the ceiling. She was so grateful nothing bad had happened at the event. Well, besides the guy asking to buy all the books and Rima passing out. But those were easily handled. Her imagination had led her to the possibility of a much worse incident. A gunman coming in and leveling the place, for example.

She sighed. Overactive imagination.

It was over. Her body relaxed. Now she could rest. As soon as Mimi left, all would go back to normal. People would forget about the murder and the book, and everybody could get back to living their quiet lives of desperation. She laughed. Hildy hated it when Summer used that phrase.

She closed her eyes and slipped away. Hildy stepped in front of her, flailing her arms. She was trying to get Summer to understand her, but Summer's ears couldn't hear her. Finally, the word *Danger!* came out.

Summer awakened with a jolt. Dreaming about her mother was unnerving enough, but for her to say *Danger!* in such a way chilled her. She pulled the covers in closer, knowing she'd have to get up soon to get ready for the dinner.

Her subconscious must be working through all of this murder business. And her mom was linked to it all. But how?

She lifted herself from the bed and made her way downstairs to make a pot of tea. As she was descending the stairs, she felt a draft.

A clattering noise erupted near the door as she walked down the hallway to the kitchen. She rushed to the door—it was wide open, blowing back and forth in the wind.

Her heart dropped to her feet. Had she left the door open? She recalled entering the house, dropping her bags on the table. Still there. But something was missing.

The box.

The box that Sam had given her, filled with photos of her mom and biological father when they were young.

Her heart raced. Someone had been in here. Someone had stolen her box of photos, the photos she had yet to even glimpse. A burning sensation rushed to her chest. *Summer, why? Why didn't you just peek through them and commit each one to memory? Why?*

She dug through her bag for her cell phone. Three messages. They would have to wait. She needed to dial Ben. *Ben again, for god's sake.*

But someone had been in her house . . .

She walked to the kitchen with her phone in her trembling hand. The other box was still there—the box with the clippings and the scrapbook. That must be what the person had been after when they picked up the box of old photos instead.

She pressed the number for Ben.

Clammy hands.

"Ben? It's Summer. I need you to come here right away."

"Where's 'here'? What's going on?" He sounded as if he'd been sleeping.

"I'm home, and someone broke in and stole a box of photos off the table. They left the door wide open."

"You want me to come over because somebody took a box of photos?"

"They entered my home while I was napping and took it. They entered my home."

He paused. "I'll be right over."

She wished she didn't have to deal with her ex-fiancé's father every time something terrible happened. But the other officer in town was on vacation. They didn't seem to have a substitute for when he left. In any case, she didn't know him—and this felt personal.

She set the phone down and heated the water for tea. Still trembling, her stomach queasy. Someone had been in her house as she slept. And her mother had warned her. Hadn't she?

Illogical. It went against every fiber of her rational, educated being.

But she couldn't explain it.

Maybe her mom was right: some parts of the universe could never be understood. Summer resisted that notion.

Danger! She recalled her mother's voice in her ear again. It had sounded so real. She shuddered away the chill creeping up her spine.

She turned to the box on the table and spilled the contents, searching for answers. Perhaps she'd find answers in this tragedy that had happened years ago. In why her mom had kept these pieces of the past.

She cracked open the scrapbook, and a few yellowed articles slipped out, the glue giving way. The pasted articles left on the pages were in chronological order. She slipped the others back in their places.

A rapping on the door startled her. She stood and walked over to it.

"Ben," she said. "I left the door as I found it."

"Where were you when this happened?"

"I was upstairs sleeping."

"You didn't hear anything?"

"Nothing."

He walked over to the table where the box had been. "Is this where the box was? I remember seeing it yesterday."

She nodded. "It was a box of photos of my mom and biological father. It had *Bellamy* scribbled in bold letters across one side and *Omar* on another side. My brother had given them to me a while back. They found them when they were cleaning through their dad's belongings after he passed."

"What were the pictures of?"

"My parents. I didn't even look at them."

"What?"

"It seemed . . . personal. I wasn't ready to . . ."

"Okay." He said it to shut her up. She was sure of it.

In the meantime, he examined the door. "Someone was very clever with a pick. You had the door locked, right?"

"Absolutely."

"I've got a fingerprint kit in my car. I'll be right back."

Summer stood and waited. The chill from outside was invading the house.

Ben came back and started taking fingerprints.

"Why would someone take your mom's photos?" he asked as he worked.

"I have a feeling they were after the other box."

"Other box?"

"Yes. Mom kept a box with a scrapbook and clippings in it all about the murder at Mermaid Point."

His chin lifted, and he dropped his tools. He went back to it. "She did what?" He eyeballed Summer again.

"I know, right? It's not like her at all, and I can't figure out why she did it, except the family connection."

"Family connection?" He stood.

"My biological father was a Bellamy. Omar Bellamy. Did you know him?"

He reddened. Summer had never seen him so flustered.

He nodded. "I did. But I didn't know he was your father." He placed the test strips in a plastic container. "There."

"Can we shut the door?"

He nodded, coming into the house and closing it.

He looked Summer in the eye. "We need to talk."

Her heart nearly stopped. Ben Singer was not her biggest fan. He had liked her mom. Well, everybody had. But he didn't like Summer. His son's heartbreak was probably the least of it. Why did he want to talk with her?

"Well, sure," she said.

The teakettle whistle pierced the air. Both of them flinched.

"Would you like a cup of tea?"

He gazed into the distance, as if making a big decision. "I believe I would."

Chapter Eighteen

A part of Summer's grown-up self found it amusing that Ben Singer, a man who didn't like her and made no bones about it, was sitting across the table from her, stirring cream into his tea.

He cocked a wiry gray eyebrow. "I'm probably wasting my breath."

"That depends."

"The Mermaid Point case is best left alone." He lapsed into a thoughtful silence.

"That seems to be the case. It seems like it's brought unwanted attention. But to whom?"

He shook his head back and forth. "It's a case that haunts me." His voice cracked. "I was young, with fire in my belly. I wanted to catch a killer and wanted justice."

Summer sipped her tea and set the cup back down on the table. Ben Singer. At her table. Drinking tea. And reminiscing. She didn't respond.

"The devastation that hit that family was painful to watch. It hurt so bad that I almost walked away from this job. Almost decided I'd become the wrong thing." His square jaw flinched.

Summer leaned forward. This was a revelation. "Are you talking about the Bellamy family?"

He nodded. "A very old-school family. Muslim. And I mean that in a good way. I learned a lot about the religion, their values, and I was impressed. Family is everything to them, and they're, you know, just very tight."

"Sounds wonderful." Summer kept her own counsel.

He leaned back in his chair, and it squeaked. "There's a flip side to that. Expectations are high. You can't deviate from the family plan. Do you know what I mean?"

Of course she did. It was a culture where marriages were still sometimes planned by parents. Children grew up and became what their parents wanted, no matter the personal cost. She'd seen that as a professor—kids coming to college and studying a subject only because their parents had told them to do so. But some American families did the same. "Yes, I absolutely do."

His face reddened a bit. "We were all a little in love with your mom then."

How had the subject switched to Hildy? Before Summer finished her sip of tea, she set her cup back down and scooched up on the end of her chair.

"I didn't know she was involved with Omar until just now. But now it makes sense and is fitting into place. She wouldn't date anybody. We figured she must be seeing someone, but it was a secret. It drove us crazy." He smiled, as if remembering a private joke.

"So, my mom had a baby. Me. She kept it a secret for years. He's dead. She's dead. And his wife is dead. I'm here trying to make sense of this, trying to make sense of why Mom kept all this stuff."

"Knowing that she was in love with Omar and probably carrying his child when all this happened adds an interesting twist to it. I didn't suspect she was acquainted with the Bellamys. I never asked her anything about them. Young know-it-all that I was." His lips curled to the side.

Not for the first time since she'd been home, Summer perceived his age and wondered why he hadn't retired yet.

"But that man today at the event is a relative of Bellamys. A very disgruntled relative. When the murder happened, it split the family. Shattered it. Sometimes that happens. There were four brothers, two were quite young, but the older brothers were Omar and Bashir. Bashir broke away from the family and took his money with him. It was his son at the event today."

"Interesting. So let me get this clear. What you're saying is the guy at the event today was Sam's cousin. My cousin. Named after his father."

"Sam may not even know him." Ben drank his tea, set it down. "This is the part that I wonder if you will heed. Sam's cousin is dangerous."

Summer's breath hitched. "What? What do you mean?"

"He has a record a mile long. A lot of it is international terrorism related, like bomb threats. Espionage. He doesn't visit here often, thank god."

A chill traveled up her spine. "Okay. But why the interest in the murder that happened here all those years ago?"

"That's the million-dollar question. I'm guessing he knows something about it and wants to keep it hidden."

Made sense.

"I want you to stay away from him."

Summer's well-trained hackles rose. It was an automatic response to Ben, to any man who tried to tell her what to do. To "protect" her. She didn't need his or any man's protection. She drew in air and calmed herself. But at the same time, the guy Ben was referring to was an international terrorist. He was out of her league for sure. "I have no reason to have anything to do with him. I didn't seek him out."

"Don't. I know you're a curious person, and I get that you want answers. We all do. But be careful, please. This guy is no joke." His phone rang, and he stood. "I have to take this."

"Certainly," she said.

The Bellamy family were an interesting bunch. Summer looked forward to learning more. But pieces were coming together in her personal life from all this. Her birth father had been kept a secret from everybody, even her mother's sister, and they had always been close. Maybe there was more reason than the fact that he was promised to another woman. Maybe Hildy had figured it was dangerous for her family to know anything about him. Or maybe Summer's overactive imagination was at play again.

In any case, someone had entered her home and taken a box of photos of Omar and Hildy together, along with letters and notes the couple had saved. Summer wished she'd even glanced at them now. But she hadn't had the heart until now. Now, when it was an act of reclamation.

The past is a prologue. A quote from *The Tempest* sprang into Summer's brain as she waited for Ben. A murder committed decades ago had led to all the recent weirdness. She recalled Rima passing out and wondered if one could ever truly heal from losing someone to murder.

Ben entered the room. "I've got to go. But I want to reiterate that you will not contact that man at all."

"Of course I won't," she said. "I'm not an imbecile."

"Of course not, but—"

"I know, Ben. I poked my nose in with Mom's case."

"I'm glad you did." He drew in air. "But it may not have gone as well for you. Or for Agatha."

"I realize that." She stood to walk him out.

"I'll run the fingerprints ASAP and report the robbery."

"Those pictures are the only thing I have of Mom and Omar together. They mean a lot to me." But she had yet to even look at them. "I guess the question is, who else do they mean something to? Or did they pick up the wrong box?"

"One of many questions."

Chapter Nineteen

Summer spread out the scrapbook and poured herself another cup of tea.

Just as she settled in, a knocking came at her front door. She opened it to Mimi and Glads.

"Hello, ladies," she said, waving them inside. "I'm having some tea. Join me?"

"Sounds fabulous," Mimi said. "A cup of tea, then I need to get ready for dinner."

Dinner? Summer had forgotten. One more social event for the day. She drew in air. One more event.

"What a lovely island. Glads showed me around a bit. I've been to the bookstore before, of course, and the boardwalk. But we went out to Mermaid Point, and it was gorgeous."

At the mention of Mermaid Point, Summer bristled.

"What's all this?" Glads sat at the table where the scrapbook lay open.

"That's the scrapbook that was in the box Marilyn and Poppy pulled out from the back of the shop the other day."

Glads leafed through it with Mimi observing over her shoulder.

"This is weird, right?" Glads said.

Summer filled their cups with hot tea and placed them on the table. "Yes, Mom saved all the clippings and followed the case. I supposed it had to do with Omar. You know, a link to my biological family and her one true love."

Mimi's chin lifted hard. "What?"

"Omar Bellamy is my father."

She gasped. "I had no idea!"

"Nobody did." Glads sat down at the table.

"I suppose I'm super glad to have this now. Someone broke in and stole the other box. The one Sam gave me, full of their letters and pictures."

"What?" Glads said.

"Broke in, stole the box, and left."

"Didn't take anything else?"

Summer sipped her tea. "No. I'm betting they will be back when they find they've got the wrong box. I think they were after this one."

Silence filled the room as the women drank their tea and sifted through clippings and scrapbook pages.

"Maybe this wasn't the safest place for me to stay," Mimi said.

"Maybe not," Glads said.

"Feel free to leave anytime," Summer said, trying not to sound as enthusiastic as she felt. "I mean, if you feel unsafe here. Break-ins are not the usual."

"Yes, but you've had two since I've been here."

"Ben called a locksmith to come over and change the locks and to put on a dead bolt. Both are supposed to be the kind it's hard to pick."

Mimi's eyes widened. "He must think there's a reason for it." She paused. "There's nothing that I can see here that's news. I mean,

I've read all these clippings myself in library archives. Why would someone want this particular box?"

"Good question." Summer changed the subject. "What time do we have reservations?"

"Six." Glads set down her drink.

"I better get a move on, then. Excuse me ladies." Summer left the room and went to her bedroom, which used to be Hildy's. All this talk of the past had unsettled her. Poor Hildy had known these people. Loved at least one of them. And she'd followed the case for what? For news of a break in the case? To maintain a connection, no matter how tenuous?

Summer opened her wardrobe. Oh, to have walk-in closets instead of half closets and overstuffed dressers. "What to wear?"

As she picked through her clothes, finding nothing inspiring, she considered Mimi. If the woman felt unsafe here, maybe Summer could offer to find her another place. Wouldn't it be good to have her out of here? She'd been there only one night, but her presence filled the house with unpleasantness.

Summer stopped herself from inwardly apologizing for not liking this particular mystery author. Mimi had stirred all of this up, and now she was a bit scared of staying here?

Summer laughed out loud.

After dressing and before leaving her room, Summer texted Fatima to ask about Rima. Her sister texted back and said Rima was fine. *But how are you? I'm sure this situation is a lot for you in one day. The event. Meeting Grandma, and then her passing out.*

That wasn't the half of it. Someone had broken into her home twice in the past twenty-four hours.

Are you processing everything? Her therapist's voice rang in her head. *I'll do that tomorrow*, Summer answered.

She texted Fatima back. *I'm fine.*

But was she? Maybe. Maybe it was all over now. Perhaps whoever was behind all of this had attempted to scare her off from having the event. It hadn't worked. But it was over. Maybe now things would get back to some semblance of normalcy. Whatever that was.

She gave herself the once-over in the mirror. Her jade silk blouse lightened her black eyes. She added a necklace and earrings and a smear of lipstick, and she was ready to go.

When Summer entered the kitchen, both Glads and Mimi were still there. Mimi, in another outfit, was poring over an article. "This is new information to me."

"What's that?"

"The body was found with several bracelets on it."

"And?"

"One of the bracelets had a Bellamy seal."

"What does that mean?"

"It means that either this young woman stole the bracelet or she was a secret Bellamy."

Summer refrained from rolling her eyes. "Maybe someone in the family gave it to her as a gift. It could be that simple. I read that she was very close to them."

"They never gave away jewelry with that insignia on it. It was a Bellamy thing."

"How do you know?" Glads asked.

"I've studied the family. When researching for the book."

Summer wondered if she was familiar with the cousin who'd visited the event today. Lovely man.

"What does it look like?"

"Like this." Mimi held up her phone as she scrolled through the pictures.

Summer recognized it. A fleur-de-lis with swirls and flowers around it. In the center was a ruby. Her heart skipped a beat. Her mom had given her a necklace with this very thing on it for her sixteenth birthday. Her heart fluttered more. How to say it? Where were the words? Her mom had been giving her pieces of her family for years.

"Summer, you've just gone pale. Are you okay?" Glads asked.

"I'm fine. Just a bit surprised. I have several pieces of jewelry with this design on it."

Mimi gasped. "I don't believe it."

"Don't be so melodramatic. He was my father. He loved my mom very much. It makes sense that I have some family jewelry." Her last words caught in her throat. A connection. Her father had known about her. Had he loved her? Had he given the jewelry to her mom to give to her? Or was it her mom's jewelry that she had bestowed on her daughter?

"Let me get you some water," Glads said.

"No need. We need to go if we're going to make those reservations." Summer straightened up. The emotions that had arisen in her were tempered by the confusion playing out on Mimi's face. New information had been delivered. And Mimi didn't like it.

Chapter Twenty

The Beach Shack sat along a cove near the eastern part of the island, on the side opposite where the boardwalk ran. This part of the island was beginning to see some slow development. As the women sat at their table, they caught views of the water and the moonlight, and in the distance, lights from Raleigh sparkled.

"Evidently the name is ironic," Lucy said, running her hand along the smooth linen tablecloth. "This is no shack."

"It's lovely," Mimi said, as if in awe. "Very understated, but I love all of the chandeliers. I wonder if they are antique or replicas."

Aunt Agatha, Piper, and Mia hadn't arrived yet.

"Good question. They are lovely, like something out of a fairy tale. Shall we order drinks?" Marilyn said. "I'm paying tonight, ladies, so drink up."

"How kind!" Summer said. "Shall we order a couple bottles of wine to start?"

"More than two, I'd say." Aunt Agatha's voice came up from behind her. Mimi looked away. The two of them were like oil and water.

"Oh, great," Mia said. "I get to be with a bunch of drunks tonight."

"Aren't you lucky?" Piper said, placing her arm around Mia.

Everybody took a seat, and Summer ordered the wine. After it was poured, she stood, holding her glass for a toast. "Thank you all. Every one of you played a part in the success of today's event. I know my mom would be proud to see the crowds and the brisk sales of books. And more than that, the way we came together, worked together, to spread her vision of community around books." Her eyes stung. "Here's to all of us." She lifted her glass. She was going to be okay. She'd get through this night and see Mimi off in the morning and slip back into normal. She'd have a decent Christmas. And she'd go on. She'd go on one day at a time. Without Hildy.

She sat down next to Lucy just as the salads were being brought to the table. Queasy, she rested a moment before eating. "So, you taught Shakespeare?"

Lucy took a bite of lettuce and nodded. She chewed, swallowed. "But that was years ago. You taught as well?"

"Yes. I'm on sabbatical." She picked up her fork.

"Will you stay here or go back?"

"I've been trying to decide."

"A part of me misses teaching. Of course, now I sometimes teach writers' workshops, and I love it." She stabbed her tomato. "But I don't miss academia."

"Cheers to that." Summer lifted her glass. "But I do love Will."

"Cheers to him." Lucy raised hers as well. "Where would we be without him?"

Summer nodded. "So true. Now tell me, how did you get from there to here? I've read the bios, but I want to hear it from your mouth."

Lucy smiled. Her earring sparkled against her white hair. "I was fired. I had an affair with the dean's wife."

Summer almost choked on her salad. Then she laughed. "They don't warn you about that in grad school, do they?"

Lucy laughed. "No. It's one of those unspoken rules: don't sleep with the dean's wife. Most especially if you're a woman."

"Goodness," Mimi said. "The lesbian is out of the bag."

"It's closet," Mia said. "She's out of the closet."

"I've never been in the closet—or the bag," she said. "Flora and I have been together for twenty years and recently tied the knot." She paused, glared at Mimi. "What do you suggest, I put 'lesbian' in my bio?"

Mimi chortled. "Absolutely not."

"You do have a very interesting gay character," Glads said. "I've always liked her. What's her name? Leah. That's right."

A gay character in a cozy mystery? How intriguing. Summer drank more wine. She'd had cozy mysteries all wrong.

"You remember Leah? They dropped that series years ago," Lucy said.

Mimi shifted around in her seat, as if bored with the conversation. Or maybe it was that the attention wasn't on her. She finished her salad and pushed the plate aside. "Are those flowers real?" She reached out and stroked the centerpiece, made up of miniature white poinsettias and tiny pinecones. "Yes, they are. Aren't they wonderful?"

The server cleared their table. He glanced around the table, and as he did so, his eyes landing on Mimi. "Are you the author of *Mermaid Point Murder*?"

"Yes," she said and nodded.

Summer bristled. She could almost see the pall descending over the table.

"I loved the book," he said. "I'm no fan of the Bellamys."

Summer's heart raced. "Why not?"

His face went stony. "They don't tip well, and yet they have more money than God."

"They do?" Summer asked. She wasn't completely surprised.

"Goodness, yes. Have you ever seen their house?" Mimi said.

Summer shook her head. As a girl, she'd clung to the side of the island where she'd grown up. As a teenager, she'd ventured out more—but that part of the island had held little interest for her. There was nothing there to lure her.

"We need to remedy that," she said.

The server collected plates and moved off into the kitchen.

Summer had assumed the family were comfortable, since they owned a shipping company. She wondered if the server had been exaggerating.

Mimi pulled out her phone. "Hang on. Wait until you see this. I took pictures today."

She handed Summer the phone.

Summer examined the photo of a house. Or was it a castle? Made of stone, it settled into the cliff where it sat, the only feature giving it visibility being the turrets. Yes, turrets. "It's a castle."

"They call it the Bellamy Palace. But yes, I'd call it a small castle. We walked halfway up the cliff today. There are stairs up to it. Scroll over one picture."

Summer did so.

"That's the view."

Her stomach flipped. Mermaid Point. But something else tugged at her. A memory? A dream? She examined the rest of the landscape. Then it dawned on her. The photo of her as a baby with her mother on the beach, the one her mom had kept on her desk—it had been snapped here. A chill spread through her. She'd been there, playing with her mom in the sun. It must have been Omar who'd snapped the photo—which meant that she'd met her dad, even if she couldn't remember it.

Chapter Twenty-One

The mental place between dreams and memory was sometimes slippery. Summer recalled picking up that photo of her and her mom and studying it. She also recalled the way it made her feel. The landscape was unfamiliar, but an unnamable emotion tugged at her.

"I'd love to see this," Mia said, eyes wide, as they passed the phone around the table.

"Why don't we go over there tonight?" Mimi said.

"Okay," Mia replied.

"Whoa!" Piper said. "I'm not so sure that's a good idea. First, it's getting late, and you won't be able to see much, since it's dark. And second"—she paused and glanced at Summer—"there's been way too much weirdness over this book. I'm not sure it's safe for you to go poking around over there."

"Mom!"

"I have to agree," Agatha said.

"Come on now. We went over today, and it was no big deal," Mimi said.

Glads nodded. "I hadn't been over there in years. But it was fine."

"The Bellamy's don't own the beach. Anybody can go over there," Marilyn said.

"But maybe they watch the beach. Or maybe the person who broke into Summer's place lives over there. Imagine if they saw us over there," Piper said.

Summer was ambivalent. But Piper was becoming overprotective. Mia had taken Hildy's death hard—harder than she'd let on. Piper had become a zealot for her daughter's health, safety, and happiness. Summer felt defensive. Maybe Piper was right, but if she kept on like this, Mia was going to be afraid of everything. Afraid to take any risks.

Summer had a similar dynamic with Hildy, who'd written the book on overprotectiveness. Looking back, Summer saw the way her mom had often manipulated situations to protect her—including keeping her away from all things Bellamy.

"I agree it's too late to go over there," Summer said.

"But the moon is full. I'm sure we'd be able to find our way," Glads said.

"I'm out," said Lucy. "I'm exhausted and am turning in early." She pushed her plate away.

Peg drank a long pull from her wineglass. "I'm up for it." Her words slurred. "Why not? What else is there to do on this island?"

Summer's face heated. She'd always considered the off-season peaceful, but she could see how an out-of-towner might think it boring. Was it her responsibility as host to entertain these writers during their downtime? Another instruction her mom hadn't left her. She scooted around in her chair. Her eyes met Marilyn's.

Marilyn's eyebrows lifted as if to say, *Why not?*

"I'm happy to take you over there, Peg," Summer said. "But Mia? That's up to your mom. She's the boss of you."

"Mom!"

"I'll take you over there sometime, Mia. But just not tonight. Now let's please drop it," Piper said.

The table quieted as the women finished eating and drinking. Mia's eyes pleaded with Summer.

Summer shrugged.

She wanted to go home and sleep. She was a weary, emotionally drained hostess. "I suggest we go in the morning. So we can see everything better." She looked at Peg. "Unless you really want to go tonight?"

Peg took another sip of wine. "Oh, fine, let's go in the morning." She held up her glass. "Field trip?"

"Mom, can I go in the morning?"

"I'll think about it."

"Very well then." Mimi slapped her hands together. "We'll head over to Mermaid Point in the morning."

The never-ending weekend.

Piper caught Summer's eye and rolled her eyes. She recognized when she was beat.

A little of the tension dissipated. Piper had been like a sister to Summer. She hated the stress between them—and over a misunderstanding. Summer wouldn't have it. She needed to make it right. And she would.

Seized with a sudden longing to leave everybody at this table, to sit at her kitchen table with Piper and laugh over customers at the shop or the latest werewolf romance, she drew in a breath. The season held no joy for her. She just needed to grit her teeth and get on with it.

Too much of Hildy filled the season. Too much of Hildy filled this table. Definitely too much of her filled the shop. Maybe Cash was right: the only way to get over the horror of her mom's death was to leave the island—and these people—behind.

But did she want to run away again? It had never done her much good in the past.

And now that she knew her biological family was here, her ties had deepened. But at the same time, she still didn't know them. As had been made clear by her shock at seeing the castle.

Her family had a secret castle. But she also had to wonder if she was the only other secret they had.

Chapter Twenty-Two

Summer tossed and turned that night. Finally, she turned the light on and fetched her laptop. She'd not researched her biological father's family. Guilt caught in her throat. She swallowed it. Hildy hadn't wanted her to know who her father was, but Summer imagined she would've told her someday. Still, a slight pang of disloyalty stung her.

She searched on the Bellamy family. A string of articles about the murder appeared. Most of which she'd seen.

Here was a new one: *The Bellamy Maid and Her Murder: Twenty Years Later.*

> *Someone shot Jamila Bastana in the heart and then dumped her body into a boat, hoping she'd simply drift off. But the tiny maid of the Bellamy family did not go off into the night sweetly. She washed up, nearly intact, but with no clue as to who had killed her left behind. And, twenty years later, still none have come forward.*
>
> *"Even though Jamila was an employee of the family, they were quite close to her," says Deputy Chief Ben Singer. "Her death almost destroyed the family."*

That's what he'd said when they had talked earlier.

She continued to read the rest of article—nothing more from the young Ben.

The family refused to make public statements and will talk only to members of law enforcement, which is one reason the story has been surrounded by so many rumors, such as that the victim had been having an affair with one of the famous Bellamy brothers. We'll never know. But what we do know is that Bashir, the second-oldest brother, left the family and the business and moved to England to strike out on his own.

The Bellamy clan in England is even more difficult to reach than the one in Brigid's Island.

Summer sat back in her chair. If Jamila had had an affair, it would have been scandalous. She was only twenty-two. The brothers, then, must have been in their fifties or sixties. One of them was Summer's grandfather, Hassam, Rima's husband. Poor Rima. Not only had she discovered the body, but she'd endured rumors of her husband stepping out on her with the help.

No wonder she'd passed out when she saw the book. The poor woman had been through a trauma, and it kept circling back.

She continued to read.

Of course, if she were having an affair with anybody in the family, it would more likely have been with Omar, the son of Hassam, who is already engaged to billionaire heiress Arwa Gibran. And there is absolutely no evidence of any of this. It's pure speculation. But it's the kind of rumor that crops up when people aren't forthcoming.

Arwa was Fatima and Sam's mom. A billionaire heiress? Hmm. *And maybe people aren't "forthcoming," Mr. Reporter, because it's too painful to revisit.*

As Summer continued to read, she learned that Jamila was from the same small town in Egypt that the rest of the Bellamys had come from. She'd recently graduated from college and was working for the family to save up money to go to medical school.

Impressive.

She'd been with the family off and on for years, working summers and breaks until she graduated.

The arrangement sounded like a sweet deal for both the family and Jamila. What had happened? What had gone wrong? Who would've killed her? Brigid's Island had been even less populated then. No one had been murdered there in forty years. That, plus the fact that Summer's mom had been so enthralled with it, led her to believe there was more to the story.

Summer's eyes burned, and she shut the laptop. Maybe now she'd get some sleep. She couldn't believe she'd been hoodwinked into going to Mermaid Point tomorrow.

She pulled her nylon mask over her eyes to keep all spiders away from her face and went to sleep.

* * *

The alarm rang way too early for a Sunday morning, but Summer rose from her bed smiling and almost skipped downstairs, as this would be her last day of hosting. As soon as Mimi left, she'd be able to get on with her Christmas plans. The gifts. The decorations. The baking. All of it. She just wanted to get it all over with.

She made her way to the kitchen and made coffee. As it was brewing, she went into the living room and uncovered Mr. Darcy.

"Good morning, Mr. Darcy."

He lifted his wings and rocked back and forth. "Darcy loves Hildy."

Summer's stomach turned. The bird had had such a hard time when Hildy died.

"Hildy loved Darcy," Summer said. She reached in and rubbed the bird's head. "Summer loves Darcy too."

He purred—a noise that Hildy had taught him. Summer laughed every time he purred.

Thirty minutes later, bird fed, coffee made, and breakfast on the table, Summer went up to Mimi's room and knocked on the door. "Field trip!" she said.

No response.

"Mimi?" Summer knocked again.

She opened the door. Mimi wasn't there.

Her bed appeared as if it had been slept in. All of her things were still there—phone, gun, everything. But she was gone.

Summer's heart banged against her chest. *Calm down. Maybe she's in the bathroom. Or she went for a walk.* She ran to the bathroom—the door was open. Mimi wasn't inside.

She ran downstairs and went out onto her front porch to view the beach. It was empty.

"Mimi, where did you go?"

Chapter Twenty-Three

Summer sent out a text to the Mermaid Pie Book Club's inner circle. *Has anybody seen Mimi?*

She dialed Piper. "Mimi is gone."

"What do you mean?" Piper's voice ratcheted up a decibel or two.

"Not dead. Just gone. She's not in her bed." Her voice quivered.

"Maybe she went for a walk. Let's calm down," Piper said.

Summer's jaws twitched. "I looked, and I can't see anyone on the beach this morning."

"I'll be right over. We'll find her," Piper said, and clicked off.

Summer paced as text messages came in from the Mermaid Pie Book Club members. Nobody had seen her. Was the field trip canceled? *There's no point in going without Mimi*, Summer texted back to the group.

Where could she have gone? After prompting a trip to Mermaid Point, why just take off? Why leave all her things? And if she had left the place, why hadn't Summer heard her? She used to be such a light sleeper. But these days, when she finally drifted off to sleep, it seemed as if she could sleep through an earthquake.

That scared her—that she hadn't heard someone moving around in her own house. A chill raced through her as her hands balled into fists.

A rapping came at the door. Piper and Mia walked into the house.

"Good morning," Summer said. "Should we comb the beach for her?"

Piper nodded. "I can't think of anywhere else she'd be. It's Sunday morning. Nothing is open."

"Could be she went to church," Mia said. "That's the only place open."

"I'm sure she'd have left a note or something. Besides, we had plans," Summer said, as all three of them walked outside into the winter air. Nothing like a winter beach.

"Mia, please stay here in case she comes back. Text us and let us know. I'll go north and you go south," Piper said.

Summer and Piper walked the paths to the beach, as they had perhaps thousands of times. "If we don't find her, then what?" Piper asked.

Summer drew in a breath. "I guess we call the police."

"She's not missing unless twenty-four hours have passed or something, right?"

"I don't know, honestly, but since she was threatened, the police might want to search for her."

They stopped walking. "Let's hope that's not the case," Piper said, as her blond hair blew in the wind.

Summer wanted to hug her but refrained. "Thank you for helping me out."

"No problem." She stiffened. "Let's get to it, shall we?"

The cousins went off in their separate directions. The beach appeared empty in every direction Summer squinted. It was hard to imagine anybody awake and active this early on a Sunday—and on a dreary, windy day at that. As she walked, a figure came into view. Her heart sped up. Could it be Mimi? But as she got closer, disappointment set in. It was a man. Not just any man. Cash.

And he had spotted her. There was no turning back.

"Morning!" he said over the sound of rushing waves.

"Good morning." She walked toward him.

"What are you doing up so early?"

"I'm searching for someone. Have you seen a short, round lady wandering around here?"

He shook his head. "I've been here since sunrise." He gazed out toward the sky, over the ocean. "I've not seen anybody."

Her heart sank.

"What's wrong?" His hands went to his hips.

She explained.

"If I were you, I'd call the police. People think you need to wait a day or two, but it's not true in all cases. There's some crackpot out there threatening her."

Summer didn't tell him the rest of the story. That her home had been violated twice in the past two days.

She frowned at him.

He laughed. "He's not that bad, Summer."

She crossed her arms. "Whatever you say, Cash."

There was a somber air about him. She'd once known him so well. She could still read him. "Are you okay?"

"What? Who me?" He said, shoving his hands into his pockets. "Don't worry about me. I'm fine. You better get home and call Dad."

His tone was familiar to her ear, as if all the years hadn't gone by. It was as if they were still together, walking along the beach, dreaming about their future.

A lump formed in her throat. She suspected something was wrong, but she was the last person he'd talk to about it.

"You're probably right." She pulled her jacket tighter. "Have a good day."

"You too. And good luck with the old man." He grinned, showing off those dimples, now deeper with time.

As she walked away, she felt as if she were walking away from something important. The vibe grabbed at her back. She'd need to ask after him. In a place like Brigid's Island, the grapevine was active, small, and correct.

Summer walked along the water's edge, eyes peeled for any people anywhere. Nothing. It was just her, the ocean, and the sky. As she walked closer to her place, she spotted Piper walking back toward her.

"I saw a couple and an old woman I thought was her, but—" Her hands went up, and she shrugged. "How about you?"

"I ran into Cash. He'd been up there since sunrise, and he said he'd not seen anyone."

Piper's eyebrows lifted, and she leaned closer. "Cash?"

Summer nodded. "It's the second time we've talked."

Piper's mouth dropped.

"Oh, don't be so surprised. It's a small island."

Piper crossed her arms. "I'm glad to know he's getting out."

"What do you mean?" They ambled toward the house.

"His wife left him and the kids, ran away with Levi. You know who I mean?"

"The delicious firefighter?"

She nodded.

"Left him?" Summer's heart hurt. Poor guy. No wonder he was so down this morning.

"It's been rough," she continued. "The talk of the island. I'm sure he's humiliated, devastated. And the kids . . . I'm sure people haven't mentioned it to you because . . . well . . . the past."

Mia walked up to them. "I've not heard or seen anybody," she said. "Any luck?"

"No." Summer grimaced. "I guess I need to bite the bullet and call Ben."

Chapter Twenty-Four

"We need a forensics team," Ben said into his phone and then hung up, slipping it in his pocket. He turned back to Summer. "You didn't hear anything?"

She shook her head. "Nothing."

"They must have come through the window."

"But we locked the window the other day, remember?"

"It was unlocked. She must have reopened it."

"Why would she do that?" she said, more to herself than to Ben.

"Good question. She may have known the person." Ben shook his head, as if holding an inner conversation.

An officer interrupted. "I've not been able to reach her husband. I'll keep trying."

Ben nodded.

"But why would a friend come in through the window?" Summer persisted.

He clicked his tongue against the roof of his mouth. "Yeah. We've also found blood."

Summer went cold. Mimi was in trouble, and it had happened on her watch.

"Summer, let me get you another cup of coffee," Piper said.

"Aunt Summer?" Mia said. "Let's go sit down." She grabbed her by the elbow and guided her into the living room.

Soon, cops—a forensics team—had invaded her childhood bedroom. Heck, why should she care? It was like Grand Central Station. Someone had broken into her home at least three times. The new locksmith couldn't fix her door fast enough, as far as she was concerned.

Summer's phone alerted her to a text message from Poppy. *I hate to ask, but who's working today? I can usually handle a Sunday by myself, but not the Sunday before Christmas.*

I'll be there, Summer texted back. *Maybe Mia will be too.*

Thanks, Poppy sent back. *Any word?*

None.

Piper brought in the coffee just as Agatha stormed into the house. She found them in the living room. "How's everybody doing?"

Piper continued to pour Summer coffee. "We're okay. Somewhat frazzled, but that's to be expected."

"Mimi was kidnapped? That's crazy." She opened a plastic container. "I bought orange-cranberry muffins." She set the container on the coffee table.

"Not kidnapped, Mom. She's just missing," Piper said.

Summer swore she could smell the muffins right through the plastic. Her stomach growled. "I'm going to need one of those."

"She was sort of asking for it," Mia said.

"Who? What are you talking about?" Agatha said.

"I'm talking about Mimi. I don't like her."

"Mia!" Piper said.

"I'm serious. She's stuck-up. Plus, that book sucks. Have you read it?"

"I have." Piper sat on the overstuffed chair near the couch. "You're right. It's pretty bad."

"What's so bad about it?" Summer asked, handing out muffins and napkins.

"Where do I begin?" Mia said, and rolled her eyes. "Starting with an ancient Middle Eastern curse and ending with an implausible murder."

"I know, right?" Piper said. "I found the whole Middle Eastern thing to be very offensive. As if they are backward, superstitious people. The Middle East is rich with culture, science, history."

"So she was writing about the Bellamys." Summer bit into her muffin.

"Thinly veiled, I'd say."

"No wonder someone is angry," Mia said.

The muffin was still warm, and the orange flavor exploded in Summer's mouth. It was heaven. She refrained from shoving the whole thing into her mouth.

"That's no excuse," Agatha said. "I'm no fan of Mimi's, but to kidnap her? This is ridiculous! It's a made-up tale!"

"But there's enough real stuff in that book that makes me nervous." Piper took a bite of her muffin.

Once again, Summer resolved to read the book. "Like what?"

"Just the whole correlation between the Lalemay family in the book and the real Bellamy family."

Summer snorted. "She didn't attempt to hide it very hard, did she?"

"In the book, the murderer is a member of the family. I don't want to spoil it for you, if you're going to read it. It's ludicrous."

"Maybe they did have something to do with the murder," Mia said.

"That is categorically untrue," Ben said as he walked back in the room. "I was there. The family had nothing to do with the murder. They were devastated."

The room quieted.

"Do you think Mimi's disappearance is linked to her book? About the murder she wrote about?" Piper asked.

He put his hands on his hips. "I won't speculate."

Summer finished her muffin and considered eating another. "It seems likely. But then again, maybe we should approach it from another angle."

"We?" he said.

Summer ignored him. "If the book isn't the cause of her disappearance, what else could it be?'

"We'd have to dig into her background to find that out," Piper said.

"Precisely."

"Wait a minute." Ben stormed across the room. "I warned you, Summer. You need to just back off."

"You warned me about the guy at the event. You said nothing about Mimi's background. What else could it be, if not the book?"

"It's definitely the book," Mia said. "Any idiot could see that. She's stepped into something she can't scrape off her shoe."

"Mia!" Piper said.

Summer smiled. Agatha rolled her eyes.

"I don't think you ladies need to worry. Leave the investigation to us. We'll find her and get her to safety."

Summer shivered at the word *safety*. What if Mimi wasn't all right? What if she was hurt—or worse? Her stomach felt queasy. She looked up at Ben. "When do you start searching?"

"We've got a team on its way from Raleigh."

"Can we help?" Mia asked.

He splayed his hand out. "I appreciate the offer. But we don't know what's going on here. So let's hold off on any community organizing until later today. We're trying to reach her husband. If any of you know a better number than what we have, please let me know." He paused. "We'd like to hold off on publicity until tomorrow, if she doesn't show up tonight."

Tomorrow? Was it possible they wouldn't find her today? Of course it was. She might be gone forever. Summer dropped her face into her hands.

Chapter Twenty-Five

Summer had a feeling that Mimi wouldn't be leaving today. She had been so looking forward to her peace and quiet, and now here she was, wishing Mimi would walk through the front door.

"Maybe you should come and stay at my place until this all blows over," Agatha said, sitting next to Summer on the couch.

Summer's brain was foggy. She didn't want to think about that right now.

"Your place has been broken into three times. I think it's safer for you somewhere else." Aunt Agatha placed her bony arm around Summer and rubbed her back.

"I think she's safe now," Piper said. "With Mimi gone."

"That may be true," Agatha said. "But who wants to risk it?"

Summer didn't want to leave her home, but maybe Aunt Agatha was right. Recalling her mom's voice in her dream—*Danger!*—Summer shivered. Perhaps she was buckling under the stress of the circumstances.

"What if Mimi comes back?" Mia said. "Someone should be here."

Summer reached for a muffin. "I need to think about this. But thanks, Aunt Agatha, for the offer."

"You know you always have a place with me."

She did. And it warmed her heart. Summer gazed across at her cousin, who still emanated chilly vibes. She'd say she had a place with Piper, too, if push came to shove. She was going to make it right with Piper. But first, they needed to find Mimi.

Summer's stomach clenched. *Mimi.*

She glanced at Mia. "Didn't Ben say something about community organizing?"

"He said not to do it yet," Piper answered with an edge in her voice.

"Oh." Summer knew better than to argue with that tone.

"I don't think it would hurt for us to look around, you know, some places on our own. They don't have to know," Agatha said, never one to be deterred by her daughter's tones. "We won't put flyers up or advertise it, for god's sake."

"Don't be ridiculous. She could be anywhere, from one of the coves to someone's house. We'd never find her. We have nothing to go on." Piper drank her coffee.

The doorbell rang, and Mia went to answer it.

Peg and Lucy entered the living room.

"So it's true, she's actually missing," Lucy said.

"Not a publicity stunt," Peg said.

"Absolutely not."

"She's pulled some doozies," Lucy said.

"I hope she's okay," Peg said. "She's no spring chicken. Just the fear and anxiety she must be feeling . . ."

"Has anybody contacted her husband?" Lucy asked.

Summer shrugged. "Ben has been trying. There's a problem with the number."

"I have his number." Peg went off in search of Ben.

"I see the police are here. Are they searching?" Lucy said.

Summer nodded and explained the details.

Peg walked back in. "I figured she chose to write about Mermaid Point to get attention, but now I'm curious," she said. "Aren't you?" She directed the question at Lucy.

"What do you mean?"

"It seems personal. Like she was on a mission."

"If that's the case, it's certainly failed."

A group of men marched through Summer's living room, directed by Ben.

"The forensic team?" Peg asked.

Nobody answered.

* * *

Mia and Summer stole away from the coven of amateur sleuths to go to Beach Reads.

"Any word?" Poppy said, peeking up from straightening the register counter.

"Nothing," Summer replied.

"Gram thinks we should all be searching for her," Mia said.

"But Ben said to hold off." Summer went into the stock room, then into her office, and dropped her purse into her chair. Poppy and Mia followed her. "In fact, Ben wants us to keep quiet. He wants time to work on it before the press gets wind of it."

Poppy appeared in the doorway, looking festive in a Christmas sweater and white fur boots. "Well, Glads and Marilyn have launched their own search. Nothing the cops can do about that."

"I guess not." Summer stood with her hands on her hips. "Where do you even begin to search?"

Poppy shrugged. "I have no idea."

The bell above the door rang, which meant the first customer of the day was entering the store.

"The show must go on," Summer said, even though she had no idea how she'd make it through today. Usually, the day after an event, the group gathered right after work for a discussion. But today Summer just wanted to get home and see if the police had found Mimi. But she had the whole day to get through first.

Her phone alerted her to a text, making her jump a little. Was she that on edge?

Good morning, said the text. Sam. *Are you working today?*

She recalled she'd told him she'd not be available until Monday. But man, she'd love to see him and maybe run some of this Mermaid Point stuff by him as well as ask about the family castle. Castle, for god's sake. Summer's biological father had lived in a castle tucked into the side of the mountain. Between that, all the break-ins, and Mimi's disappearance, Summer was feeling like she was living in a gothic novel.

Yes, she texted back.

I might stop by, he texted back. *I know you're busy and we talked about getting together tomorrow. But I have some gifts to get.*

Great, Summer replied. *This is the place for gifts.*

Poppy reentered the stock room. "Have we gotten the new Deanna Raybourn in?"

"It's on back order." Summer followed her out to the store. Mia was already straightening shelves and cleaning up a bit. Even though they'd cleaned the store yesterday, somehow they'd missed some things. Books were out of place and needed to be straightened. Hildy used to say the book fairies came in the middle of the night to have a party. Summer cracked a smile. Book fairies. That was so Hildy.

Summer regarded the customer eagerly awaiting news about the book. "We're hoping to get it in tomorrow."

"I hope so," she snapped. "I need it for a gift at the office." She paused. "I like to support my local bookstore. But I may have to go to Amazon for this book. They deliver quickly."

Summer gritted her teeth.

"I'm sure we'll have it in tomorrow," Poppy said.

The woman huffed off.

Thus began the Sunday-before-Christmas shopping day at Beach Reads.

Chapter Twenty-Six

A few hours later, Marilyn and Glads bounded into the crowded store just as Summer was checking out the last person in a long line of customers. They came and stood near her.

As soon as she was finished, she glanced up at them. "What's up, ladies?"

"We've not been able to find her." Glads shoved her hands into her jacket pockets and rocked back and forth.

"We've searched everywhere," Marilyn said.

"Everywhere? Really?" Summer cocked an eyebrow.

"Well, not in houses, of course. Whose house would we even look in?" Marilyn said.

"Start with that creepy guy who wanted to buy all of her books," Mia said. "Where does he live? What's his name, even?"

Summer reached down behind the desk and slid out another box of the mermaid Santa pins, then added them to the few that were left. She didn't think it was a good idea to give Mia details. "I can't remember his name. Besides, Ben says he's very dangerous."

"Well, that does it, then—we need to find him. He might have Mimi," Marilyn said. "I'm going to cancel my tat appointment."

"Another tattoo? Do you have any space left?" Summer asked.

"Never you mind."

"If he's not local and he's rich, which I assume he is, then he must be staying at the Foster Inn," Glads said. "I have a few connections there with the staff. I'll make a few phone calls."

"But this guy is very dangerous, according to Ben," Summer said. "Maybe we should leave this up to the police."

"Please," Glads said. "You know what our local cops are like. Besides, Ben needs help."

"He's called in help from Raleigh," Summer said. Here she was, defending Ben Singer.

Glads walked off into the stock room, her phone to her ear.

"Excuse me." A customer came up to Summer. She held a handful of books. "Can you tell me if this is the latest book in the series? It's so hard to tell. I don't know why they don't make it clearer, like with numbers or something."

"Sure, let me look." Summer flipped through the pages to the series page in the front of the book. "It's not listed here, so I assume it's the newest one."

The woman beamed. "Thank you."

"Anytime." Summer's heart lightened just a bit. If she focused on the task at hand, helping customers and selling books, she could almost pull herself away from worrying about Mimi's disappearance.

At this internal reminder, her stomach sank. If someone had entered her home and taken Mimi, Summer wasn't sure she would ever feel safe there again. She checked her phone messages to see if the locksmith had called. Nada. She wondered about getting a security system. That idea blew her mind. A security system for her little pink beach cottage?

Life kept getting stranger and stranger.

"Excuse me." A voice came up behind her, startling her.

"I'm sorry. I didn't mean to scare you." The woman smiled. "Where is the ladies' room?"

"Upstairs," Summer said. "When you get to the top of the stairs, make a right past the huge green mermaid painting. You can't miss it."

"Thanks," she said, and took off for the stairs.

"You seem kind of jumpy," Mia said as she came up to her. "Are you okay?" Her niece observed her with concern in her eyes.

"I am a little jumpy, I suppose."

"If I were you, I'd stay with Gram. I'd be jumpy too."

"Well, I guess I'm a bit stubborn," Summer said.

"I'll say that again," Mia retorted, rolling her eyes. "Even Aunt Hildy used to talk about how stubborn you are."

Summer cracked a smile. "What else did she say about me?"

"What is this? Third grade? You'll get nothing more out of me." Mia smiled.

Glads came back. "He's there. The guy."

"What guy? Who?" Summer said.

"The man who wanted to buy all the books. He's staying at the Foster."

Summer's heart jumped. "Is he alone?"

"My friend thinks he's alone, but she's going to snoop around a bit."

"Did you tell her we're searching for Mimi?"

"I did. She knows to be careful."

"Maybe I should let Ben know . . ." Summer said, more to herself than to Glads.

"I shouldn't think so," Glads said. "My contact is someone he's not very fond of."

Summer harrumphed. That wasn't unusual.

Glads excused herself and went upstairs. Marilyn was making a pot of fresh coffee. Poppy was behind the register. And Summer and Mia were walking the floors, cleaning up, and asking if the customers needed help.

Just as Summer straightened a wreath, Sam came up behind her. "Hello, sister," he said.

She turned. "Hello," she said, and hugged him. "It's good to see you."

"I know it must seem strange, the way I left the island. But I'm back now for a good long while, now that Grandma is here. She's getting senile, and we had so much business to take care of with her. We needed to wrap it up and bring her back here. Better doctors."

"Ah, I see. Well, what can I help you with?"

"My nephew is about Mia's age. Fifteen? I'm trying to get him interested in reading. I thought maybe you knew something that would do the trick."

"Let's ask Mia, shall we?" Summer said.

The two of them went off in search of Mia and almost ran into Glads. "I found out the name of the man staying at the hotel. It's Bashir, all right," she said. "And he's got another man and a boy with him. No Mimi."

Sam's face fell. "That's my cousin. What's going on here?"

"We've got some catching up to do." Summer took him by the arm and led him to the back.

Chapter Twenty-Seven

After Summer gave him the rundown of all the events, Sam sat at her desk chair, stunned.

"So the box with the photos was stolen?"

"It breaks my heart."

"Mine too."

"Do you know anything about any of this?"

He shrugged. "Not really. I do know that Bashir is—well, 'eccentric' is what we call him in the family. His father is quite ill. I'm not sure what he's doing on the island. I've heard about the murder my whole life. Not directly, but I caught bits and pieces about it growing up, when the adults were talking. I've never been curious enough about it to ask questions. I guess it was always just a scary thing that happened a long time ago in my mind. Nothing to do with me."

"Well, Mimi is missing. I assume someone took her. If it's not Bashir, who could it be? Any idea?"

He knit his eyebrows. "None. If it has to do with her book and the murder—well, I've not even read it."

"Neither have I."

"Maybe her vanishing has nothing to do with the book or the murder."

Mimi seemed like a character out of a book herself. Perhaps somewhere in her life she'd come across the wrong character. "That is a possibility. But with all the publicity and threats and break-ins, I think it's more likely it has to do with the murder at Mermaid Point. And unfortunately, that brings our family into the spotlight."

"The only people still alive who'd know anything about it at this point are our grandmother and our uncle in England, and neither one is well. When Mimi came to us, we told her that. My father and mother are both gone. My sister and I weren't even born when it happened."

"I hear you. I was born shortly after the incident. My mom saved clippings about the murder for years."

His head tilted. "Maybe your mom knew something about it."

"I think she may have known the young woman who was killed. Surely our dad did as well. I'm sure it affected them both greatly."

Mia came bounding into the room. "I need more water. It's getting so warm out there." She reached into the small fridge in Summer's office. "Hi," she said to Sam.

"How are you, Mia?"

"Thirsty." She took a long slug of water.

"Sam is looking for a delightful book for his nephew, who's about your age and not much of a reader."

"What does he like to do?" she said.

Great question. Best question ever. What a smart kid.

"He likes to play computer games. Day in and day out. I'm very worried about him."

"What kind of games?"

"I don't know . . . one of them is very sword and sorcerer."

"Follow me," she said. "I've got you covered."

Summer was glad Poppy had beefed up the rather small YA section in the store. She planned to get more books in than just romance and mysteries, though those books would always be the cornerstone of Beach Reads.

He stood and turned to Summer. "Are we still on for lunch tomorrow?"

"I wouldn't miss it," she said. She watched her brother walk off with Mia. *Her brother.* Life was full of surprises. Would she have known about him if her mom hadn't died? Would he have had the courage to confront her mom with his boxes of photos and memories?

Hildy had agency, but she was easily approached. Summer liked to think she would have welcomed him. But maybe not. Dread came over her. Her mom had gone to great lengths to keep Summer from knowing her father. She probably wouldn't have liked this turn of events at all. Summer shivered and reached for a sweater.

But what could be the harm in Summer's having a relationship with her biological family?

She'd always wondered why her mom had been so secretive about her father. These days, unmarried women often had babies and even collected money from their baby daddies without issue. But the 1980s were just the cusp of all that starting to happen. Hildy had been vigilant with her secret. Nobody knew. Nobody. Not even Agatha.

Summer's phone buzzed. She picked it up and read the text. It was from Ben. *We're all done here. The locksmith is here. I'm going to run the new key over to you.*

Thanks, Ben, she texted him back.

She walked back out into the fray of the bookstore.

Two hours later, a few straggler book buyers were browsing and the crew was starting to clean up and get ready to close. Mia was straightening the books, Poppy was behind the register, and Summer was walking the floors downstairs. She loved this part of the day, even though she was usually exhausted. As she picked up a few out-of-place books, she felt more pressed than ever to get out of the store today. With Mimi missing, a feeling of unwarranted anticipation moved through her. It was as if she expected Mimi to walk through the door any minute.

Instead, Ben walked through the door.

He nodded a hello.

"So, what's going on?" She took the key from him.

"We have search crews on it. It's obvious someone entered your house and took her. And with everything leading up to that, we thought it best to start searching right away."

"Why would someone take her?"

"That's a good question, but one I'm not qualified to answer." He grimaced.

"Attention, shoppers. The store will close in fifteen minutes. Please make your purchases now." Poppy's voice came through the speaker and briefly drowned out the Christmas music that had been playing.

He started to walk away.

"Ben?"

He turned back to her.

"What about this Bashir? My sources say he's still on the island."

"We are on him. Don't you worry. If he had Mimi, we'd have found her by now. He's on probation, and we always know his whereabouts."

Relief washed over Summer. Even though Sam had said Bashir was just "eccentric" and not dangerous, family could be completely blindsided. "That's great to know."

"You're not 'investigating' this case, are you?" He used air quotes.

"No." A wave of nausea threatened to overtake her. "Not yet." Summer hadn't enjoyed investigating her own mother's death. And she wouldn't enjoy poking her nose into this one. But she felt as if she was missing something that might be right in front of her face. And she felt obligated to help as much as she could, since it was Beach Reads that had brought Mimi to Brigid's Island and her house she had been stolen from.

"We've got a team of experts on this, not just us, so it's in good hands. In the meantime, we're not going to the press with this yet. Please keep it under wraps. We'll find her. If she's on this island, we will find her."

If she's on this island. Summer shivered. Mimi, the uncozy cozy mystery writer, could be in Mexico or California by now.

Chapter Twenty-Eight

"What did he want?" Glads sidled up to her as she was packing up her things and getting ready to go home.

"Just to touch base." Summer lifted her bag, noting that *Mermaid Point Murder* was still there. She had yet to read it. Now she didn't know if she ever would.

"The other writers are still here," Glads said. The two of them walked out of the office and stock room.

Summer stopped walking. "What? Why?"

"They're staying on their own dime. Don't worry. They're staying because they're concerned about Mimi."

"Didn't seem like there was any love lost," Summer said.

"No. But she is one of their own, I suppose."

Everybody else had left. Summer and Glads were alone. Summer flipped off the stereo system and welcomed the quiet. She and Glads stood a moment among the books, soaking in the silence. Christmas. Books. Mermaid paintings.

"They say if they don't find a missing person within twenty-four hours, their chances of survival are slim," Glads said, walking toward the door.

"Well, aren't you the bearer of good news?" Summer stepped out, locked the door, and pressed in the code—a new alarm she'd had installed since she'd taken over managing the shop. Hildy had been way too trusting of people.

"Seriously." Glads stood beneath the mermaid arch over the door, her face resolute. "She must be so scared."

Summer's stomach dropped. "Yes." They started walking down the boardwalk. "I don't mean to be flippant. I'm very concerned. We brought her into obvious danger."

Glads frowned. "We need to find her."

"Did you and Marilyn look in places like the cove? Where else?"

"Yes, everywhere we could think of. But it was like trying to find a needle in a haystack. It's a small island, but too big for two women to completely cover."

"Besides, what would you do if you found her?" Summer and Glads walked past the arcade, which was closed on Sundays during the off-season.

"That's a good question." Glads laughed. "But I'm sure we'd figure something out. But I feel like we need to be doing something." She snapped her finger. "Flyers. We need to blanket the island with them."

"Ben has asked us to keep her disappearance quiet for now."

"That's odd. I mean, I'd think we should announce to get all the help he needs."

"It seems strange. But he has his reasons, I guess."

They stood at the end of the boardwalk, the point where they would part ways—Summer to walk the beach toward home and Glads to go to the parking lot. But Glads stood, appearing lost.

"Are you okay?" Summer asked. "Do you want to come to my place for a cup of tea? Maybe some supper?"

Glass looked toward Summer's home and then back the other way. "I'm not sure you should be alone."

"I have a new lock," Summer said. "Ben dropped off the key. I'll be fine."

"Hildy would never forgive me if I let something happen to you." She blinked hard.

"Oh Glads." Summer stroked her shoulder. "I miss her too." She paused. "If it would make you feel better, why don't you come over and spend the night?"

Glads's face cracked into a smile. "Okay. I'll go home and get some stuff."

"Good. I'll order pizza. How does that sound?"

Glads nodded. "Very good." She walked off. "See you soon."

Summer hefted her bag onto her shoulder and headed down the beach for home. Her pink cottage with turquoise shutters awaited her.

Dusk was coming on, and the glassy water rippled in the glowing light. The empty beach felt menacing tonight, even though she usually liked it. She had to admit—she was on edge. Someone had come into her home at least three times, and the last time they had stolen Mimi right out from under her nose.

How could she sleep through that?

She stood and contemplated her house. The Christmas lights were lit. The timer worked.

A shadow moved across them. She blinked. What was that? A cat? No, it was big. A person?

She kept moving toward her house. Another movement came from the shadows. She stopped. Prickles ran up and down her spine. There was someone on her porch. She reached for her cell phone and approached her house.

"Hello?" she said out loud.

As she came closer, she perceived that it was more than one person. Peg and Lucy, the cozy mystery writers, were in a confab on her front porch.

"Oh, there you are," Peg said. "We've been waiting to talk with you."

"Oh, nice," she said, thinking otherwise. "Please come on in."

Summer stood at her door and fiddled with the new key. It worked without effort, and she twisted the doorknob to open the door. She couldn't shake an awkward feeling. What were these two up to? What could they hope to accomplish by staying on the island?

Lucy had a bottle of wine tucked under her arm. "We need to talk."

"Okay." Summer eyed the bottle. "Glads is coming over, and I was going to order a pizza. Is that okay with everyone?"

"Then we better get to it quickly," Peg said. "Glasses?"

Summer reached into her cupboard and pulled out the wine-glasses. Peg poured.

The women both bore a serious countenance, as if they were getting ready to drop bad news. "What's going on?"

"First, promise to not get the police involved," Peg said.

"What?" Summer's prickles came back. "I will do no such thing, ladies."

"Okay," Peg said, sipping her wine. "We had you pegged wrong. Never mind. We won't get you involved."

"Does this have something to do with Mimi?"

They nodded.

"Well then, you should tell the police." She couldn't believe that had just come out of her mouth.

"We absolutely can't do that," Lucy said, fiddling with the collar of her red turtleneck.

Summer's brain clicked into action. If these two had news they couldn't tell the police, then someone must have reached out to them. "Is there a note?"

Neither woman answered her, which was answer enough.

Clearly, they were not going to talk until she promised not to tell the police. "Okay. I promise to keep this a secret. What's going on?"

Lucy's hand trembled as she lifted her glass to her lips.

Peg pulled out a note from her bag. It was printed on Christmas stationery etched in gold.

Mimi is alive and well. But she won't be for long. It's up to you to deliver my instructions to Summer Merriweather.

Summer's heart beat fiercely against her rib cage. She gasped.

She needs to put the bookstore up for sale. The moment she does that, she'll get an offer from my lawyer. We will pay her in cash. And deliver Mimi back to her. Do not get the police involved. Or you will never see Mimi again.

Chapter Twenty-Nine

Sell the bookstore. At one point in Summer's life, that was exactly what she'd planned to do. She needed the money and wasn't fond of the place. But even though she'd not officially resolved to keep it, Beach Reads had grown on her, and the idea of selling it to a stranger, especially the one who'd kidnapped Mimi, sickened her.

"Summer?" Lucy said. "Are you okay?"

"I'm not selling the bookstore. I'm not doing business with a person who kidnapped Mimi."

"Are you crazy?" Peg said. "You have to. They'll kill her if you don't."

"It's just a bookstore," Lucy said. "We're talking about a woman's life here."

Summer's throat tightened. "It's not just a bookstore. My mom built that business. It's a place for the community of readers . . . and coffee drinkers . . . and mermaid lovers . . . and . . ." She drew in air.

Peg reached out and touched her hand. "It's a very special bookstore. And I get why you don't want to sell it."

"We sort of have a plan." Lucy clutched the Christmas tree charm on her necklace, sliding it back and forth.

"Sort of?" Summer wanted to call Ben, the FBI, and the CIA. These two had a plan?

Lucy's hand went still and she took a sip of wine, leaned forward. "Her kidnapping is linked to the murder on Mermaid Point. If we solve it, we've got the person who has Mimi."

Summer refrained from screaming. She concentrated on keeping her voice low. "Is that all? So many people have tried to solve it over the years, and the police couldn't solve it. What makes you think you can?"

Peg shrugged. "It's what we do in our books. Why not in real life?"

Summer's ears burned with fury. How absurd. A woman's life was in jeopardy. Someone wanted the bookstore in exchange for Mimi's life. And two cozy mystery writers were going to save everybody? Her chest tightened.

"We need to figure it out. It's obvious that the killer is still alive. The killer didn't want Mimi writing the book, and now they have her. So it's clear that if we figure out who the killer—"

"Then what?" Summer leaned forward. "What do you expect to do? Make a citizen's arrest?"

Lucy frowned. "We'd not gotten that far. But you see the logic, correct?"

"It's book logic. Things don't unfold like that in actual life. Murders go unsolved. People convicted of murder get out of prison and kill again. It's a sloppy system, not something that could be finished by page three hundred and twenty." Summer's pulse rushed in her ears.

The two women quieted and drank their wine.

Peg sat her glass down. "Have a better plan?"

Summer wilted. "Not yet."

"The one thing we have going for us is there's no date on this. No deadline. But I assume they want the sale to happen ASAP."

Summer brought her wineglass to her mouth with a slightly trembling hand. "How could they expect to buy a bookstore and remain anonymous? The logic is flawed."

"I assume it would all be done through lawyers. Attorney-client privilege and all that. People with money can do whatever they like." Peg tapped her fingers on the table.

Summer detected a bitter note in her voice. "So you're thinking the kidnapper and perhaps the murderer has money."

Peg nodded.

"Why do they want the bookstore? It would mean nothing to them. A drop in the bucket."

Peg leaned in. "Precisely. Why the bookstore?"

"Sounds personal to me." Lucy slurred her words. "But then again, what do I know?"

"Maybe." Summer's brain ran through reasons, but it couldn't find one that made sense.

"If we dig a little, we might find a link between the bookstore and the killer," Peg said.

"Don't be absurd," Summer said, but a nagging sensation plucked at her. Her mother had kept clippings and followed the case. Hildy could never have been involved in a crime. This much Summer understood. But maybe something else was going on here. Hildy had her own sense of justice.

"You're a Bellamy," Peg said.

The words hit her with a rush. "Only biologically. I know nothing about those people."

"But you could find out." Lucy lifted her glass. "You have every reason to snoop around."

True. And she had planned to do that anyway. The Bellamys were a mysterious bunch. They'd been torn apart by the murder of a young employee. The brothers had gone their separate ways. And one of their sons had gotten a local woman pregnant. Summer's own heritage had been kept secret from her. Her, the daughter of a local bookstore owner. *Bookstore.*

Maybe Lucy and Peg were right. Perhaps there was a link. But if so, it was tenuous.

How would she find out? Sam seemed unaware. Fatima probably knew even less. But Rima? She knew something. Of course she did. That's why she'd passed out when she saw the book. She'd been there. She'd discovered the body of the young woman. Summer needed to speak with her, but it would be tricky. She didn't want to dredge up what were obviously painful memories. She needed to approach her carefully. She didn't have time to develop a relationship and build trust with her. But Sam and Fatima had one. She'd talk with them first about how to bring this up to Rima. "I'm having lunch tomorrow with my half brother and sister—my father's other children. I will ask Rima, my grandmother. If anybody has any helpful memories of the murder, it's her."

Peg straightened. "That's a good idea. I'm going to the courthouse and getting the police records tomorrow, first thing."

"And I'm going to the library." Lucy set her glass down.

A knock sounded. Summer rose from the table and answered the door. "Glads!" She'd forgotten about her coming for the night. "Come in. I have company."

"Oh?" Her eyebrow lifted. "It's not the cops, is it?"

Summer scoffed. "No."

Glads left her bag in the hallway. "I'll get that later." She walked into the kitchen. "Where's the pizza?"

Chapter Thirty

After a fitful night, Summer readied herself for the day. She wished she could transport herself and move time forward. She was having lunch with her new family. It seemed like the strangest of dreams. Surreal, even. Between that and Mimi's disappearance, Summer's reality was a thing of the past.

Glads sat at the kitchen table with Aunt Agatha and Piper, who had, evidently, brought quiche.

"Good morning, sleepyhead," Aunt Agatha said.

"Did you sleep at all?" Piper asked.

"Off and on. Good morning, Aunt Agatha. I know it's a bit late, but—"

"No worries. I'm not your keeper. We just came by to check on you and to feed you. Glads said you didn't eat last night."

Summer glanced at sheepish Glads. "You told them everything, didn't you?"

"She absolutely did!" Agatha said. "You should've called us last night."

Summer groaned. "Nobody is supposed to know!"

"We can help," Agatha said.

"How?" Summer poured herself a cup of coffee. She had wanted to single Glads out. Why she'd brought the rest of them into this, Summer would never know.

"Anyway, you need us to," Agatha said.

Summer drank her coffee. "Good to know. Right now, I think we're covered. The police are searching for Mimi, and that's the most important thing."

"But the bookstore—" Glads said.

"Is going to be okay." Summer drew in air and let it out slowly. "I'm not selling the bookstore."

"Unless maybe you should." Piper stood and took her plate to the sink. "You know, get the cops involved and set up a kind of a sting."

"Last resort." Summer scooped a slice of quiche onto her plate. Her stomach growled. She hadn't eaten anything since yesterday around lunchtime.

"So, you're going to question Rima today?" Glads asked.

"I'm going to have lunch with my new family." Summer took a bite of the quiche and swallowed. "And Rima will be there. I hope to be able to bring the subject of the murder as tactfully as I can."

Piper snorted. "Good luck with that. Tact isn't your forte."

Summer took another bite, steering clear of the goading. "Where's Mia this morning?"

"She doesn't have to be at the store until noon, so she's sleeping in."

"That kid is something else," Glads said. "She's been such a huge help at the store."

Piper beamed.

"Of course she has," Agatha said, with a chiding tone.

"Speaking of the store, I better get going. Sorry to eat and run." Summer stood and placed her dish in the sink. "Please lock up when you leave."

She was on a mission. The busier she kept herself this morning, the quicker time would go and the sooner she'd be eating lunch with her new family. But when she opened the door to leave, Ben Singer was on her stoop.

He nodded. "Good morning, Summer. Can I come in?"

"I was just leaving. I need to get to the bookstore."

"I won't take long." He stepped around her and walked into the house.

Summer's heart raced. She didn't need him in her home. What if the person who had Mimi was watching? Would he think she'd called the police?

She followed him back into her house.

"What's going on here?" Ben said as he walked into the kitchen.

"Breakfast?" Agatha said with a slightly sarcastic tone.

He frowned.

"Do you have news?" Summer stood, impatient. She wanted to get on with her day, and she wanted Ben out of her house.

He sat down at the table.

"Would you like some coffee?" Glads asked.

He smiled. "Always."

Glads rose from her chair and went to the cupboard to find a coffee cup as Summer's throat closed and her head spun. Why would she do that? The kidnapper didn't want the cops involved.

"Now?" Summer prompted.

"The bad news is, we still haven't found her," he said as Glads slid the full cup over to him. "Thanks."

"You have good news?" Summer asked.

"Yes. We've gotten good prints from both your doorknob and your windows. We're running them through the system. We also have a few leads." He slurped his coffee.

"Leads?" Piper said.

He nodded. "Yes, I'm not at liberty to discuss those with you yet. But we are moving along in the investigation. I wanted to let you know." He glanced at Summer. "You don't look so good. Are you okay?"

"Thanks." She folded her arms. *I want you out of my house.* "I didn't sleep much last night."

"Of course you didn't," Agatha said.

"Have any of you heard from anybody? Seen anything odd?" he asked, setting his cup down on the table.

The women stilled.

"What do you mean?" Glads asked with a voice two octaves higher than usual.

The others went back to their coffee and quiche and avoided looking at Ben.

"I mean, in cases like this, often some little odd thing will be what breaks them. A stranger walking somewhere they don't belong. A weird phone call." He paused. "Also, if this is a kidnapping, often there will be contact from them. They want something. Usually money." He gazed around the table. "If you received word from a kidnapper, you'd be obligated to tell the law. Or you'd be implicated in the crime."

Piper stirred her coffee. Glads stood, took her plate to the sink, and rinsed it off.

"Of course we would tell you, Ben," Agatha said, looking directly at him, her chest moving up and down. Summer was impressed. Her aunt lied well.

"The longer we don't find her . . ."

"We know, Ben," Summer said. "We know and we're all a mess about it. Can't you tell? We brought her here. If something happens to her . . . it would be awful. Just awful. What exactly do you hope to do by scaring us like this?"

"I'm glad I scared you. It's a very serious situation. You should be scared." His eyes were full of warning. There was more to the story than he was telling them. More than he could tell them. Maybe he knew about the note. Maybe he was trying to warn them. He stood. "I want your word. If anybody reaches out to you, you'll let me know."

If they told him, they might lose Mimi for good. They couldn't risk it. But to lie to the police was serious business.

"Of course," Summer said, wishing she could tell him, wishing he'd swoop in and take care of it all with his magical police superpowers. But Summer had given up on fairy tales a long time ago.

Chapter Thirty-One

Summer walked Ben to the door. Just as she opened it, a thud and the sound of breaking glass came from the kitchen. She ran into the kitchen, Ben trailing her.

Agatha and Piper were helping Glads off the floor.

"Are you okay?" Summer said.

"Just clumsy." Red-faced, she dusted herself off.

"That was quite a fall." Piper scooped up pieces of the broken cup as Agatha helped Glads to a chair.

In that split second, Summer spied vulnerability in Glads. She appeared older, tired, and stressed. "You better get going," she said, looking at Summer. "I'll be okay. Just tripped over the chair leg."

"Are you sure?" Summer caressed her shoulder.

"We'll take care of her. You go ahead and go to work." Agatha said.

Summer turned to go and almost ran into Ben. "Didn't realize you were still here."

He just smiled. "I better go too."

The two of them walked out of the house into the cool air. Summer wished she'd worn a scarf this morning.

"I'll be in touch," Ben said as Summer walked off down the path toward the beach.

"Okay," she said, and kept moving. She felt his eyes still on her. As she turned and started walking along the beach, she could see him with her peripheral eyesight. He was still standing there, watching her. How odd. A sinking sensation crept into her gut. He knew. He knew they'd heard from the kidnapper. But how? Was it just his intuition, or was it something more tangible? Had someone leaked it to him? Piper, Agatha, and Glads were at her kitchen table this morning. Where were Lucy and Peg?

That was all she needed—to get arrested if he found out she hadn't told him everything. Would that truly be aiding and abetting?

She continued walking down the beach and breathed in the cool air. The ocean shimmered in the new morning light. A few people walked in the distance. But other than that, Summer was alone with the sea, sky, and sand. Just like she loved it.

The hot dog truck stood empty at the edge of the beach and boardwalk. Sometimes Summer could swear she smelled those hot dogs, even when the truck was closed. She stepped up onto the boardwalk, rounded the corner, and ran into a man. She was thrown off-balance and tried not to lose her footing, but it was no use. As she landed on her rear, she blinked and turned—the man kept running, and all she spotted was his bare behind.

Even though she was on the boardwalk, splayed out for all the world to see, she exploded into laughter. The streaker! She'd finally caught a glimpse of him. As she lifted herself up, a group of women sauntered down the boardwalk. "There he is!" one of them said, and pointed off in the direction he was running.

"Honestly, why doesn't someone arrest him?" one of the women said as they walked by Summer.

"He's depraved," another said. But Summer noted that she still watched him.

"We'll catch him next time."

Summer kept walking. While it was probably true that the man was depraved, she wondered what these women were going to do if they did indeed catch him.

She walked past the arcade and into Beach Reads. The familiar scent of patchouli and coffee wafted toward her as she entered.

Poppy stood at the coffee station, filling her cup. "Good morning." She stirred in some sugar, then looked up and caught a glimpse of Summer. "You look as if . . . I don't know . . ." She put her cup down and turned to brush dirt off Summer.

"Oh, I took a tumble. Ran into the masked streaker on the boardwalk. I mean, literally." Summer took off her jacket and went into the back to hang it up. Poppy followed.

"We're getting in our last big shipment before Christmas this morning," she said. "I've called Marilyn and Glads to see if they can help. I left messages."

"Glads is at my place, and she didn't mention it."

Poppy's eyebrows rose in surprise.

"She insisted on staying with me. She didn't want me to be alone."

"I'm glad. I was worried about that too. Any word on Mimi?"

"Not much. The police have a few leads, and they lifted some good prints from my door and window. But they've been unable to find Mimi. It's like she vanished into thin air."

"It's a small island. You'd think they'd have found her by now," Poppy said.

"Maybe she's off the island?" Summer shivered when she said it. If that was the case, they might never find her. Unless Summer sold the bookstore.

Not going to happen. She would not negotiate with a kidnapper. But then again, she didn't want any harm to come to Mimi.

"Are you okay? You're very pale."

"I'm fine, just tired, stressed. You know. The most wonderful time of the year."

Poppy frowned. "You don't need any of this."

"True." But her mind had been occupied with a million things other than this being the first Christmas without her mom. Maybe that was good. She didn't know. She used to think she understood so much. But that was before the world turned upside down.

Today, in just a few hours, she'd be sitting and dining with her new family. The ever-mysterious Bellamys. She had a million questions for them. Starting with the castle. Who lived in a castle in this day and age? And why a castle?

Of course, she had to find out more about them—and about the murder that haunted the island and had nearly destroyed the family. Surely Rima would talk with her about it.

Summer drew in air and released it slowly. She would have to be very careful in unearthing the past. Rima had passed out at the sight of the book. What would she do when a long-lost granddaughter questioned her?

Chapter Thirty-Two

After checking in with Ben one more time about Mimi, Summer walked into the restaurant, her pulse racing. She'd not been this nervous about meeting anyone since . . . well . . . ever. This was all so surreal. Mimi was missing, and here she was meeting the only family with ties to the murder at Mermaid Point—and they were *her* family.

The restaurant was one that Sam had chosen and Summer hadn't been to before. Housed in an old hotel, it reeked of class, with its chandeliers and white linen tablecloths.

The Bellamy clan were already seated.

Sam smiled as he spotted her from across the room. He stood. Fatima and Rima rose as she approached the table. Sam embraced Summer, then Fatima gave her a bear hug. She stepped away and waved to Rima.

Rima reached for Summer's hands, clasped them, and looked into her eyes. "I knew your mother. She was a remarkable woman. I'm so sorry to learn of her death."

Summer's mouth dropped. She gathered her wits enough to say thank-you just as the woman embraced her. She was thin, and Summer swore she felt her ribs as they hugged.

They situated themselves at the table, and Sam cleared his throat. "So here we are."

Summer managed a smile. "Yes." Here she was at a table full of Bellamys. A half brother and half sister and grandmother. All a part of the secret her mom had kept from her her whole life.

"How are things at the store?" Sam asked.

"Very busy with Christmas in a few days. We got our last shipment in before the big day this morning."

The server appeared at the table and handed them menus.

"What do you do?" Summer said.

"You don't know? We're in shipping. Have been for generations." He focused on the menu.

Summer glanced at Fatima. She smiled. "I work for the company too. Legal."

"She's such a smart girl," Rima said, then turned to Summer. "I hear you're a Shakespeare scholar."

Summer nodded. Or she used to be. Was she still? She ruminated about the Bard every day and needed to make a decision about her job at the university soon. "Yes, but now there's Beach Reads. That's keeping me very busy."

"Will you go back to university?"

"I don't know." She read the menu, hoping they'd pick up the cue to drop the subject.

After they ordered, a harp rendition of "Silent Night" played. Summer scanned the room and spotted a harpist in the corner.

"That's lovely," Rima said.

"I feel like I know so much about your mom, but you must have questions about our father," Sam said, fingers rapping on the table.

"I do. Mostly, what was he like? Was he strict? Was he smart? Handsome? Was he a good dad?"

They all laughed. “Slow down,” Sam said. “Hmm, yes, he was very strict with me. Not with Fatima.”

“No fair, Sam!” Fatima poked at him.

“I think there’s a measure of truth in that,” Rima said in a joking tone. “He doted on Fatima.”

There was a moment of awkward silence.

“But he was a great father,” Sam said wistfully.

Fatima lifted a glass. “Hear, hear!”

“I have a few pictures,” Sam said, reaching into his pocket.

“What happened to the box of pictures Sam gave you?” Fatima asked.

“It was stolen.” Summer set her glass down to handle the pictures Sam handed her.

“What?”

“My house was broken into, and the person who broke in stole the box.”

She studied the photos of her father. A square chin—which she hadn’t inherited, thank god. Startling black eyes—which she had inherited—along with sweeping black hair. “Handsome,” she said.

Rima beamed.

“Wait a minute! Someone broke into your house?” Fatima said.

If she only knew. Summer needed to be careful with her words. “Yes, all sorts of weird things have happened over the past few days while Mimi stayed with me. Someone broke into my house at least three times.”

“Mimi Sinclair is trash,” Rima said.

“Grandma!” Sam said. “We said we’d not get into this. This is supposed to be a pleasant visit.”

But Summer seized the opportunity. "It's quite all right. I don't know much about her and haven't even read her book." Rima sat back in her chair. Fatima blinked nervously. Sam rapped his fingers on the table. "But she did stay with me for several days because of the cozy Christmas event. That's when all the weirdness took place."

"The book is a pack of lies!" Rima said.

"It's fiction," Summer replied. "It's not meant to be a true-crime nonfiction book. She spoke about this at the event. She just took the bare bones of the story from reality and then embellished."

"I know some writers who've gotten into legal trouble for that. But as long as they are forthright about what they're doing, it's fine." Fatima turned to her grandmother. "I don't understand what the big deal is. Why this upsets you so much." Her voice softened. "I know it was a difficult time for you. For the whole family. But why bother with this? Why even pay any attention to it? It will all blow over."

Rima cleared her throat and fiddled with her bright-yellow scarf. "There are things you don't know about. And as far as I'm concerned, you never will. It was a dreadful time."

"I understand," Summer said, reaching out for her hand and gently squeezing it.

"I know you do," Rima said, just as the server brought their salads.

Murder was a terrible bond. But there it was.

"You know, my mom kept a box of clippings. She followed the case for years. It was so unlike her. Hard to make sense of." Summer stabbed her lettuce with a fork.

Rima frowned. "She was as devastated as the rest of us."

"You've never talked about it with us," Sam said.

Rima swallowed her salad. Her dark eyes watered. "And I never will."

Resolute. Regal. Not a person you could push. All of that came through in just those few words.

But what she didn't know was that Mimi Sinclair's life hung in the balance. Summer needed to prod more. Perhaps she'd wait until dessert.

Chapter Thirty-Three

Summer's appetite waxed and waned as she sat at the table, feeling as if she was on the edge of tears one moment and filled with unbridled joy the next moment. The Bellamys were lovely. How could her mother have kept them from her all these years?

"I wish I'd known you all growing up," she said impulsively. They silenced as they gazed at her.

"Was it difficult without a dad?" Fatima asked.

Summer nodded as tears threatened to surface once again. She blinked them away. "Oh, my mom was a fantastic mother. But yeah, it would have been great to have a dad." She paused. "She went totally silent when I asked about him. She wouldn't say a word."

"Sometimes wounds are so deep that you simply can't talk about them," Rima said, gazing off into the distance.

But it wasn't lost on Summer that Rima was probably one of the reasons her mom and Omar had not married. "Can you tell me more about what happened between them?"

Rima's chest rose and fell. "It wasn't that long ago. But it was a different time. Our son was promised to another."

"In the 1980s! It's not that long ago, and yet . . ." Fatima said.

Rima nodded. "You know this better than most, Fatima. Even today, it's difficult to marry for love sometimes. But if your family doesn't like the person you love, it's impossible."

Summer's heart dropped. "Is that what happened with Mom?"

"No." Rima held her hand up as if to say *stop*. Rings on her fingers glittered. She turned to Fatima and Sam. "You both know that your parents' marriage was arranged. Between two old families. These promises cannot be undone without horrible ramifications."

"Money," Sam said. "It all came down to that, didn't it?"

"Well, that was a part of it," Rima said slowly. "Our families were quite entwined businesswise; other members had married one another. I hated to see your dad so torn apart over this. But he and your mom made the best of it, and they suited one another."

"Were they happy?" Summer asked.

"Eventually," Rima said.

"We didn't know about your mom and you until he passed away." Fatima set her plate aside, her red nails gleaming against the white tablecloth.

"Of course your parents would not have told you about that," Rima said. "That he'd gotten a local girl pregnant and wanted to go against his family's wishes and marry her?"

There it was. A note in her voice that rubbed Summer the wrong way. *A local girl.* That girl had been her mother. A woman who loved Omar so much that she'd kept this secret from her daughter for years. But why? Was it because it hurt too much? Or was it anger? A sense of shame and regret?

Sam glanced at Summer and quickly looked away. He'd caught that.

"They came to us wanting to marry." Rima shrugged her bony shoulders. "It was impossible."

"How well did you know my mom?" Summer's jaw tightened. Her stomach turned as she considered her half-eaten pasta salad.

"Not well. All we knew was that our son was never around that summer."

Summer. It had been a summer romance.

Rima drew in a breath and let it out slowly. "It was a shock when they came to us."

"I didn't know they even tried."

Rima nodded. "Your mother was beautiful and very sweet. But your grandfather . . . he was unmoved. And I'm afraid he was unkind." Her voice cracked. "I sometimes wish I could have spoken up." Her chin lifted. "But I did the best I could under the circumstances."

"You were aware she was pregnant?" Fatima asked, incredulous.

"Yes, but we understood that if they didn't marry, she would not have the baby. Then the next thing we heard, she was going to give her up for adoption."

The baby was thirty-two years old and sitting at the table, taking in as much as she could and trying to feel something now. Feel anything. She was disassociating. Which was not necessarily a bad thing.

"It's all behind us now," Sam said. "We have a new sister. Let's be grateful we found one another."

Summer's stomach seized. "Excuse me." She stood. "I'll be right back." They watched as she found her way to the restroom, where sickness came over her hard and quick.

She splashed water on her face. As she dried the water off, she caught a glimpse of her rough and raw face. She couldn't shake the ominous feeling that Rima beamed rotten vibes.

But come on, Summer, you wanted to know. You've always wanted to know the truth. Now you do. And it's not pretty. She stared at her reflection. Of course. That was why Hildy had never talked about it. They'd wanted her to get rid of Summer, as if they could shove away the past, their son's indiscretions, with an abortion or an adoption. But Hildy had listened to her heart. She'd kept Summer. She'd loved her daughter with a ferocity that Summer was only now just beginning to understand. Hildy against the Bellamys.

Summer presumed there was more to the story. More ugliness. She didn't need to know anymore. Not now. She needed to know more about the murder. The other part of this sordid tale.

Not only was Mimi missing, but her mom had been interested in the murder case beyond what was normal for her.

As Summer walked over to the table, she spotted a young woman talking with the family. Voices were raised. She blinked, then bristled as she recognized Yvonne Smith, the reporter. Summer grabbed the woman by the shoulder. "I think you'd better leave." She glanced around and eyed a waiter who was making his way toward them.

"Is there a problem?"

"Please escort this person out of here. She's disturbing us."

"Yes, ma'am," he said.

"Wait a minute," Yvonne interjected. "I just have a few questions about Mimi's disappearance from your house."

Summer's face heated as all the Bellamys eyed her. "Please take her out."

As the waiter left with Yvonne, she sat back down. Coffee and dessert had arrived.

"What's this about Mimi?" Rima asked.

"I promised the police . . . it's imperative to keep it a secret." But it was no longer a secret if Yvonne was asking questions. Was it going to be all over the papers? “She disappeared from my house yesterday. It’s true.”

“You didn’t mention this?” Rima’s voice was steely cold.

“She couldn’t,” Fatima said. “You heard her. The police asked her not to.”

Rima stood. “Family is more important than the law.” She took her bag off the chair. “Sam, take me home.”

“Grandma—”

“I need to go home.” Her chin lifted as her voice deepened.

“Well, okay,” he said, standing. “I’m sorry, Summer.”

But Summer sat, allowing it all to sink in. The old woman was upset by Summer’s holding back information—not quite as upset that Mimi was missing.

Chapter Thirty-Four

Now that the news was out of the bag, the island was buzzing. Search groups were being formed. Amateur sleuths and Mimi fans were gathering to discuss their theories.

Summer, Peg, and Lucy congregated in Summer's Beach Reads office after closing to compare notes on their day.

"What was it like, meeting them?" Peg asked.

"Weird. And I found out nothing about the murder case. Rima has never talked about it and never will," Summer said.

"I get that," Lucy said. "It must have been traumatizing for her."

Summer had felt sorry for her grandmother, but now she didn't know how she felt. "She was very upset when she found out about Mimi because I hadn't told her. She said family is more important than the law."

"That's not surprising." Peg slid a file toward Summer. "The family has been linked to terrorism and Egyptian crime gangs, for a start. In the weeks before the murder, some stuff was going down in Reda, their hometown. A gang war of sorts. Two of the families involved were the Bellamys and get this, the family of the young woman who was killed."

Summer's heart almost stopped. "Did the police know about this?"

"I doubt it. They probably just focused locally, of course. It's a trick I use in my writing. I research current events during the time of the murder to add some context, and in this case, I looked at both London and Reda. London because that's where the other brother settled." Peg leaned forward across the table and opened the file. She pointed to the first copied article. "Bashir has been linked to a number of bombings in London and one murder."

"What do you mean by *linked*?"

"He was a suspect, but the authorities were unable to pin anything on him." She sat back and sighed. "Take your time reading those files."

"But what does this tell us about Mimi's disappearance?" Summer closed the file and brought it closer, planning to read it at bedtime.

"I guess it could mean that she was taken by the family. Or at least part of the family." Peg drank her water. "It's just a theory. But I'm sure her books stepped on some toes."

"But why? The murder happened a long time ago."

"Not long enough ago that people don't remember it," Lucy said. "And not long enough ago that whoever killed that young woman couldn't be alive and well and living on this island. Heck, might even be someone you know." She opened her files. "The police records on this are spotty."

"Ben's first murder case," Summer said. "He was quite moved by the reaction of the family."

"That's no excuse for sloppy police work. One mistake after the other. The person who discovered the body—Rima, your grandmother—well, she never gave a statement. She was deemed mentally unsound." Lucy lifted an eyebrow.

"I'm sure she was horrified," Summer said. "Shocked. Maybe she *was* mentally unsound."

"For a few days, weeks even, but the police have to get statements from everybody, even victims, rape victims, assault victims. It's very difficult on them, but the police do it. Why not this time?"'

"Good question." Summer made a mental note to speak with Ben about it. He was prickly, but it seemed as if this case still interested him.

"Rookie mistake," Peg said.

"So we have several avenues to explore here. Who has Mimi upset the most by this book? The police? The gangs? The family?" Lucy said.

Summer mulled all of that over as she drank her water. "There is another possibility. She seems rather disliked by you two. Maybe her disappearance has nothing to do with her book. Are there others that don't like her?"

"She's loved by publishers and readers. I can't speak for all writers in the mystery writing community, but I don't think she's highly regarded by most of us. She's a 'mean girl,' if you know what I mean."

Summer nodded. "Unfortunately, yes."

Peg frowned. "I caught her cheating on a game once during a reader event. I've never trusted her since."

"She does a lot for her readers. Has special events, like mystery train rides and reader luncheons," Lucy said. "They'd be shocked to know what she's really like."

Summer glanced from Lucy to Peg. Author politics. Hildy used to steer clear of it. As would she. She very much doubted an author would kidnap another author. They took their angst out on the page.

"We'd better go," Lucy said, standing. "I hope that all helps. If I can think of anything else, I'll let you know."

Peg stood too. "We'll be around until they find Mimi, or as long as we possibly can."

Summer's intuition pricked at her. If these women didn't like Mimi, why were they so concerned? Could it be some kind of Munchausen by proxy? Could these women have kidnapped Mimi and now be working to solve the case to throw the police off?

"Do you have someone staying with you?" Peg asked.

Summer nodded. "My cousin is going to stay with me tonight." People were taking turns so Summer wouldn't be alone until this all blew over.

Peg smiled. "Good. I don't think you should be alone."

But alone was exactly what Summer wanted to be. She needed to sort through the files on her table, but more than that, she needed to sort through what had happened today at the restaurant. She'd hoped to be welcomed into the family with no problems. But the Mimi situation was sticky and revealed that the family had serious ghosts in their closet.

Her stomach sank. When she'd first learned of Sam, it was as if her mother had left her a parting gift. But now she wasn't so sure. Her mom had kept them out of her life for a reason. It was more than pride or hurt. It might have been for Summer's own protection.

Chapter Thirty-Five

Back at home, Summer shuffled through the blog posts, articles, and reports Peg had left with her. She read over the police report one more time. When a knock came at the door, she assumed it was Piper coming to stay with her. But when she opened it, she found Aunt Agatha and Mia.

"Hey, where's Piper?"

"Sorry to disappoint," Agatha said, pulling her bag into the hallway.

"Mom's taking a shift tonight at the community center for the search." Mia picked up her grandmother's bag. "Where should I put this?"

"Someone will have to sleep with me and someone on the couch. Take your pick."

"I'll sleep on the couch," Mia said.

"Why's Piper at the community center?" Summer helped Mia with Agatha's bag. They started up the stairs.

"She's helping with the search for Mimi," Mia answered. The two of them slid Agatha's bag into Summer's room. "Putting flyers up tonight, I think she said."

Good old Piper, always doing the right thing. So much the opposite of Summer. She felt like the bad guy. She should be helping too. But then again, she had a bookstore to run, and it was a busy time of the year. "What does your gram have in that bag?" Summer's hands went to her hips.

"I have no idea." Mia shrugged. "They haven't found one clue about Mimi. They think she might be off the island."

They started back down the stairs. "Are they calling off the search here?"

"No, they're intensifying it—at least for a few days."

Summer and Mia walked into the kitchen to find Agatha brewing some tea, as was her habit. Chamomile before bed.

"I saw the police report there. Anything interesting?" Agatha said, placing cups on the table.

"Not really. I just need to talk with Ben. There was no interview with the person who found the body."

"Rima?"

Summer nodded.

"That doesn't sound right."

The teakettle went off, and Aunt Agatha plopped a tea ball into the pot to let it steep.

"I plan to ask Ben about it in the morning."

"Good luck getting a hold of him. The man is incredibly busy." She learned against the counter. "How did your visit go with the Bellamys?"

Mia sat down at the table and began sorting through the research materials. She dropped them. "Did you go to the castle?"

"No. We met at a restaurant. And to answer the question you're about to ask, it didn't go so well."

"What's all this?" Mia gestured to the papers on the table.

"It's all research on the Bellamys. Peg and Lucy did it and brought it here earlier. They think the Bellamys have something to do with what happened to Mimi."

"Crazy talk," Mia said. "Those people are so rich, why would they care about Mimi Sinclair?"

Summer cracked a smile. If only life were that simple. Not all rich people were happy and content. Just like not all poor people were sad and discontented.

Agatha bobbed the tea ball in and out of the steaming brew. "Because Mimi wrote about something that hit very close to home. I read the book." She looked at Summer. "You should too. There was an allusion to an out-of-wedlock baby. At first I figured it was you, but then the numbers didn't quite add up. Then I told myself that if we didn't even know who your father was, how would Mimi? It was just a coincidence." She shook her head. "I don't think any of this has to do with a baby—or your mom, for that matter."

She poured the tea into cups and set them on the table.

But Aunt Agatha hadn't been at that table with Summer's family today. Summer tried to talk herself out of the feeling that her grandmother knew something she wasn't saying. And Rima hadn't told the police anything at the time, which was very strange. She hoped Ben could clear that up. It doesn't seem like a mistake someone like him would make, even as a rookie cop.

Summer finished her tea. Weariness swept through her. "Thank you both for offering to stay with me. I feel a bit foolish having people stay with me every night."

"I think it's prudent," Agatha said. "Until we know about Mimi, we need to keep an eye on you."

Maybe I'm too tired to feel afraid, Summer reflected. No, that wasn't it. Or at least, she wasn't afraid for herself. She was afraid for Mimi. She'd been gone for more than twenty-four hours. Summer feared for her life. Those fears bubbled in the quiet, which Summer hadn't had much of—between the Christmas season, Beach Reads, and the whole family thing.

"I made vegan pumpkin bread for Christmas. Your mom loved it. I made a special loaf for you. We can have some in the morning," Aunt Agatha said. "You look exhausted."

Summer nodded. "I'm going to bed. Do you need anything?"

"No. I know my way around." Agatha winked. "You don't need to worry about me. Now go to bed."

A few minutes later, Summer melted into her bed, making sure to leave enough space for her aunt, who would quietly slip in later, no doubt. She willed away the images of the day: Ben at her kitchen table. Sam and Fatima at the restaurant. Peg and Lucy and all their research. But the last image in her brain before she nodded off was Rima and her cold, black eyes.

Chapter Thirty-Six

The next day, Beach Reads was already packed when Summer arrived. Poppy was behind the register and needed a break. Summer slipped right in and took over, with barely a break in the flow of people buying last-minute Christmas gifts.

"Will you be getting more copies of *Mermaid Point Murder* in?" a customer asked as she was being checked out.

Summer wanted to scream. "Not until after the holidays. I'm sorry. We have all of Mimi's other books."

The woman wore a Santa pin on her coat and a red velvet bag flung across her shoulder. Festive. Why did she want Mimi's book?

"You know that poor woman is still missing." She leaned across the counter. "I have a theory."

Summer cranked her head around to let her know that another customer was waiting.

"I think the spirit of the young victim is back and haunting the island." The woman stood back up and placed her fingers on her lips. "That's all I'm saying."

Summer smiled and waved. "Well now, you have a lovely holiday."

The woman smiled back and left the store. The next customer plopped a book on the counter. "What a nutjob." She rolled her eyes. "Everybody knows who killed her. It was the brother."

Summer rang up the book and hoped there wasn't steam coming out of her ears. "Brother?"

"The one who left the island, of course. He left right after the murder. My ma says he was having an affair with her." She handed Summer a credit card.

Summer's ears pricked up. "Your mother?"

The customer nodded. "She worked for the family then."

Summer's heart raced. "Really? Doing what?" She slid the card through.

"She was the cook, let go soon after the incident."

Summer tried to tamp down her excitement. "I'd love to talk with you more."

The woman's face fell. "The police have already been around. Mom knows nothing about Mimi."

Summer placed her book in a bag. "I have personal reasons. Nothing to do with Mimi."

"Ah. Well sure, then. Let me give you my card."

Finally, someone who was familiar with the family, had even worked with the family. Summer's family. She could probably offer insight into the dynamics of it. And if she had been there during that time, maybe she'd known Hildy.

The woman handed Summer her card. *Sally Lawson, beekeeper.*

"Thanks, Sally. You'll be hearing from me soon." Summer felt lighter, even as her feet and back ached from standing for hours.

At long last there was a break in the stream of customers, and Summer popped off to use the restroom.

When she went back out on the floor, Glads and Marilyn were there, next to the register, chatting with Poppy.

"Any news?"

"None. It's like she vanished into thin air," Marilyn said. "How are you?"

"Any more break-ins?" Glads asked.

"I'm fine, and there've been no break-ins." Summer kept a watchful eye on the now-smaller crowd in the shop.

Glads's head tilted. "I think that's the third time I've heard that version of 'Silent Night' today."

"Has Ben been at the search center? With the search parties?" Summer straightened the few mermaid pins at the register display.

"I've not seen him at all," Marilyn said. "Someone said you just can't get to him. He's either working or sleeping."

"I don't think he's sleeping much." Glads hooked her thumbs on her jeans.

A young woman walked up to the register, and Summer hopped behind the counter as the others dispersed. Poppy went over to the coffee station.

Summer reached for the next customer's book and then glanced at the woman's face: Yvonne Smith. "What are you doing here?"

One eyebrow lifted. "Buying a book for my dad."

Summer glanced at the J. D. Robb book. "Your dad has good taste." She bit her lip. *Get out of my bookstore. And don't come back.* She forced a smile as she rang the reporter up.

"I'd love to talk with you, Summer." Yvonne handed her a credit card. Didn't anybody pay in cash anymore?

Summer concentrated on checking her out as quickly as possible. She didn't want anybody to see her talking with Yvonne. Especially not the person who had Mimi—the person who had conveyed to Summer that she shouldn't talk with the police and needed to sell Beach Reads. "I'm sorry. I'm just so busy. 'Tis the season."

Yvonne frowned. "It's too bad. I think you and I have a few things in common."

Summer tried not to laugh, but a strange bubble of something like a sinister chuckle came out of her. She craned her neck to look behind Yvonne. "Next!" She handed Yvonne her package.

Yvonne stepped aside as the next person stepped forward, then stood a few moments, watching the transaction.

Summer completely ignored her. She'd once respected reporters. Those days were long gone. Yvonne Smith had no scruples and could have ruined everything for Mimi. Summer's stomach sank. With each passing minute, she wondered if she'd ever see Mimi again. And she was starting to think selling the bookstore might be the only way.

Or at least pretending to sell it.

Chapter Thirty-Seven

With the last Christmas shipment of books shelved, Glads, Mia, Marilyn, Poppy, and Summer plopped down in the storage room.

Mia, sprawled on a huge box, sighed. "Who knew shelving books was so hard?'

"We did." Glads sat down on the box next to her.

Poppy groaned. "A few more days of this madness."

"Someone, please, shut off the Christmas music. It's getting embedded into my brain," Marilyn said.

Poppy flipped off the switch and laughed.

Summer threw her the keys. "Would you all lock up? I need to go home." Peg and Lucy would be there soon.

"What? Why?" Mia stood. "I'll come with you."

"Don't you need to get home?" The last thing Summer needed was for her niece to get wind of the ransom note.

Mia eyed her as if she'd lost her mind. "Why would I? Mom is staying with you tonight, and so am I."

"Maybe I'll call her and tell her to stay home. I know she's got to be tired, since she's been working with the search teams."

"She's done with that. They've stopped searching for now," Mia said.

"Besides, you need someone to be there." Glads stood and stretched.

"Do I?" Summer was so done with people. She felt the need to be alone to sort through everything she understood about the case—about Mimi, about her family, about the ransom note. After Peg and Lucy left, she wanted a bath and bed and to get up in the morning to sit with her thoughts. She didn't want to have to deal with anyone.

"Yes, I think as long as Mimi is missing, you need to have someone stay with you. I'll come over if you don't want Piper and Mia to," Marilyn said.

Mia crossed her arms.

"It's fine for Mia and Piper to come over. But how long can this continue? We all have lives, and it's Christmas. I'm sure everybody has things to do." Summer glanced at her watch. She was sure Peg and Lucy were waiting for her. "I need to go."

"What's your hurry?" Glads said. "We need to chat about the book club party. Let's have a drink."

"Not tonight. I'm sorry. I'll see you tomorrow." Summer walked out of the room. Was she being too suspicious?

As she walked out of the store, she felt the eyes of the books on her. She stopped, drew in some air, and took it all in. The overstuffed chairs, the romance authors' signatures all over—the walls, the floors, the mermaid decor. Everything about this place was carefully geared toward readers. Her mom had loved the place, and you could feel the passion for reading in every crack and crevice. It was so different than what you experienced walking into a huge chain bookstore. This place had been carefully crafted for readers by a woman who loved reading.

Summer sighed and opened the door to the night. She'd been trying to make her decision—whether to go back to work or to stay here with the bookstore, her family, her friends. She kept putting off the deliberations. It was too much in the middle of her grief. It took so much energy just to get through each day.

Summer walked along the boardwalk, past the dark arcade, and into the night. She stepped out on the beach, heading for home. The dark, slate-blue sky was reflected in the glassy, shimmering water.

She breathed in the cool air and stopped to take in the full moon. If her mom were here, she'd tell Summer to ask the moon for anything and it would be granted in some form or another. Summer whispered a little prayer that Mimi would be found alive and well.

She walked toward the house. Things didn't just happen without a lot of work, without a lot of compromise. Maybe she'd have to compromise on the bookstore for Mimi's safety. It was just a store. Mimi was a person whose life was in danger. There shouldn't even be a choice.

Pangs of guilt tore through her. Hildy would have sold that store in a minute if it would help someone. Maybe Summer's decision had been made for her by the universe. Perhaps it was time to let it go and get back to her life in Staunton, teaching, wrangling with academia.

As she turned down the path toward her house, she saw three figures on her porch. She had been expecting only two, and of the female variety—not a third, male visitor. Her heart skipped around in her chest as she approached the porch. The women sat on her porch swing opposite her Christmas tree. The man sat on the stoop. They all stood when she approached them.

Summer's heart nearly stopped when she detected who the man was, and her mouth dropped.

Peg walked forward. "Summer, we've hired a lawyer."

Summer eyed Peg, then the man, who was standing, moving toward her.

"I told them you might not be too thrilled with this," Cash said.

"We thought it was our best option, to get the sale of the bookstore under way ASAP. The clock is ticking," Peg said. "Cash here can handle the sale for us."

He nodded. "Real estate law is one of my specialties."

Summer grabbed Peg's arm and dragged her closer. "How much does he know?"

"Only that you need to sell the store and that it will all be handled without the buyer's presence."

Still. Cash's father was the chief of police. Would the kidnapper even go for it? Or would they think it was a setup?

"I'm sorry. I don't think this is going to work." Summer shook her head.

"He doesn't need to know the rest. He just needs to know that it will be handled quickly," Peg said.

"It's just not a good idea. Can you find another lawyer?"

"We tried. He's it. The only real estate lawyer on this island."

Summer grimaced. The Cash she knew would never be involved in any illegal activity. She had to believe it was still true. "His father is the chief of police. Did he tell you that?"

Peg's face fell.

"I didn't think so. Just him being here, if we're being watched, is not good," Summer said, then stiffened as Cash approached them.

He cleared his throat. "I understand if you don't want to use me." He smiled that crooked, dimpled smile of his. "It's fine. I'll be moving along, ladies. Thanks for your efforts."

He started to walk away.

"Cash—" Summer said. He turned around. "I'm, ah, just not sure about any of this. Please don't tell people I may be selling the store."

He leaned forward and his mouth opened, then closed. "Fine."

"You know how people are."

His eyes locked with Summer's. "I do. Believe me, I do."

As he walked away again, the years melted, back to the day she'd left him standing at the altar. For days and weeks after, the islanders had talked of nothing else. Now Cash's wife had deserted him for another man, and he must be getting sick of feeling like everybody was always talking about him.

She followed him. "Cash?"

He half turned.

"Would you like to come in for a cup of coffee or a beer?'

He turned toward her, took her in. "Another time. You've still got those two to contend with. But soon?" A softness came over him.

She lowered her head and then raised her chin. "Absolutely."

Chapter Thirty-Eight

Peg and Lucy sat on Summer's living room couch, Mr. Darcy observing them. He was a happy bird when he had an audience. The two could hardly concentrate on the matter before them because he was such a distraction.

A knock came at the front door, and Summer opened it to find Piper and Mia with their bags. "Hey, I forgot you were coming." Summer yawned.

"Excited to see us, I see," Piper said, and smiled. "I'm sleeping with you, just like old times."

Summer's heart danced. Was everything okay between them now? Maybe tonight she could talk with her about Mia. They walked into the living room.

"But someone is sitting on my bed," Mia said.

"Oh, sorry," Peg said, and she and Lucy started to get up.

"I was just kidding," Mia said. "I'm not going to bed anytime soon."

"What's all this?" Piper said, gesturing to the papers strewn about the floor and table.

"We've been trying to figure a few things out about Mimi's case," Lucy said.

Piper lifted an eyebrow. "Funny, I've not seen you at the search center."

"Speaking of that, have you seen Ben? I have a question for him," Summer said. "We've gotten the police report from the murder at Mermaid Point, and either there's a section missing or he never talked with the woman who discovered the body."

Piper set Mia's bag down next to the recliner and plopped herself into it. "I've only seen him fleetingly. He's like a dog with a bone. I don't think the man has slept since Mimi disappeared."

"He's got a crew in from Raleigh, right? The man should get some rest," Peg said.

Piper lifted her chin toward Summer, ignoring Peg. "Ben's a careful cop. I doubt that he didn't interview the woman who found the body. That's cop 101, isn't it?"

"Yes, but here's the report." Summer handed it to her.

"Can I go watch TV in your room?" Mia asked Summer.

"Sure. Just don't go near the guest room. The police asked us to not disturb it." Summer turned back to Piper. "Yes, that's cop 101. But that was his first case, and he told me how much he felt for the family. I wonder if he was just a nervous wreck about it and got sloppy."

"I don't think so," she muttered, flipping a page back and forth. Back and forth again. Her eyebrows gathered over her blue eyes. She handed Summer the report. "Look at the page numbers."

Summer studied them. Why hadn't she seen this before? Two pages had been taken right out of the middle of the report. "There's pages missing!"

Piper nodded.

"How about that?" Peg said. "The three of us have been studying this report for two days and hadn't noticed that."

"Someone must have taken it," Lucy said.

"Or it was misplaced," Piper said. "That's more likely, knowing the clerks at the courthouse." The room silenced for a few beats. "What's going on here?" she said, looking from face to face.

"Just as I said, we're trying to figure out where Mimi might be," Summer replied.

"I feel like you're hiding something," Piper said. "Is there something else I should know?"

"Nothing," Summer said, with a reassuring note in her voice. "Pinkie promise."

"Darcy loves Piper!" The bird suddenly squawked. And a shiver moved through Summer.

Piper's chin tilted; her voice lowered. "Have you learned more?"

"Piper, I love you, but no, we've learned nothing else."

"Summer, we need to go to the police."

"I can't. I'm sure they will kill her if we do."

"We're being watched," Lucy said in a loud whisper. "So you see, we can't go to the police. We need to figure this out."

"How is all this going to help?" Piper gestured toward the papers on the table. "Look, I'm sorry, but you need to take this to Ben."

"If we do . . ."

"I'll do it. I'm not being watched," Piper said.

"You don't know that," Summer said. "It could be dangerous. I can't allow it."

Piper cocked an eyebrow. "Allow it? Honestly, Summer."

The tension hung in the air like thick soup.

"I think it's time to go." Lucy stood, pulling Peg up beside her. "It's getting late."

They gathered their belonging and started to leave, but when they opened the door, a bedraggled Ben Singer was already there, about ready to knock. "Hello, ladies," Summer heard him say. She and Piper exchanged panicked glances. Summer gathered up the article and reports about the Bellamys and stuffed them under the couch. "Can I come in?"

"We were just leaving," Peg said.

"You may want to stay for this. I'm sorry," he replied. All of them walked back into the living room.

"Ben! I've been trying to reach you." Summer stood. "Please come in and sit down. Can I get you something? Water?"

"No." He hung his head. "I'm here on official business."

The room silenced.

"What is it, Ben?" Summer's voice quivered. "Have you found her?"

"Not exactly." He held up a bag and pulled out a shiny object. "Can you identify this? Any of you?"

It didn't look familiar to Summer, but she wasn't one to notice jewelry.

Peg gasped, her hands going to her chest. "It's Mimi's."

The room silenced again. Lucy's arm wrapped around Peg. Summer's eyes moved from Ben to Piper and back to Ben again.

"Where did you find it?"

"Near the water," he said with a hoarse voice.

"Mermaid Point?"

He nodded, eyes watery. The man was bone-tired and very near tears.

Summer went to him, touched his shoulder. "Ben, this all has to do with that first murder, doesn't it?"

His face fell. "The same one that's haunted me for years." He nodded. "It's back. Just as I was getting ready to retire." He drew in a breath and eyeballed Peg. "Thank you. We were pretty certain it was hers."

"She could still be okay," Lucy said. "She could have lost that ring when she was out there earlier. She visited Mermaid Point earlier."

"She was wearing the ring on Saturday. That was after she'd visited it," Peg said.

"When did she visit? She didn't get to my place until late. Did she go there Saturday morning?" Summer twisted her hands together. The longer Ben was here, the longer the kidnapper would have the chance to see he was here. Were they watching? She walked to the window and looked out, seeing nothing but the lights from the Christmas tree on her porch and the sand, sea, and night sky beyond.

"Yes, she went that morning," Peg said. "We thought she was crazy going out there, after she'd been threatened and everything."

"She could still be okay. She could have slipped it off as a clue for those of us looking for her," Piper said.

"She could still be okay," Lucy said, as if trying to convince herself.

They all glanced at Ben, who dropped his head.

"Ben? Is there something else?" Summer asked.

"We found the ring on a finger."

"Mimi's finger?" Piper asked after a few beats.

"Pretty certain."

"A person can survive that!" Lucy said. "I've researched and written about that in one of my books. It could depend on how it was taken off and how the bleeding stopped."

"Correct." Ben regarded her. He straightened. "I need to get going. I'll touch base with more news. We've still not been able to reach her husband. Do either of you know where he could be?" He looked at Peg and Lucy, who both shook their heads.

"I'll see you out." Summer took his arm. When they were in the hallway, she lowered her voice. "Ben, I've been reading the police report from the murder on Mermaid Point, and Rima's statement is missing. Why would that be?"

He lurched back, and his white eyebrows hitched. "I've no idea. Are you sure?"

"Positive." Summer let his arm go. "Do you think someone took it?"

He smiled. "Highly unlikely. It's one thing to go to the courthouse and ask for public records. But for someone to get to the actual records would be almost impossible with the security in place."

"Could it be lost?"

"Maybe. Misfiled, more like it. I'll get Cash on that."

"I thought he was a real estate lawyer."

He nodded. "Yeah, but he does a bit of investigative work for me on the side now."

There was more to her old boyfriend than she'd discerned. Imagine that.

"Thanks for pointing it out. We need to keep our records accurate."

Summer bit her tongue. She wanted to unburden herself. To place the entire matter in Ben's hands. She needed a hero. But as she considered the weary cop in front of her, she wasn't sure she could tell him what was going on with the ransom note and the bookshop. He didn't need one more problem. Not tonight while he stood there clutching the bag with Mimi's ring in it. And, truth be told, she needed the time to figure this all out. And to make a decision.

Chapter Thirty-Nine

Soon Piper and Summer were the only two in the living room.

Piper searched through all the papers containing articles and research on the Bellamys. "Interesting family," she muttered.

"Right."

Mr. Darcy rocked back and forth, whistling a tune.

When her cousin said the word *family*, warmth bubbled up in Summer. And not for the Bellamys but for the family she'd grown up with. Would she ever feel anything like that for these new relatives? Just because they shared a father didn't make them family.

"What does it have to do with Mimi's case? Anything?" Piper held up an article from 1987, when the murder had taken place.

"We don't know for sure. But it seems likely. It seems like someone didn't like her writing about the murder. Dredging up the past, right?"

"But what if that's not the case? What if someone just wants it to look like it? Is there anything else about her we should know?"

Summer's mind drifted. The other writers disliked Mimi. Maybe she had a sordid past. "It's possible."

"Bedtime, Summer!" the bird said.

"Yes, I know, Darcy." Annoyed that a bird was telling her to go to bed, she turned back to her cousin, wanting to broach the subject of Mia and their tiff a few days ago. "I love you, Piper. And I love Mia. I'd never want anything to happen to either one of you."

Piper's jaw twitched. "I know that."

"Aunt Summer?" Mia came down the stairs, holding a cloth bag. "Do you know anything about this?"

"What is it?" Summer asked.

Mia stood in front of her aunt and opened the bag. Summer peered into it. And blinked a few times. "Is that—"

"Hair and teeth!" Mia exclaimed, eyes almost as wide as her face.

"What? Where did you find this?" Piper said.

"Under Aunt Summer's bed. I dropped my pen, and when I went to get it, I saw this. And it appeared—I don't know—odd, so I pulled it out of there."

"Could it be Hildy's?" Piper asked.

Summer's heart beat hard in her chest. "No. I just cleaned under there last week. She wasn't much for keeping things under her bed."

She peeked into the bag again—the hair looked real. It wasn't a wig. The teeth were different shades of gray, white, and yellow, but definitely authentic.

"Where did it come from?" Piper's voice quivered. "What does it mean?"

"It's voodoo, Mama," Mia said, as if her mother should know.

Piper crossed her arms. "Right."

"It is!" Mia examined.

"Calm down," Summer said. "I agree that someone wants to make it look like there's a voodoo thing going on. I have no patience for such things."

"But Aunt Hildy knew about it," Mia continued.

"But voodoo is very different from what Aunt Hildy practiced. She was pagan, a Goddess worshipper. She had nothing to do with voodoo," Piper said.

Summer's mind leaped to Mimi. Did the hair and teeth belong to her? Was this a message? How long had it been there?

"We should call the police," Piper said.

"The police just left here," Summer muttered.

"You know what? I'll take it down to the station myself. You should stay here and get some rest." Piper stood. "Maybe they are scattering pieces of Mimi. Is that the color of her hair?"

"Yes, but that's a popular hair color. Mousy brown. Nothing unusual about it."

"Gross," Mia said.

"Indeed," Summer said, then turned back to Piper. "Let's wait to give it to the police? I'm afraid—" She looked at Mia and shut her mouth. Mia didn't need to know about any of this, did she?

Piper caught Summer's drift. "Okay. But we do need to take it to them. I think it's best if I do it."

Mia glanced back and forth between Piper and Summer. "Oh, brother. What are you two up to?"

"Nothing to concern you," Piper said in a tone that said not to argue.

Mia shrugged. "Whatever." She shifted her weight. "Can I lie down? I'm exhausted."

Summer rose from the couch, where Mia was going to sleep. The girl had been working hard for days. Summer was sure she was tired.

As Summer and Piper went upstairs to bed, Piper whispered to her cousin that she had an idea. When they went into the bedroom, she spilled it. "Let's call Posey."

"Posey!" Summer said. Posey was the local psychic and a close friend of Hildy's. She'd been dealing with diabetes and had had to slow down. Since she was eighty-four years old, maybe it had been about time. But it vexed the spirited woman.

"She knows all about voodoo and can at least tell us if this maybe has something to do with it. If so, that should narrow things down quite a bit."

Summer reached for her phone, which was plugged in next to the bed. She pressed on Posey's name.

Her call was answered quickly. "Summer? Girl, how are you doing?"

"Not so good, Posey. You heard about Mimi, right?"

"That writer? Yes. Is that what you're calling about? Do you need my help to find her?"

Summer hadn't considered it. Maybe that was because even though she loved Posey and Posey had helped during her mom's investigation, Summer didn't buy into the psychic thing.

"Sure, but that's not why I'm calling."

Posey laughed. "My favorite skeptic. What do you need?"

Summer paused. It was an odd thing to say to somebody. Best to just spit it out. "We found a bag with teeth and hair under my bed. I'm certain it wasn't there a few weeks ago, because I cleaned under there. Is that a voodoo thing?"

"I'm not sure I'd classify it as a voodoo thing, but a witch bag. It depends on the intent of the person. It could be a protective talisman or a hex."

"A hex or protection?"

"Yes, as far I know. My next question, is who's been in your bedroom?" Posey laughed.

"Well, tonight it's Piper," Summer responded. "Nothing exciting going on in my bedroom."

Not in a very long time.

"I know you're worried about Mimi," Posey said. "I can feel it. She's not passed. If she had, I'd know it." She paused. "But seriously, who has access to your room?"

Summer recounted the situation for her.

"All I'm sensing is confusion and fear. I'm not getting a clear picture. But if I do, I'll let you know."

Summer and Posey said their good-nights.

Summer slid under the quilt. Piper did the same and sat up on her elbow. "Here we are again. You and me in your mom's bed."

Summer laughed. "The more things change?"

Soon enough, the two women drifted off to sleep.

Summer dreamed of mermaids, books, and a lone woman walking along the seashore. She tried to catch up with her, but she couldn't. The woman wouldn't stop. Her strides were long.

Wait! Summer yelled. *Please wait for me!*

There was something important that the woman held in her arms. Summer needed her so much.

But she kept walking into the mist. Summer followed through the mist, blindly, and when she reached a clearing, the sun startled her. She shielded her eyes. The sea. The sun, the shade. Where had the woman gone? Who was the woman? She eyed the coast, squinting, and made out the form of a huge structure. She blinked several times. It was the Bellamy castle.

Her heart raced. Should she move forward? Had the woman gone into the castle?

She drew in a breath and stepped forward and sank into the sand. It was deep and turned into a mud pit. Her legs stuck there. She pulled and yanked. It was no use. She sank deeper into the pit, even as she thrashed.

Someone had her by the shoulders and was shaking her. "Summer! Summer! Wake up! You're dreaming."

Her eyes popped open. She was drenched in sweat.

"Are you okay?" Piper said.

She nodded, mumbled, "Sorry," and rolled over to descend into an even deeper sleep.

Chapter Forty

Day three of Mimi missing, and the stasis dragged on. For Summer, time was moving forward only by chance, as if everybody were living in some strange time warp.

Was Christmas in two days? Or was it three? Summer drank her coffee while sitting at her table, trying to be quiet. She didn't want to wake Piper or Mia.

She sat with a tablet and doodled, as it sometimes helped her to think. She drew swirly flowers and planets. Then she turned the page, drew a straight line, and began marking dates.

She had been born in April 1988.

Her mom and Omar had gone to his parents in August of the previous year. Which must've been just after Hildy found out she was expecting.

The murder had taken place on August 30, 1987.

Summer envisioned Rima when her son came to her and her husband with this wide-eyed island girl, expecting a baby.

Whatever they said had upset Hildy so much that she'd cut them off. And cut Summer off from them. As a baby Summer had been taken out of the Bellamys' lives—not that she'd ever been in them, because her parents' affair had been kept secret until that moment.

Her father's brother, Bashir, had left the country the month after the murder and settled in London. She drew a little clock tower. Big Ben. She grinned.

Could he have killed the young woman at Mermaid Point? Had he been running from the law? If his son was anything like him, Summer could imagine it. Bashir Junior was cold. A shiver ran up her spine. Her deliberations kept turning to him. How closely were the police watching him? It made perfect sense that he knew something about Mimi's kidnapping. But why would he be interested in the bookstore?

She drew lines out from the timeline. She wanted to find out Sam's and Fatima's birthdays. Sam seemed a good bit younger than her. But she was terrible at guessing ages.

And how old had Rima been when this was all happening? Sam had said she was seventy now, so she must have been in her thirties. And she'd had a son preparing to marry.

Summer shrugged it off. It was a long time ago and the Bellamys' culture was complex and nuanced. Yet it seemed important that Rima had been very young when she had Omar.

"Good morning," Piper said. "There's coffee. I love you."

Summer laughed. She continued to study the timeline.

Piper observed over her shoulder. "You know what that needs?"

"What?"

"Mimi's timeline."

Summer looked up at Piper. "Why?

"Call me crazy, but I keep thinking Mimi has something to do with the Bellamys. Like, why else was she so passionate about that story?"

Summer hadn't even considered that. "Makes a certain kind of sense. But she's a writer, and sometimes they're drawn to stories. You just can't make sense of why."

Piper held her phone and keyed something in. "Mimi was born in March 1988."

"Seriously? A month before me? Now that's weird." Summer took a sip of her coffee. "I thought she was much older than me."

"So did I." Piper sat at the table. She read over the text on her phone. "She was brought up in Pittsburgh, adopted by an older couple."

Summer's heart sank into her stomach. "Adopted?"

"Says so right there in her Wikipedia bio."

"So what does that mean?"

"It may not mean anything. But then again, maybe she was the baby in the book."

"What baby? What book?"

"Haven't you read Mimi's book yet?" Piper asked. "There was a baby one of the brother's girlfriends had, and the family rejected it. I thought it might have been you. But the timeline didn't work." Summer remembered that Aunt Agatha had made a similar note earlier. "But now that I think about it, it could be Mimi."

Her cousin was talking crazy. She was making wide jumps in logic. What was the possibility of something like this being true? "I don't know, Piper. Seems farfetched."

She grunted, placed her elbows on the table. "Yeah. Probably. But then again, how farfetched is it that your father lived in a castle on the other side of the island and you were completely unaware? Or that your brother would walk into Beach Reads one day? Stuff happens. That's all I'm saying."

Summer had to admit that Piper was right. "Okay. Let's roll with this hypothesis. If she is a long-lost child of someone in the Bellamy clan and she writes the book as a sort of revenge, who would care? Thirty years later? Care enough to kidnap her?"

"To cut her finger off . . ." Piper stared off.

Summer's stomach roiled and waved. Someone had Mimi. Someone had been in Summer's home. Stolen her pictures. Left a bag of hair and teeth. Someone wanted the bookstore.

Maybe she should involve the police. She, Piper, and the writers weren't getting anywhere. Oh, there was a ton of information, but nothing holding it together. It was all scattered bits and pieces. Mimi's past. The Bellamys' past. The murder. The bookstore.

She needed to make a decision. Sell the bookstore clandestinely and give the kidnappers what they wanted or tell the police, who might have another plan entirely.

"I think the finger was a warning," Piper said. "It was a warning that these folks aren't playing. I suggest we tell the police."

"But—"

"I know they warned you against it. But you're just a Shakespeare professor, not a cop. You're not equipped to deal with these people. If you continue to do nothing, who knows what body part will turn up next?"

Chapter Forty-One

Summer agreed to allow Piper to take the bag of hair and teeth to the police. She was still on the fence about telling them the rest of it. If she told them and the kidnapper killed Mimi, she wouldn't be able to live with that. But the alternative was selling the bookstore.

"Nothing will come of nothing," she muttered. A quote from *King Lear.* One of her favorites. But how could Summer continue to do nothing? She needed to talk with someone other than cozy mystery authors and her cousin. But who?

Someone educated in the law.

Would it be possible to fake the sale of the bookstore just to lure the kidnappers out? She racked her brain, trying to recall someone, anyone she knew, with a law specialty back in Staunton. She wondered if she could use her own lawyer. Cash came to mind, but she'd be asking him to keep it all from his father. That would not be cool.

Summer called Sally, the beekeeper whose mom had worked at the Bellamy estate years ago, and left a message. One thing off her list. She hoped to hear back soon.

Her phone buzzed, and Piper's name came across the screen. "Hello."

Piper was breathing hard. Was she crying? Summer gripped the phone. "What's wrong?"

"All of the flyers have been torn down! All of them!"

"What?" They were angering someone with their search for Mimi.

"Yes! All ripped to shreds. And poor Ben . . ."

"What happened?"

"I handed the bag to him, and he gave it to forensics. But—"

"What? What happened?"

"He looks like death warmed over. And the guys from Raleigh were making fun of him and his old-fashioned techniques. It was awful. I don't even pretend to know what they were talking about. But Ben sort of shriveled right before my eyes." She paused. "I know you don't like him, but I don't think his heart can take much more."

"His heart?"

"Yes, didn't you know? That's why he's retiring. Bad heart. He's been trying to keep it on the down low, but I found out from a mutual friend."

Summer's stomach sank. For most of her life, he had been her sworn enemy. But these days, they were getting along. And she certainly wished him no harm.

"I think we may need to handle this on our own."

"I think you're right. Let's just help him and the case as much as we can without—"

"Without what? Breaking the law?" Summer drew in a breath. "Do you know a good lawyer?"

"Cash."

"But—"

"I know what you're going to say. But he's a damn good lawyer."

"We'd be asking him to go against his dad."

"I know. I considered that too. But we'd be helping his dad, right? We need to do something. Mimi's life is in danger. You're being harassed. I say we call him, hire him, and invoke attorney-client privilege." Piper breathed heavily into the phone.

It could work. "We'd need to be very respectful of the fact that—"

"Of course."

"Do you want to call him? I need to get to the bookstore."

"I will," she said. "But you need to promise me I have your support."

"Of course you do. We need to do something. Whatever we can without involving the police or Ben."

"You won't lose the bookstore," Piper said. "We will finesse the whole thing."

"Legally."

After she hung up, Summer's stomach knotted. So much could go wrong. She owned a popular bookstore, one that had meant the world to her mom, and she didn't want to lose it. Summer didn't know if she wanted to be there forever to run it, but she knew she wanted to keep it.

Her jaw tightened. Kidnappers. *Really, Summer? Trusting criminals?* She could see no other way.

Summer gathered her things, said good-bye to Mr. Darcy, and locked her door as she left her house.

She stood for a moment taking in her Christmas decor on the front porch, trying to let it lift her spirits. It was Christmastime, damn it, and she'd just wanted to get through this first year without her mom. That had been her focus. Just get through.

Summer, the queen of self-delusion! Her therapist kept telling her to be still, to feel her feelings. But if she did that now, she'd take to her bed for days with the covers over her head.

She didn't want to deal with the Mimi situation.

She didn't want to deal with the Bellamys' sordid past.

She didn't want to deal with her ex-fiancé helping them out.

As she moved along to the sandy beach, wishing she'd worn a heavier coat, she envisioned the patchy timeline she'd been piecing together. She needed to place other people on that timeline. She needed more info about her grandmother. Rima had been here, on the island, then. She'd discovered the body. If the Bellamys or anybody in their circle had had anything to do with the kidnapper, Summer was certain Rima had the key to unlocking that door. If she could only find a way to get the old woman to trust her.

She stepped up onto the rickety boardwalk and spotted a group of women pointing into the distance. As she approached, she saw what they were pointing at: the masked streaker was at it again.

A woman turned to face her. "My child is inside the bookstore. Thank god she didn't see this. What are you going to do about this?"

The masked streaker had just become way less charming.

Chapter Forty-Two

After explaining that the local police were extremely busy because of a missing-person case, Summer walked into the store and made a beeline for her office, where Lucy and Peg were waiting for her.

"We have news." Peg lifted her chin.

Summer slipped off her jacket and hung it on the back of the chair, half afraid to ask what the news might be.

"We've heard from the kidnapper again," Lucy said, handing Summer the note.

For sale sign in two days or her arm is next.

Summer gasped.

"What are we going to do?" Peg's eyes watered.

"We?" Summer dropped the note on her desk. "This is my bookstore."

"But nobody wants to see you sell it, of course," Lucy said.

"Well, someone does," she muttered, sinking into her desk chair. She pulled out her phone and texted Piper. *Got another note. They've given us two days to sell the store.*

She received a text back almost immediately. *Here with Cash. Don't tell anybody anything. We're on it.*

Summer's stomach crawled with butterflies. *Okay.* She turned to Peg and Lucy. "Thanks for dropping this off. How did you get this?"

"It was on my car this morning. The same as the other one," Lucy said. "Why me? I have no idea. We are not the best of friends. I'm not the owner of the store, so I don't know why they've reached out to me."

The hair on the back of Summer's neck prickled to attention. Did Lucy despise Mimi so much that she'd kidnap her? How ridiculous. She'd been so helpful. Doing research. Brainstorming. Summer shook off her paranoid suspicion. But she still kept her own counsel. No need to let them in on specifics.

"It's odd, but the whole thing is odd," Lucy continued. "In this day and age, who cares about a murder that happened thirty-some years ago? Hardly anybody it affected is still alive!"

"That's not true. Ben is still alive," Peg pointed out.

"Rima Bellamy is too." Summer clicked on her computer.

"But you know what I mean," Lucy said. "It's such a long time ago. "

"People don't get over murder." Summer keyed in her password. "They just don't. And evidently Mimi pushed just too hard."

"The killer got away with it years ago. He's still worried that he'll get caught. I still say if we solve that first murder, we'll find our kidnapper and the killer," Lucy said.

"I agree," Peg replied. "But we've covered a lot of ground, and we've gotten no real leads except the brother that left, and he has a rock-solid alibi at the time of the murder and the time of the kidnapping."

"A little too rock solid, if you ask me," Lucy muttered.

Summer was only half listening, as she was checking over books orders online. "What was his alibi?" She didn't remember that anybody had mentioned this earlier.

"Thirty years ago, he was out at sea. And of course, he's living in London now," Lucy said.

"But his son isn't. He's here. In fact, both of them are here, right?" Peg said. "And he could hire someone to do his dirty work."

The room silenced. It was a little too coincidental for Summer's liking that Bashir Senior's sons had shown up just before Mimi disappeared. What business did they have here? Maybe Sam would know. She had learned during lunch with her newfound family that it was Sam and her father who had stayed behind and run the U.S. operations of their family shipping business. And perhaps Sam would know why his father and his uncle had fallen out. Did it have to do with the murder of the young woman, or something else? Once again, Sally's name popped into Summer's head. Surely her mom could shed light on this. But Summer hadn't heard back from her.

"It's hard to imagine a hired criminal on Brigid's Island," she said. "But I suppose you're right. He could have hired someone."

Mia bounded into the office. "Reporting for duty." She said hello to the two women lurking in Summer's office, then returned her attention to her aunt. "Where do you want me this morning?"

"Please check out upstairs. I'm sure it needs straightening. The book fairies always come out at night." Summer said it without thinking.

Mia laughed as she exited the room.

Peg and Lucy eyed each other as if Summer were crazy.

She cleared her throat. "That's what Mom always said." She smiled. Not that she owed them any explanation at all. Book fairies were . . . books fairies. If they thought that was strange, there wasn't much she could do about it. In truth, Summer had always thought it a strange turn of phrase too. But now she liked it, as it was just another one of those strange and quirky connections she had to her mom.

Her mom was full of quirk. She could kick herself for not dipping into the box of photos of Hildy and Omar. Now that it had been stolen, she might not ever see them together. Disappointment hit her in the gut. Nobody to blame but herself. Most people would've torn into it at once. But it had been too much for Summer. Just too much. It had felt so deeply personal, as if by inspecting the secret photos she'd be betraying her mom in some strange way. She'd betrayed and disappointed her mom so much already just by the way she'd lived her life. Which, in principle, seemed to be the very opposite of the way Hildy had lived hers. But at Summer's core, she was Hildy's daughter, through and through.

How would Hildy handle this situation?

Summer leaned back in her chair and closed her eyes: Hildy Merriweather would start off by taking a plate of vegan cupcakes or brownies to her long-lost grandma.

Chapter Forty-Three

After making sure everything was running smoothly at Beach Reads, Summer popped home to whip up some Christmas cupcakes. Peppermint-chocolate, perhaps. Rima wasn't Christian and wouldn't celebrate Christmas, but she couldn't hold Christmas treats against Summer, could she?

Summer dug in the kitchen drawer for her mom's notebook of recipes and pulled it out. A rush of nostalgia swam through her. She opened the book to the first page. Her mom's handwriting jumped off the page. Tears stung Summer's eyes. *Get a grip. You have a job to do.*

She flipped through the pages, her eyes catching glimpses of the other recipes: *Santa's Favorite Brownies. Twinkle Star Cupcakes. Hot Chocolate Marshmallow Cookies.* And there was the one she was searching for—*Peppermint Patty Cupcakes.* She cracked a smile. Her mom was so creative with naming the recipes. Summer used to roll her eyes at her mom's borderline cutesiness, but now she considered it endearing.

Summer spread the book out on the counter, warmth spreading through her. Here was another thing Hildy had left her. She was everywhere, even though she was physically gone.

She gathered the ingredients, pleased that she had everything on hand. She unscrewed the top of the peppermint extract and drew in the scent. It popped through her nose into her head and sparked a memory. "Peppermint sparks, that's what you're feeling," Hildy had said when Summer did the same thing as a child.

As she placed the cupcakes in the oven, her phone rang.

"Where are you?" Piper said.

"At home."

"We're at Beach Reads."

"I need to bake cupcakes."

"What did you just say?"

"I said I need to bake cupcakes."

"You've never baked cupcakes in your life."

"Yes, I have. With my mom."

Pause. "Okay, we'll be right there. Don't go anywhere."

She clicked off.

We? Was she bringing Cash over here?

Summer glanced around the place. It was clean already. But the kitchen was a bit of a mess. Of course—she was baking. You couldn't bake without a mess.

Since she had her phone in her hand, she tried calling Sally again. Left another message.

Then she texted Sam. *I have a little something for you all. I'd like to stop by and drop it off. I need to make sure I have the right place. The castle?*

She set the phone down and reached for the paper towels, wet them, and cleaned flour from the counter. She rinsed out the apple cider vinegar bottle and placed it in the recycling bin.

Since Piper was on the way over, she turned on the electric teakettle. The room was starting to smell like Christmas.

Summer planned to drop off these cupcakes and perhaps be invited inside. She'd sit and chat with her new family and find out more about the brothers who'd split up after the murder of their hired help. She didn't have to bring up the murder at all. She just needed to frame it as questions about her new family.

A rapping came at her door, and it creaked open.

"We're here," Piper's voice rang out.

"I'm in the kitchen!"

Piper and Cash entered the kitchen.

"My god, it smells heavenly." Cash opened his arms and drew in the air.

Summer beamed. "Mom's Peppermint Patty Cupcakes."

"You're baking?" He grinned.

She nodded. "I didn't realize you were bringing Cash. But sit down. I have the teakettle on, or would you rather have coffee?'

Both agreed to tea as they sat at the table.

Summer opened the oven to check on the cupcakes, and a swirl of scent escaped.

"I hope we can taste those!" Piper said.

"Well, maybe one. I'm taking them to the Bellamys." She closed the oven door.

"What? Why?" Piper said.

The teakettle whistled. Summer made the tea and placed the steaming cups in front of Cash and Piper. "Things didn't go so well at the restaurant. I want to smooth things over. What better way than Mom's vegan cupcakes? Besides, I have questions."

"I bet you do," Cash said. His skin was still pink from the cold, which made his blue eyes look ever bluer. "We need to talk about the 'sale' of Beach Reads," he said, used air quotes.

Summer picked up her cup of tea. "Can this be done? Can we pretend to sell it just to lure them out of hiding?"

"I'm certain I can draw up a contract with so many loopholes they think they will be buying the store, but it won't be official. Or they will come back with so many questions, it will drag things out."

"But time is not on our side. They have Mimi."

He frowned. "Have they given you any sign of when they will let her go?"

"Not at all."

He drew in air and let it go slowly. "The more time goes by, the less likely it is that she's going to survive. I hate to say it, but it's true." He picked up his cup and blew on it. "She may already be dead."

Summer gasped. "Don't say that!"

"Okay. I agree that we have to go ahead as if she's still alive. But kidnappers are not upright folks. They rarely come through." His voice was calming. But his words made Summer's heart race.

The three of them sat in silence for a few moments.

"I'm sorry we dragged you into this." Summer's chin lifted toward him. "We had no choice."

He nodded. "I get it. But I can only go so far, as a representative of the law. I can't and won't do anything illegal. We have to be careful."

"How can they maintain secrecy? And how do we get beyond that?"

"Dummy corporations. Layers of bureaucracy. Their legal team would be representing them, and they don't need to disclose who the actual buyer is."

The timer buzzed, and Summer popped out of her chair to open the oven door. "Done!" She shut off the oven and pulled out her two pans of Peppermint Patty Cupcakes. "What do you know about the Bellamys?" she asked Cash.

"Not much, unfortunately. They've always stuck to themselves."

"That can be said for many of the south islanders," Piper said. It was a more rural area with fewer people and businesses. Some of them didn't see the point of venturing into town to do anything other than get supplies.

Cash sipped his tea. "True."

Summer shuddered. Her family were south islanders. Her father had been here all along. She just didn't know it.

Her phone dinged, alerting her to a text message from Sam. *We've never lived in the castle. It used to be offices, but now it sits empty. Our address is 1325 Windy Surf Drive. Come by this afternoon or evening. We are all here.*

Summer read it aloud.

"Well, that's disappointing. They don't live in the castle?" Piper grinned. "I guess you're not a princess after all."

Summer snorted. "More like a toad than a princess."

Chapter Forty-Four

Once they'd decided to place a FOR SALE sign in front of the store in the morning, the happy little meeting dispersed. Summer left her home with a tin of goodies in hand—after she, Cash, and Piper had carried out a taste test.

As she drove to the south side of the island, she rehearsed what she might say to Rima. *I'd like to know more about why Uncle left the island.* Was that too cold? *Why didn't my father and his brother get along?* Too nosy?

As she pulled into the driveway of the large house, she gripped the steering wheel, fighting off the impulse to leave. The house wasn't a castle, but it was stately. She'd been in large houses in Virginia, of course, but nothing quite this big. She found a space to park and drew in a breath. Her dad's family had a lot of money. But they were just people. She'd taught kids from families like this. She'd talked to their parents. She'd been to her dean's home, also large. So she could do this. She wasn't rich, but she was skilled with language and could talk about anything to anyone.

Summer's legs trembled as she walked to the door, cupcakes in hand. What had she been thinking? She had so much to do in the bookstore and at home to get ready for Christmas. She hesitated at the door. Why was she here?

She needed to find out about her dad and his brother.

It might be the key to the whole murder case, which might lead them to Mimi.

She pressed the doorbell, and it buzzed. A dog barked inside. The door opened.

Sam stood there, holding a fluff ball of a dog against his chest. "Hi. Come on in!"

"What a cute dog!"

"Yes. He won't hurt you. I just didn't want him to jump up on you," he said as he placed the dog back on the floor. The dog sniffed at Summer approvingly. She held her hand out and petted him. "What a pretty dog."

She stood and handed him the tin. "I just wanted to drop these by. My mom made them every year for Christmas. I know you don't celebrate, but I hope you'd still accept them."

"Oh, sure." He took the tin. "We're not Christians, but we love Christmas." He placed his arm around her and led her through the vast hallway into an expansive great room with a wall of windows facing the beach.

The view drew Summer to the windows. "Gorgeous." They were high on a hillside, perched above the beach. It was a bit more rugged here, with patches of sand between coves and rocks.

"Yes, my grandfather designed this house. He wanted to be an architect, but he went into the family business instead." He paused. "If you look off to the left, you can see the castle. It's funny that you thought we lived there."

"Mimi told me that." Her face heated. She hadn't planned to mention her name.

"She had a lot of things wrong about our family. Please have a seat. We'll have tea brought in. Grandmother and Fatima will be with us momentarily."

She and Sam sat on an overstuffed couch, facing the window. Summer's gaze drifted to the window and the beach beyond.

"How's business?" Sam asked, placing the tin on a shiny coffee table.

"Booming." Summer almost mentioned that she was selling the bookstore but caught herself. The less he knew, the better. And Cash had told her to not tell anybody. If all went as planned, the sign would be up for a short time and the phony sale made, luring in the kidnappers. " 'Tis the season."

Fatima came in with a large tray and set it on the table. "Welcome to our home, Summer." Summer stood, and they hugged. Fatima smelled of honey and cloves.

"I warn you. After you drink my special tea, it will ruin you. You'll want no other tea ever again." She beamed and poured a cup, filling the room with the scent.

"We all love it," Rima said, entering the room and sitting on a chair opposite the couch. She wore a cream-colored silk pantsuit with gold scarves and jewelry. She gazed at Summer. "Welcome."

"Thank you. Magnificent view you have."

"My husband designed this place."

"Sam told me. Must have been very talented."

"He was. But he was also very loyal. A dutiful son, father, and husband."

"I wish I'd known him." Summer's throat squeezed. "I wish I'd known them all." Despite her best efforts, her voice cracked.

An awkward pause permeated the room.

"Of course you do. Must have been hard growing up without a dad," Fatima said. "And without your dad's family. I can't imagine."

Summer had never found it difficult. She'd had her mom, Aunt Agatha, and Piper. They had more than filled her days. But there were times she'd wished she had a dad. "There's so much I'd like to know."

Sam laughed. "Well, let's start slow. There's a lot to tell. We have an enormous family."

"There's just you two?"

"Yes, Mom and Dad just had the two of us. But Rima and Hassam had six kids. Four boys and two girls. They're scattered over the world."

Summer held the tea to her mouth and smelled the brew. Spicy. She sipped.

Fatima watched for her reaction.

It was like nothing Summer had ever tasted. The flavors were deep and spoke of the East. The tea was spicier and warmer than chai, which Summer loved. "Oh my god! This is fantastic!"

Fatima beamed. "Thank you. I'm glad you like it. One of my uncles has a tea shop in Paris, and he sells my tea there. I've been thinking of bringing it to the States."

"You should! We could sell it at Beach Reads! I'd love to," she said.

"We can talk about that later," Sam said.

"Absolutely." Summer sipped more. She turned to Rima. "You had six children?"

She nodded. "Your father, Omar, was the oldest. Then there was Bashir, Ehab, and Zouhir. My girls are Khadija and Mizzayam. Both married well and are living in Paris."

Married well? Summer refrained from rolling her eyes. *Oh, brother.* "What about the others? Where do they live?"

"Bashir was my second son. He went to London to run the business from there."

He was the one who'd left on bad terms, whose sons were here on the island now. "Does he have a family?"

"Yes," Sam interjected. "You met one of his sons at your book event."

"So ridiculously dramatic," Fatima said.

"Just like his father," Rima said.

Interesting. "I'm very confused," Summer lied. "What do you mean about his father being dramatic?"

"He and Dad had an argument, and he left the island. They didn't speak to each other ever again. I know Dad regretted that."

"You father reached out to him many times over the years." Rima lifted her chin, her gold earrings jiggling. "He should've had no regrets."

Summer prepared herself. "What was it about?"

The room went silent.

"I suppose it's okay to tell her," Fatima finally said. "It happened such a long time ago."

Summer's stomach knotted.

Rima nodded. "Bashir wanted to marry Sam and Fatima's mother."

"Yes, and she was promised to the oldest Bellamy son. Her family wouldn't hear of her marrying a younger son. They were very old-school."

"Did she love Bashir?" Summer asked.

"She claimed she didn't." Rima shrugged. "But we'll never know. She'd certainly not have opened up to me about it. And she's long gone." She clapped her hands together. "I'd love to try a cupcake."

The oldest tale in the world. The brothers had split over a woman. Summer tried to hide her disappointment.

"She was not just any woman," Fatima said, opening the tin. "Our mother was an heiress to a huge oil fortune."

"Fatima! You act like it was all about money. But it involved love." Sam reached for a cupcake.

"It's just as easy to love a rich person as a poor person," Rima said, and cackled.

Summer almost choked on her tea.

Chapter Forty-Five

"Have they found the writer yet? What's her name? Fifi? Mimi?" Rima asked.

"You know her name, Grandma. It's Mimi Sinclair," Fatima said.

"This old brain . . ."

"No. They've not found her yet." Summer drank her tea and sat back further into the soft couch, even though each of the tiny tendons in her neck seized at the mention of Mimi. She glanced at her watch. She'd need to be going soon. All she'd found out was that the brothers had split over Arwa Gibran. Having a falling-out over a woman wasn't so rare or suspicious. And she couldn't connect it to the murder of Jamila. Yet all of it had happened within the same month. "I haven't read her book. I suppose I should?"

"Pshaw. You could live the rest of your life without reading that trash." Rima leaned forward and shoved another cupcake into her mouth. "These are so good. I can't believe they are vegan."

"Yes, but—" Summer started.

"It's pure fiction. And bad fiction at that," Fatima said.

"But it's a bit coincidental, isn't it?" Sam set his cup and saucer on the side table, which held a display of fresh winter flowers. "She writes the book, causes a stir, and then disappears."

"Precisely," Summer said. "The police have been asking questions about . . . the past." She didn't mention Jamila. Or the murder. But they all grasped what she was talking about. "Like, who did she offend so much that they wanted to kidnap her and maybe hurt her?"

Rima gasped and held her hand to her mouth. "She offended everybody!"

"I see what you mean," Fatima said to Summer. "Like maybe whoever killed Jamila wants it to be continually swept under the rug."

"They got away with it all those years ago. Of course they want to continue to evade justice, so they kidnapped Mimi," Sam said.

Rima *tsk*ed. "Absurd."

"They solve cold cases all the time," Fatima said. "Maybe they will solve this."

"I hope so," Sam said. "I know it would mean the world to her family."

"Or dredge up a very painful time," Rima said, red-faced, voice cracking. She stood. "I'm sorry. I'm not feeling well. Thanks for the delicious cupcakes, Summer."

"Oh! I'm sorry you're not feeling well." Summer stood and hugged her politely.

"I'll walk you to your room," Fatima said.

"No need." She rushed out of the room, not like an ill woman at all.

"I apologize. I had no idea this would upset her so much." Summer rose from the couch. "I should go too."

"Wait," Sam said. "We'd love to show you Dad's library."

"I'd love to see it, but I need to go." Summer felt as if she had swallowed cement. Rima knew more than she was telling. It was like Summer had just stepped into an episode of one of those old nighttime soap operas: *Dynasty*, *Dallas*, *Brigid's Island* . . .

Sam's face fell. "Okay. It's a date. I know you love books, and he was quite a reader."

Summer's heart almost stopped. "He was?"

Fatima helped her with her coat. "He loved the classics and even had a thing for Shakespeare. Like you."

Summer felt as if her heart might tumble out of her chest. "Really?"

"There's so much I want you to know about him." Her lip quivered. "And so much I want to know about you."

Tears stung Summer's eyes. Heat rose on her cheeks. She hugged her half sister with abandon, and they cried in each other's arms.

* * *

Of all the things Summer had been expecting, bonding with her half sister had not been one of them. But as she drove away from the house, she left knowing a few more things. She didn't think any of them would help with the murder case—but then again, perhaps figuring it out was just a matter of engaging in a process of elimination.

The brothers' spat had been about Arwa and not the young woman who was killed. But Rima Bellamy? She was hiding something. Summer made a hard right onto the main highway. How to penetrate the older woman's icy walls?

Maybe there were other ways of finding out about the matriarch. Maybe Cash could help with that. Maybe there was a database he could access.

She turned left off the highway and headed toward Beach Reads. She needed to warn everybody about the sale of the store. She didn't want them to be surprised by a FOR SALE sign in the morning. And she was hoping to alleviate any fears around the sale of the store. She, Piper, and Cash were the only ones aware it would be fake. It absolutely had to stay that way until Mimi was home safe and sound.

Rudy, the grouchy guy who owned the arcade next to the bookstore, had been wanting to buy Beach Reads for years. But, if Summer remembered correctly, during the few weeks around Christmas he and his family went out of town. Maybe he wouldn't be around. And that was an excellent thing.

As she pulled into the parking lot, the sky darkened. Were they expecting a storm? She'd not been paying attention to the weather at all, but the wind was picking up. As she walked from her car to the bookstore, a fierce, stiff gust embraced her. She ran for the comfort and warmth of the store.

It surprised her to find a relatively empty store. Poppy, with a bored countenance, lifted her chin when she spied Summer. "We're expecting a severe storm. The customers cleared out. So here we are."

Summer's heart sank. "How bad?"

"Maybe hurricane bad. It depends on which way the wind blows. Or something." She straightened the books behind the register.

"Perhaps we should close up shop and head home ourselves." Summer approached the register. "In fact, I'll close out. You head home."

"Are you sure? I don't mind staying, even though I'm worried."

"Go home, Poppy. I'll be okay." Summer looked around. "Are we alone?"

"Yes, the last customer left about ten minutes before you got here." She walked into the back and emerged wearing a coat and carrying her handbag and an umbrella. "See you tomorrow."

"Good night." Summer had started her count of the cash when the doorbell rang, alerting her to a customer. Poppy must've forgotten to lock the door. "I'm sorry, we're closed for the day."

But when she glanced up, she realized it was no customer. It was Ben Singer, and he didn't look happy.

Chapter Forty-Six

"Cash told me you're selling the store," Chief Singer said. "I can't believe it."

Had he told his father the rest of the story? The rest of the plan? Summer's face heated. She had no way of knowing without asking, and she couldn't do that.

"After everything? You're just going to sell this place your mom built up?" He gestured widely with his arms.

Her breath hitched. She nodded, speechless that Ben would even care.

He shook his head. "I hate to see you do it. Your mom would be turning over in her grave."

Anger flared in her. He knew nothing of the situation. If she determined to sell the store, it would be her decision. She'd do it for the right reasons. Of course he'd jump to wrong conclusions about her.

"I have no choice." She spoke the truth. Right now she had no choice. And it was a fake sale. But if it were real, Summer didn't need Ben or anybody in her face about it.

"Is it that bad? Living here? Working here? Are we that bad?"

Her heart sank. "That's not it at all, Ben. It's finances. Pure and simple. I have a job and a life back in Staunton."

His eye caught hers. In that moment, he was peering into the depths of her soul. He recognized that she was lying. And she knew it. "I don't buy this at all." An eyebrow hitched. "I don't know what you're up to."

A bubble of fear and anger welled inside her. Her jaw clenched. "I'm up to selling the bookstore."

He looked at his feet and back up at her. "I've got to go. I'm busy. Caught the streaker. He was some guy from Raleigh. But there's this missing-persons case, you know."

Summer blinked hard, then peered away. He suspected something was up and it was like he was circling his prey—and she was his prey. The tendons in her neck stiffened. "I hope you find her, Ben."

What if the person who had her was watching Ben? Watching her? What if they saw he was in the store right now? Beads of sweat pricked on Summer's forehead.

She switched off the Christmas music, clutching her bag of nightly deposits. "Closing early tonight. The storm is keeping everybody at home." Her attempt at small talk fell flat. Ben just stood there in silence. But as she moved forward to leave, he followed. She opened the door and he walked out. She turned off the lights and set the alarm with the wind nipping at her back.

"Have a good evening, Ben." She walked toward the parking lot, and he walked in the opposite direction, muttering something. It might have been a good-night.

When Summer got to her car, she finally breathed. Maybe she'd been holding her breath the whole time. Ben was a good cop. His instincts told him something more was happening. What he didn't realize was that she longed to tell him everything, to hand it all over to him, but she couldn't. He also didn't know that his only son was involved in her deception. She hadn't wanted to get him involved, but no matter which way she looked, she hadn't been able to find an alternative.

She sat in the car and watched the storm clouds move across the sky. What if the fake sale of the bookstore turned into a legitimate one? What if the kidnappers bought the store and killed Mimi anyway? It could go wrong in so many ways.

She started the car, flipped on the radio, and "Silent Night" filled her car. Christmas was in three days. She had a lot to get done. Presents to buy. The inside of her house to decorate. But more than anything, she needed Mimi back. Summer couldn't have Christmas with Mimi in danger.

The soft rumble of the engine played against the music. Car in gear, she headed home.

Just as she was pulling into the driveway, a raindrop splattered on the windshield. Her phone rang. She picked up.

"Hello."

"Hi there, this is Sally. I've got my mom here on speaker. Her name is Ruby. She's happy to talk with you."

Summer settled her excitement. "Great. Hi, Ruby." She briefly told them what little she knew of her family history, explaining that she was looking to find out more. "I spent some time with Rima, Sam, and Fatima today," she concluded. "They told me the brothers had a fight over a woman. And that woman was my father's fiancé."

Silence.

"Mom?"

"Can she hear me?"

"Yes. She can hear you."

"Oh!" Nervous laughter from Ruby. "Yes, Summer, that's true, but I've always suspected there was more to it."

"What do you mean?" Rain splattered the windshield.

"Bashir left soon after the murder of Jamila. I always wondered if he did it."

"Mom! Really?"

Summer's ear pricked up. "His son is in town, and I found him very cold."

"Cold is one word for it. I never liked his dad. But your father? He was so different from the rest of them."

Ruby's words warmed her. "Can you tell me anything about Jamila?"

"She was very sweet, a good worker, very loyal to the family. She came from the same small town in Egypt where they came from. Their families were quite intertwined."

"Tell her, Ma. Tell her what you told me."

"She was very depressed for months. Something had happened . . . with her and Rima. They had words, and she just wasn't the same after. I couldn't put my finger on it then, and I still can't. But that young woman had become so depressed that I barely recognized her at times."

Summer ran her hands along the steering wheel. "So you think something happened that threw her into this depression and may have resulted in her murder."

"I do. I've never thought it was random."

Summer shuddered. Her inkling that Rima knew more about the incident grew more intense.

"Rima was the reason I planned to quit. But the day after they found Jamila, she let everybody go. She was a difficult woman, and I'd just had enough."

"What do you mean specifically?"

"Nothing I ever cooked was good enough. She sent food back all the time. She was hard on her boys. She'd fling shoes at them to hit them. She had quite the aim."

"What? She hit them with shoes?" Summer raised her voice over the sound of the rain hitting her car.

"And once she beat one of her daughters for speaking with a man in public."

Summer gasped. It was beyond the pale.

Chapter Forty-Seven

So Rima wasn't the sweet old grandmother Summer had longed for. But was she a killer? A pang of suspicion tore at her. Why would Rima kill Jamila? What could her motive have been?

What had happened between the two of them that had sent Jamila into a depression?

"Is there anybody who worked there at the time who might know more?"

The rain was coming harder now. It pelted her car. Trees swayed in the wind.

"Anybody? I can give you a list. I was in the kitchen, but others were in the fray more. I'm sure they know more than I do. I'll text you names and phone numbers." She paused. "I hope you find something out. Not a day goes by I don't think of that young woman . . ."

"I'm sure."

That young woman had been from the same town in Egypt as the Bellamy family. She'd been saving money for medical school. *Medical* school. Her family must have been very proud of her. Working hard. Good student. Evidently, they were of modest means—or she wouldn't have had to stop her education and work.

"Do you know anything about her family?"

"She had a brother living in Chicago at the time. I think she said he was an engineer."

Summer's heart jumped. "I wonder if he's still in Chicago." Reaching out to find someone in Chicago was one thing; Egypt was another.

"Maybe. When she died, he was the one who claimed her body and took care of getting her home. It happened very quickly. Muslims prefer burial within twenty-four hours after death. They didn't quite make it, but it was very quick."

This was the first Summer had learned about any of this. It wasn't in any reports or newspaper articles. But then again, why would it be?

"You know, I gotta say I see the wisdom in it," Ruby said. "But I often wondered if the autopsy was too rushed. Maybe if they'd taken their time . . ."

Summer had wondered about that as well. "What do you think of Mimi Sinclair's book? *Mermaid Point Murder*."

Ruby whistled through her teeth. "I've not read it. I'm just not a reader, sorry to say. I'm a cook. But I've heard it's bold."

"Bold?" Summer was almost yelling to be heard over the rain.

"Yeah, that in her book one of the brothers kills Jamila to keep a family secret."

"What's the secret?"

"An illegitimate baby."

Summer wanted to laugh. That was no big deal; illegitimate babies were everywhere. But wait—this was in the 1980s. Maybe not quite as prevalent. Still. "It doesn't sound like cause for murder."

"Not for most of us. But in Muslim culture, at that time, being a virgin was of utmost importance when you married. So, if the baby was conceived out of wedlock . . ."

Summer's head spun. Mimi had probably had no idea it would be such a deep vein of embarrassment to the family to make such a suggestion.

"I do hope they find Mimi safe and sound."

"Me too," Summer said, before she said good-bye. It was getting to be almost impossible to talk over the rain.

Piper and Agatha had also mentioned a baby in the book, and they'd at first thought it could be referring to Summer until they realized the numbers didn't add up. Could someone have taken such offense to that notion as to kidnap the author and cut off her finger? Summer doubted it.

There had to be something else.

True to her word, Ruby sent along a list of people working at the house at the time of the murder. Summer was certain the police had talked to each of them already. But it wouldn't hurt to give them a call. Her eyes scanned the list. One name leapt out at her: Luna Rangoon. One of her mom's dearest friends.

Summer's heart raced and her brain sparked. Luna would tell her everything she wanted to know and more—including the astrological signs of the individual involved. Summer had always considered it complete mumbo jumbo, but she had to admit that since her mom's death and the investigation of her murder, she'd come to realize that there was something more to the universe than what she could see with her eyes.

Why hadn't she remembered Luna first? She was a wise woman with her ear to the ground and her eyes on the stars. She might know more than anybody else what was going on with Mimi.

Summer gathered her things and made a mad dash for her house, as the rain had eased momentarily. She still ended up soaked and chilled. She craved a long, hot bath and a glass of wine.

She glanced at the clock. Yes, that was exactly what she'd do, before her next "babysitter" came along. Was it Glads tonight? Piper? She'd lost track.

She didn't feel like she needed anybody there, though she supposed it was best to err on the side of caution.

As she entered the house, her skin prickled. Something was out of place. She dropped her bag on the hallway table and headed for the kitchen. As she walked along, she fell hard—pushed by a strong arm. Her head thwacked against the wall before everything went black.

Chapter Forty-Eight

Summer! Summer! A voice rang in her head. Enveloped in a mist, Summer strained to see. But she moved toward the voice. *Summer!*

I'm here, Mom. Where are you?

Here. Summer felt her mother's arms wrap around her, and she fell into them. The hug spread warmth and light through her, stemming from the center of her chest outward.

"Summer, I'm so proud of you," Hildy said, not letting go of the embrace. "So proud."

Summer sank into her, allowing the warmth of the moment to comfort her. Nobody hugged better than her mother. *Her mother.* Wait. something was wrong. Her mother was dead. This wasn't right.

Hildy was gone.

Summer cried out, "Mom!"

"Shhhhh," a voice said. "Can you open your eyes?"

Summer struggled to do so. "Aunt Agatha? What—"

"Shhh. It's okay. I came in and found you here. The door was wide open. Ben is on his way."

Summer struggled to sit. "Why?"

"Your place has been vandalized. They cut up the couch, the drapes. Some of the paintings and pictures. Someone was in here." She cradled Summer and helped her to sit up.

Why would someone do this? Had it been the kidnapper trying to warn her because they'd observed her with Ben? She recalled walking through the door and someone's hand on her. Hard hands. Strong hands. She swore she could still feel them.

Aunt Agatha blinked hard. "You were calling for your mom."

Summer swallowed. "I was dreaming about her."

Agatha helped her stand. Summer was woozy. Her rubbery legs took a minute to adjust to her feet being on the floor. "I've been dreaming about her almost every night," her aunt said, her eyes alight.

A pang of jealousy tore through Summer. How ridiculous. Silly dreams. Nobody could control them, especially not the dead people in the dreams.

Her head pounded. She rubbed the knot. "I need ice."

"I'll get it."

Agatha sat her down on an overstuffed chair, with Mr. Darcy observing her. He flapped his wings and rocked back and forth.

"Hello, Darcy. Pretty bird," Summer said weakly.

He whistled back to her.

She took in the room. The couch cushions' insides spewed everywhere. Shredded magazines were strewn all over the floor.

Aunt Agatha walked back into the room with an ice pack, aspirin, and a glass of water. "It might be a while before Ben gets here. The storm is slowing everybody down."

The storm. Right. She'd been sitting in her car and talking to a woman. Ruby. Talking about Rima. The rain was pelting the car. She gulped the water with the aspirin, lay back, and placed the ice pack on her head.

"Do you remember what happened? Did you see anything?"

"I saw nothing. I walked in and was pushed from behind."

Aunt Agatha's hands rested on her hips as she took in the room. "Isn't this awful? Who would do such a thing?"

The freezing-cold ice pack stung Summer's head. She grimaced. "I wish I knew."

"Could this have to do with Mimi's disappearance?"

"It must. I can't think of another reason someone would do this." It hurt to speak. All her nerve endings were converging in the lump on her head.

"I'm packing a bag for you. You're coming home with me." Aunt Agatha's voice held a finality that Summer was familiar with. There was no arguing with her.

Besides, as she took in the place, it creeped her out.

A boom of thunder. The bird squawked. Rocked back and forth.

"It's okay, Darcy. It's just a storm."

He cocked his head and continued to rock.

Summer started to stand.

"Whoa. Where do you think you're going?"

"I wanted to calm Darcy. Get him out of the cage and love him up."

"I'll get him." Aunt Agatha opened his cage door, and he grabbed on to her arm.

Summer offered her arm to him, and he hopped over. She tucked the bird into her neck, and he placed his head there as she stroked him. He purred as he situated himself between her neck and shoulder.

Aunt Agatha grinned. "That bird."

As Summer stroked him with one hand and held the ice pack with the other, a knock sounded at the door.

"Must be Ben," Agatha said, exiting the room.

The bird stiffened.

"It's okay, boy. I've got you," Summer said soothingly.

Ben walked into the room, and the bird curled into her even more. Darcy was not fond of Ben. As had been established several times.

He was wet, disheveled. He nodded. "Summer."

"Ben."

"Is the bird okay?"

"Slightly traumatized, I'd say. He doesn't like storms, but he'll be fine."

He looked around. "I don't like them either. What happened here?"

Aunt Agatha stepped forward and told him everything.

"Do you think this was random?" Summer asked as she continued to stroke the bird.

"Usually when we see this kind of vandalism, it's random. But other people in the neighborhood would have experienced some kind of incident as well. Nothing else has been reported. So in this case, I can't guess."

"Could it have to do with Mimi's missing-person case?" Agatha said.

"Seems unlikely, given that she's still gone and we've not heard from a kidnapper or anything."

Summer's heart nearly leaped out of her chest.

"If it weren't for the blood and the broken window upstairs, I'd almost think she just walked out of here on her own. The investigation is about to close. We've not got the resources to continue searching for her." He paused. "In any case, we'll need to write up a report about this so you can submit it to your insurance."

"Insurance is the furthest thing from our minds," Agatha said. "She's coming home with me tonight. Why does this place keep getting broken into and strange things keep happening? It seems dangerous for her to be here. None of this happened before Mimi came to this island. It seems logical to me that she has something to do with all of it. Or rather, her assailant."

"What would the point be to this?" He gestured toward the trashed room.

The women were silent.

"Unless you have been investigating on your own and have gotten very close to solving it. Summer? Is that what you've been doing?"

She drew in a breath. "I've been trying to solve the murder case."

"What murder case?"

"Jamila's."

His face reddened. "You're what?"

"We've come up with a theory that if we find out who killed her, we'll find the person who took Mimi."

"We?"

"Peg and Lucy came up with the theory. I think. I don't remember." Her head pounded. "I've been visiting with the Bellamys, talking to the help. That kind of thing."

"Hmph."

"Have you found out anything?" Agatha asked.

"Yes. All kinds of things about my family. But nothing that would help the case. I don't think."

"You have every right to question your family about all this," Agatha stated.

"Maybe more so than most," Ben said.

What had she just heard? Was Ben okay with what she'd done?

"I can't get to them at all anymore. Maybe you can."

Chapter Forty-Nine

When Summer walked into her Aunt Agatha's home, she was swept back to her childhood. Carrying a birdcage containing a cranky bird and a suitcase, she made her way to the guest room, Aunt Agatha trailing her. "I've called my friend Ted to come and examine you to see if you have a concussion. If there's anything you need, please just let me know. You've got a nasty bump. It's probably best for you to just go to bed. Get off your feet."

Summer couldn't agree more.

After Ted scanned her and pronounced her concussion-free, she slipped on her night clothes and pulled on her face mask. "Good night, Mr. Darcy."

He squawked back at her. He was not a bird who liked change.

Even though she was exhausted, Summer tossed and turned, as she couldn't seem to get comfortable. The bird also couldn't settle down. Her aunt wouldn't appreciate Darcy being in bed with her, so she refrained from calming the bird by snuggling with him.

She drifted off to sleep, only to wake back up at four in the morning, bright-eyed. She flipped on the bedside light and rummaged through her bag. She'd brought her files with her. She pored over them and added more to her timeline. Her uncle. Rima.

She spread the files out on the bed.

Rima had discovered the body on Mermaid Point in August.

A month later, Summer's uncle left the island, never to return.

Jamila's brother arrived on the island the day after they found her.

Two days later he flew back to Egypt with Jamila's body to have her buried at home.

Was he still in the U.S.? In Chicago?

She pulled out her laptop and keyed in his name.

A string of *Assad Bastana*s came up, some in Syria, some in Egypt. Some in Boston, New York. She limited the search terms by including the word *engineer*. And there he was. Yes! He was in Chicago and had his own engineering firm.

She clicked on his bio.

Assad Bastana had grown up in Reda, Egypt, the youngest son of two schoolteachers. After graduating from the University of Chicago with his master's in engineering, he'd started Bastana Mechanical Design at the same time he began Jamila Bastana Foundation, named for his sister.

A foundation named for her? This was interesting. Nobody had mentioned this. Did anybody even know? Did they care about her beyond trying to solve her murder? Had they dug into her background very much?

Tears stung Summer's eyes as she clicked over to the foundation's home page. The foundation supported young Muslim women who wanted careers in medicine. What a moving way to honor his sister.

She clicked through the photos of the many young women the foundation had helped—some wearing a hijab and some not.

Summer had taken a class on Islam years ago and appreciated the beauty of the religion. It appealed to her intellect, but she had been brought up pagan and Christian. Aunt Agatha had taken her to church, and she'd liked it. Her mom had never stood in the way. In fact, they'd often had interesting conversations about religion when Summer returned from church.

Islam was variable. Like Christianity, it had many forms—hence some women wearing the hijab and some not, for instance. Several interpretations of the Koran existed, just like the Bible. So Muslims couldn't all be painted all with one stroke. Summer kind of wished they could—it would make figuring out her family and the murder a little easier, perhaps.

She was digressing. She needed to focus on the matter at hand, not get carried away with learning everything she could about her family and Jamila.

The one thing she could take from this new information was that she needed to call Assad.

"Summer?" Aunt Agatha's voice came through the door as she rapped on it. "Breakfast is ready."

Summer couldn't believe the early-morning hours had slipped away. "Be right there." Research had always been her jam. She could lose herself in it—and had on many occasions.

She gathered up all the papers spread across the bed and shut her laptop. Her head was swimming. Jamila's brother was alive and well in Chicago.

As she readied herself for breakfast, her phone rang. It was Poppy.

"What the hell?" she said when Summer answered.

"What?"

"The bookstore? You didn't tell me you decided to sell."

Heat rushed through Summer. "I'm sorry. I meant to tell you yesterday, but with the storm and everybody leaving early . . . I just didn't get around to it."

"It's my job," Poppy said, voice cracking.

"Don't worry. I've got you covered. It'll be a part of the contract that the new owners will keep the current staff." She paused, giving herself credit for her quick thinking. "I'd not leave you high and dry. I promise."

Poppy snorted. "Well, that's good at least." She hung up.

Oh boy. This fake-sale-of-the-bookstore thing was going to be harder than Summer had imagined. But today was the day. If all went well, they should have Mimi back by the end of the day. If she was okay, Summer could get back to her home and celebrate. Summer whispered a prayer that the kidnapper would be true to their word and release Mimi.

Her phone beeped with a text message from Cash. *Where are you?*

I stayed at Aunt Agatha's last night.

I've already been contacted by the seller. Let's meet at the bookstore in an hour?

Alright. Is everything okay?

Depends on how you look at it. Talk soon.

Summer's heart raced. If this didn't work out, she could lose everything—and Mimi could be killed.

Chapter Fifty

Summer had gotten over the need to be liked years ago, which had served her well as a college professor. She didn't care that she was the least favorite teacher on campus. She wasn't there for a popularity contest. She was there to educate, which sometimes meant doing "unlikable" things, like failing a student, not allowing makeups on certain tests, and not becoming her students' "friend."

All that said, she'd gotten used to the way her mom's friends had scooped her into their circle and the way she was respected and liked as the new owner of Beach Reads.

So when she entered the bookstore and the group of them stood with their arms crossed, glaring at her, she wanted to cry. Instead, she walked by them and into her office, where Cash and Piper waited.

"Oh boy, you've pissed them off," Piper said.

"I know, and it breaks my heart." Summer set her bags down.

A disheveled Cash cradled a paper cup of coffee in his hand. He looked as if he'd just rolled out of bed. Summer quashed the stirring she felt. "Can someone tell me what's going on?"

"Sit down." Piper gestured to her chair.

Uh-oh.

She sat down. Piper handed her a check from Sealife Incorporated, certainly a dummy company.

Summer read it over. Her eyes landed on the amount: 3.5 million dollars. Her heart nearly stopped.

Piper eyed her cousin. "If you accepted this check, like really accepted it, you could be set for life."

Summer's mouth dropped open. She glanced at Cash.

"You should consider it," he said.

She'd stopped considering selling the bookstore. She'd figured she'd keep it, and even if she went back to teaching, she'd hand over the management reins to someone else. She didn't know if she'd ever have kids, but right now Mia was the person who stood to inherit the place. Could she even do that to her?

"Summer, you could do so much with this money." Piper crouched next to her. "I know what you're thinking. This is your mom's place. A part of her." She paused. "You're thinking about Mia too. But heck, you could send her to college. She wouldn't need aid and student loans . . . her future doesn't have to be here."

Summer blinked her eyes rapidly, as if to clear away the shock of having such a huge check in her hand.

"You can take the day to think it over. You have one more day." Cash leaned across the desk. She remembered his words to her last week: *How will you get over your mom's death if you're here?* She'd told him she didn't run away anymore. And she didn't.

But $3.5 million? She could run far, far, away. Was this the answer to everything? She could research and write books about Shakespeare, unencumbered. That was what she wanted, wasn't it? The teaching had turned out to not be what she'd expected. And academia was not the world she wanted. Her dreams crystallized as she held the check. To write and teach others in a different way—that was the dream.

She could certainly make it part of the contract that Poppy and Mia keep their jobs. The others were volunteers. The Mermaid Pie Book Club could still be a club—that didn't have to change.

A shuffling at the office door made all three of them turn to look. Lucy and Peg stood there. The two cozy mystery authors had figured out what they were doing, of course.

They entered the office and shut the door without saying a word. Lucy pulled out another note and placed it on Summer's desk.

The next twenty-four hours are everything.

Cash scooped up the letters and the check. "I'll take these."

Peg leaned in. "I thought you didn't want him involved."

Summer's face heated. "I changed my mind."

One eyebrow lifted, and Peg whispered, "I can see why."

Summer felt heat spread further through her. Yes, Cash was a good-looking man, and like it or not, she was still attracted to him. Or was it a new attraction? But that was neither here nor there, as she had other things to think about.

"I'd appreciate it if you two kept this on the down low," she said.

"We're not telling a soul, especially the disgruntled crew out front." Peg crossed her arms. "I've already told them how rude it is. This is your bookstore and your life. Your mom wanted to have it to do with what you wanted. This is none of their business."

"I couldn't agree more," Piper said, with a gravity the two writers wouldn't understand.

This money could change Summer's life.

"I have some thinking to do," Summer said after a few beats of silence, realizing that Peg and Lucy had no idea what she had to think about. But that was probably a good thing.

"Is that code for us to leave?" Lucy asked.

"I think it is." Piper gathered her things and ushered everyone out, some muttering good-byes.

Summer was alone in the office. She had twenty-four hours to decide. But there had been no mention of when they'd let Mimi go. She shivered. Summer was cooperating, as far as they knew, and yet there had been no communication about Mimi or from Mimi. Cold swept through Summer again. How could she trust that they'd let Mimi go, even if she accepted their check?

She pondered the money. How it would change her life. But could she even entertain accepting it if Mimi didn't survive? Even if she did, surely she'd never be the same. A hard knot formed in her stomach. It was blood money. Pure and simple.

Chapter Fifty-One

Summer took a deep breath and walked out into the store. Her employees and friends were milling around the cash register. There were very few customers in the shop, so she approached them.

"Listen, I'm sorry I didn't tell you about this. It was a last-minute decision. I need to get back to Staunton." Her voice quavered. "It will be part of the contract that employees will keep their jobs and that Mermaid Pie Book Club can meet here."

"Peg was right," Glads said. "It's none of our business what you do with the store. Hildy left it to you. It's yours."

"But a little warning would've been nice," Marilyn said.

"Agreed," Summer said. "I'm so sorry." Her heart hurt. She hated disappointing these women and hated lying to them. She wasn't selling the bookstore. It was a ruse. Even though she had a $3.5 million check, she couldn't accept it. This time tomorrow, she'd divulge everything. If all went well. Standing with the group, Summer took in their faces—disappointment, hurt, concern—until she couldn't take it anymore. "I'm going upstairs to check on things."

As she walked away, her gut pulled at her. She'd never have gotten through these last few months without them. Lying to them felt like a betrayal, even though it wasn't.

In every kidnapping case Summer had read or known anything about, the kidnapper had gotten in touch with the person who was coming up with the money. As she glanced around the second floor of the store, straightening books, throwing out empty water bottles and used tissues, her attention turned to the oddness of how the kidnapper had contacted her, using Peg and Lucy as the messengers. And Peg and Lucy had helped with the research. Peg and Lucy were everywhere, and suddenly Summer didn't like it.

They were aware of everything about the case and about what was happening with the store. Everything. They were all up in her business.

She walked by two customers who were browsing the mystery section. She stood at the windows overlooking the balcony, watching as the waves rolled in and out. The gray skies grew darker, and the ocean responded in kind. It was going to bloody storm again! She was so tired of the rain. Here it was, so close to Christmas, with no snow on the horizon, only buckets of rain.

A pang of nostalgia tugged at her. There had been snow last year in Staunton. She'd left it to visit her mom for a week. When she'd returned to Staunton, even more snow had welcomed her.

She didn't want to go back to a job she hated just because Staunton was one of the prettiest towns on the planet. She loved teaching, she loved writing, but she hated academia. She swallowed. Hard to admit. It was all she'd thought she ever wanted.

That check would allow her a major life change.

But wasn't that what this was?

Being here in this store, so much a part of her mom?

She didn't have to be a part of academia to write or teach.

She could figure out another way.

But first: to get Mimi back. She swallowed. They'd still not been able to figure out the murder at Mermaid Point. She agreed with Peg and Lucy on this. Mimi's case had to tie back to the murder.

Summer recalled her list of Bellamy ex-employees. She didn't want to chat with them here.

She tore herself away from the view and headed back to her office. Things were quiet in the store. Even Poppy and the rest of the group, now dispersed, were quiet, each off into their own things.

But just as her foot hit the last step on her way downstairs, Ben Singer stepped out of the shadows of the bookshelves. Paranormal romance.

"Ben! You startled me!"

He grabbed her elbow. "Come with me into your office."

"Okay." She pulled away from him as they walked.

"What's going on?" she asked, the moment they were behind the closed door.

"Can you get back into the Bellamy house?" His eyes were bright with anticipation.

"Probably, why?"

"We've been tailing Bashir. We're within our right to do that, since he's on probation. He checked out late last night, but he's not left the island. He's still here. We think he's staying with them."

Summer's heart raced. "They barely know him. And I don't think they're fond of him."

Ben nodded. "Yes, but he is family. I don't think they'd turn him away. Do you?"

Summer sat in her chair. "I'm sorry. I have no idea. I don't really know them."

Ben quieted and appeared to be deep in reflection. "I'm not sure they're safe with him in the house."

"Ben, for god's sake, then just check."

A pained expression played out on his face. "I'm not welcome there. I can't say I blame them. When Rima sees me, she goes limp. Or ballistic. It's unproductive."

Summer understood, but surely this was better handled by the police than by her—the secret love child of a local girl and Rima's son. "Is your assistant back from his vacation?"

"No."

"I'll just text Sam and see." She picked up her phone.

"I don't think that's a good idea. I need you to get eyes on them, to make sure they're okay."

Summer's stomach hardened. "There's something you're not telling me."

He nodded. "I think he knows where Mimi is."

Heat swirled through Summer and traveled to her face, which she was certain would pop with anger at any moment.

"Please keep it to yourself. He's our number-one suspect. If everybody else is around, I don't think he'd be dangerous to you."

Her cousin was the number-one suspect in a kidnapping. And he might be staying with her new family.

"Okay. I'll do it," Summer said.

Chapter Fifty-Two

Just as Ben left, the bookstore line rang. Summer picked up.

"Summer Merriweather, please."

"Speaking."

"This is Martina Biro from Three Lakes Press. I'm Mimi's editor. I'm calling to see if you have any word on Mimi."

Summer drew in air, then let it out. "No. I'm sorry."

"How could something like this happen?"

"She wrote about a murder that happened here thirty years ago."

"I know that," Martina snapped. "I edited the book. There was nothing in that little book that should've caused this. "

"I've not read it. But I agree, it seems ridiculous. But she was threatened before she even came here."

"She was?"

"Yes, but she was determined to come, even through a snowstorm. She had her husband drive her, drop her off."

"What? Mimi has no husband."

Summer's heart tumbled in her chest. "What? That's what she said. She said her husband dropped her off."

"Did you see him drop her off?"

"No."

"Odd. Mimi and her husband split a few years ago. I don't know, maybe they are back together, though I doubt it. But in any case, we're all very upset."

"Of course. We are too," Summer said. Mimi didn't have a husband. Even though she'd told everybody he dropped her off. Were they back together, as Martina suggested? Was it a boyfriend she'd not told anybody about? Summer had had a few of those. But those days were long gone.

"Can you please keep me informed? I'd be there right now if it wasn't so close to Christmas. You know. Family stuff."

Summer did know. Her stomach sank. Christmas without her mom. Christmas with a missing Mimi. "Yes, of course. I'll keep you posted."

After Summer clicked off, she looked up Mimi's website, clicked on the *About* section. It did still say she was married. Maybe she just hadn't updated it. Maybe she didn't feel like she had to let her readers know about her personal life. Summer could appreciate that.

The husband was always the number-one suspect in the murder of a married woman. But what about in a kidnapping? Ben was still trying to reach Mimi's husband. "No wonder he couldn't get him," she muttered. She dialed Ben and left a message.

She sat at her desk, trying to ready herself to visit the Bellamys. Her orders were to get into their house, see if Bashir was there, and survey the mood. Were the Bellamys happy to see him?

She didn't know them that well, but she'd be able to sense whether something was off.

A shiver traveled through her. She couldn't say why. It wasn't as if Ben had asked her to infiltrate a spy ring or something. This was her family. And they might be in trouble. He was the son of the man who'd split with their father. Was he here to heal? Or here to settle the score?

According to the cook, Bashir's father was deeply in love with Arwa. Much like her own father with Hildy. It had been just as forbidden for them to be together as it had been for Hildy and Omar.

As Summer shut down her computer and gathered her things, she reflected on the fact that most murder victims knew their killers. Her mom had known hers. But Jamila hadn't known many people. Just the Bellamy family, from what Summer could gather.

But maybe not. Maybe she'd had friends. Summer remembered the list of employees she had on her phone. She didn't have the time now to call them. But Jamila's friends and associates needed a voice. Had Jamila been a social butterfly on the island? Or had she stayed at home?

Summer stood and wrapped her scarf around her neck, reaching for her coat. Ben had said not to warn her family that she was coming. It was to be a surprise visit.

She rolled her eyes. Ben.

She was doing this out of curiosity. She wanted to see for herself whether or not Bashir was there.

When she turned to go, Cash was in her doorway, Piper just behind him.

"What's up?" she asked.

"We just wondered if you made a decision," Cash said. "We need to get the show on the road, since tomorrow is Christmas Eve. Some offices and banks close Christmas Eve."

Summer took in his face and then her cousin's hopeful gaze.

"I'm sorry," she said. "I can't take that money. I'm not saying that I will never sell the bookstore. But not like this. I know it could change my life. But I don't think I could live with it."

"Oh, Summer." Piper wrapped her in her arms. "Crazy. You're crazy!"

"Crazy, but filled with integrity. Per usual," Cash said, blinking hard. "I'll start the process."

"Where're you going?" Piper said after a moment.

"I'm going to see the Bellamys," Summer replied.

"Why?"

Summer looked away from Piper. "Just visiting."

Piper squinted her eyes. "Uh, interesting." She folded her arms.

"I've got to run." Summer walked through the door. "I'll see you later. I shouldn't be long."

"Famous last words!" Piper yelled after her.

Chapter Fifty-Three

Summer wrapped her scarf tighter around her neck. The temperature was dropping, and the wind was picking up. Perhaps they were getting another storm. She walked toward the Bellamy house. The place looked strange. As in, no lights on and no cars in the driveway. Maybe they weren't home? She rang the doorbell. No answer.

Hmm. Well, they weren't expecting her. She was just popping in.

She walked around the side of the house. Maybe they were outside. A short distance away, she spotted the spire of the castle. It couldn't hurt for her to check it out.

She found steps leading to the castle and started down them. As she descended, it was as if she were walking in the sky. The clouds lowered around her to form a thick mist. A storm was moving in. She folded her arms around her body and moved ahead on the rickety steps.

The castle sat lower than the house on the cliffs, and as she drew closer, its majesty reached out and grabbed her. It was a small castle but still a castle, perched on a hillside and facing the sea, Mermaid Point, and beyond.

She squinted to see the point, imagining the boat holding the body of Jamila tucked inside. One shot to the heart.

What would it have been like to grow up here with this view? This castle? A father? She swallowed a creeping sensation in her throat. It would've been nice.

But she loved the tiny beach cottage where she'd grown up. It brimmed with love. And even though it didn't offer a view like this, she'd grown up with a view of a different sort. The beach was just down the grassy path from their front porch.

When she reached the castle, she peered through the closest window. Definitely an office building. She was disappointed not to see red carpets and thrones. Or anything remotely castle-like. Instead, a conference table with chairs around it. Just like a thousand other conference rooms.

She turned to head back up the hillside and spotted a NO TRESPASSING sign. Oops.

But was she trespassing? After all, Bellamy blood ran through her veins.

She'd have a hell of a time explaining that to a security guard.

Summer rushed up the stairs and toward her car, feeling the first chilly raindrops fall just before she threw open the door and climbed inside. She sat for a few moments and listened to the rain on her car. She loved the sound.

She turned on the ignition, backed out of the driveway, and headed back to Beach Reads.

* * *

When she entered the bookstore, Peg and Lucy greeted her.

"We came to say good-bye," Peg said. "Tomorrow is Christmas Eve, and family beckons."

"Indeed," Lucy said. "But I hate to leave with Mimi still missing."

"Me too!"

Summer hated to see them go. But it was Christmas.

"I hope everything goes well," Lucy said. "That Mimi comes walking through that door any minute."

"Speaking of Mimi . . . did you know that she's not married?" Summer asked them.

"The last I heard, she was married." Lucy lifted her bag to her shoulder.

"Her publisher called me earlier and said she's been divorced for several years."

Peg's mouth dropped open. "Then who dropped her off at your place?"

"I don't know. He didn't come in. She placed her bags in the hall and I left for the store." Summer didn't know if this was an important detail, but something nagged at her about it. "Why would she lie about being married?"

Lucy cleared her throat. "This doesn't sit right. If she lied about being married, god knows what else she's lied about. She's gone to great lengths for publicity sometimes. I hate to think that's what's going on here."

"Surely not," Peg said.

But Summer wasn't so sure. Then again, she wasn't so sure about anything these days.

"God, I hate to leave," Peg said. "Please call if there's anything I can do. You have my number, right?"

Summer nodded. "Thank you both for all your help, the research, the brainstorming."

She hugged them each in turn and watched them walk out of Beach Reads to go back to their families for Christmas. Though she doubted either would have a pleasant holiday. Not this year, with one of their own missing, as vexing as she was.

She pushed ahead into her office, trying to evade the glares coming from Poppy and Glads. She dialed Ben's number and left another message. "I went to the Bellamy house, just like you asked. They weren't home."

Glads stood in her office doorway. "Are we still having a party?"

"Of course. The day after Christmas, just like always," Summer said.

"Well, I just thought I'd check. Things change so quickly around here."

"Glads. You have to believe me. Everything will continue as normal."

"Everything?"

"Well, I may not be here as much. That's all." Summer's charade of selling the bookstore and moving back to Staunton continued, though she didn't miss it there at all. The minute Cash and Piper had started talking about selling the store, Summer had felt a shift in her world, even though she hadn't quite known what that shift meant. Now she did. Telling her dean wouldn't be easy.

But she couldn't tell Glads that. Not yet.

"What do we need for the party?" Summer asked.

"We usually all bring leftovers from Christmas. How does that sound to you?"

Summer nodded. "Fabulous."

Her phone rang. It was Ben. "I have to take this."

Glads nodded and left.

"Hello, Ben."

"Got your message."

"And?"

"I checked into it. Mimi is not married. Which begs the question of who brought her here."

"A boyfriend, maybe."

"Did you see the driver at all?"

"No, I'm afraid not. I mean, she just showed up on my doorstep. When I opened the door, the car was long gone."

"Okay. Maybe a neighbor saw something. Thanks. We'll check around." He paused. "If you get a chance, go back to the Bellamys. I have a weird feeling."

"What do you mean?"

He sighed and breathed into the phone. "I have no idea what I mean. Call it old-cop intuition."

Chapter Fifty-Four

Summer would never have believed she'd hear the word *intuition* come out of Ben Singer's mouth. But life was full of surprises. Sometimes good ones.

Most of the time, they weren't.

Summer stood and walked out into the bookstore. *Her* bookstore. The rest of her crew were milling around. If she were paying Glads and Marilyn, she'd would have been pissed. But they were volunteers. Maybe she should give them a check for Christmas. Yes, that's what she'd do.

Poppy still seethed. Steam came out of her ears whenever Summer made eye contact with her. Poppy obviously felt as if Summer had betrayed her—even though she hadn't. God knew she couldn't have learned how to manage the store without Poppy. Her assistant was a keeper.

Summer hoped Cash was correct, that the pretend sale would go off without a hitch. That it would lead them to Mimi.

The floor creaked in the same spot it always creaked. *I should get that fixed. Along with the creak on the third stair. And shine the mermaid overhang on the door. All things I really should do.*

Things I will *do.*

She walked down the regency romance aisle and reshelved books, tucking them properly back into their spots. Customers often pulled them out and left them like orphans askew on the shelves. And sometimes when they did put them back, they put them in the wrong spot. Summer noted the titles as she tidied up.

Dukes.

Lords.

Princes.

She grinned. She still didn't get it. But whatever floated your boat. Piper was all about the regency romances.

She turned the corner, passing the overstuffed chair, where a woman sat with a pile of books on her lap. She glanced up and smiled at Summer. "I love this place. I come here every year to shop. I hope the new owner won't change anything."

Summer's heart flickered. "I hope so too."

She continued to walk down the regency romance aisle. She spotted the Bridgerton series, now all the rage on Netflix. The author was on Summer's list of people to invite to the store for an event. She tucked a book back into its spot.

She'd never thought she'd be here mulling over the Bridgerton series.

Nor had she ever thought she'd have a half brother, half sister, and grandmother from Egypt.

Nor had she ever thought she'd be able to stomach Ben, let alone work with him and do favors for him on a case.

Nor had she ever thought she'd know a kidnap victim. Or that she'd be the person supplying what the kidnapper wanted.

Careful, her mother's voice whispered in her head. *Careful, my love.*

Summer's heart raced. Careful was the word of the day.

She turned the next corner and almost ran into Yvonne Smith.

"Please," Yvonne said. "We need to talk."

Rage swept through Summer. "I've got nothing to say to you." She started to walk away.

"Off the record. Please," Yvonne said, following on Summer's heels.

Summer spun around to face her. "I hope you don't mind, but I don't trust you."

"Please. We have a lot in common, and I really need you to know this." Yvonne scanned the area and lowered her voice. "Privately."

Summer sized her up. "I'm not taking you into my office. We can go outside on the balcony." *Where I may push you off.*

Yvonne followed Summer upstairs and waited as Summer unlocked the balcony door. The balcony was closed off during the winter months.

Once they were outside, Summer planted her feet and crossed her arms. "What is it?"

"My father is Bashir Bellamy. The senior, of course. Your uncle."

Summer's stomach dropped into her feet—or at least that's what it felt like. She gathered herself. "That's absurd. Why would you make such allegations?"

"Because they're true. We're related, Summer. Under other circumstances, we both would've grown up surrounded by family and wealth. I don't know about you, but I certainly didn't. I was placed in an orphanage in Raleigh and adopted out eventually."

Adopted. As Mimi had been. Summer refrained from talking. Her ears burned with curiosity.

Mimi and Yvonne had both been adopted.

"I ran away at twelve and never looked back. You can guess why. I don't want to go into that. But yeah, maybe my writing skirts the truth sometimes—"

Summer harrumphed.

"But I'm a survivor. I'm smart and I'm sick." Yvonne wilted.

"Sick?" Summer asked. "What's wrong?"

"I have a rare form of liver disease. That sent me on my journey to find my parents."

The wind was picking up, and Yvonne's purple hair blew in the wind. She tucked it behind her ears. "And I found them. No question."

"And?"

"They won't even talk with me."

If Summer was making the right connections, Yvonne probably needed medical help from a relative.

"Here's the thing. I don't care if they ever acknowledge me. Or refuse to be a part of my life. I don't know about you, but I'm fine without them." She shoved her hands into her jean jacket. "But I want a chance. I want a chance to live. I don't want to die."

"Have you told them that?" Summer didn't know if she wanted to know the answer.

"I've tried. I've left messages, sent emails . . . they suspect I'm after their money," she said. "I get it. And when all this business with Mimi and the book came up, I tried to approach them at the restaurant."

"But I interrupted you." Summer's stomach sank.

She nodded.

"I'm sorry. I thought you were there for the Mimi story, and they weren't even aware of that yet."

Yvonne's brown eyes met Summer's black ones. "Are you sure about that?"

Summer shivered. She wasn't sure about anything anymore.

Now, as she recalled the lunch and Rima's becoming so upset, she realized she'd assumed it was all because she'd kept the news about Mimi from her grandmother. Looking back, what was so distressing to Rima could've very well been Yvonne's news. Which had the ring of truth.

Chapter Fifty-Five

"There you are!" A voice came from behind her. Poppy was at the door. "Someone is here to see you."

"Be right there." Summer held up an index finger. She turned back to Yvonne. "I'll see what I can do. In fact, I may head over to the Bellamys' later. Maybe you'd like to come with me?"

Yvonne's eyes watered and her mouth turned down. "Thank you. Yes, I'd like that."

"In the meantime, let's have a cup of coffee or tea and let's chat." Summer opened the door, and Yvonne walked through it. After locking the door, they went downstairs, Yvonne to the coffee station and Summer to the register, where Poppy stood with tiny, mocha-skinned Posey, who whirled around and embraced Summer. More like enveloped.

When Summer came out of the embrace, she became dizzy from the warm energy emanating from Posey—one of her mom's oldest friends, a modern-day witch, and self-described psychic.

"I needed to pick up a few gifts." She held up her packages. "I hoped to see you but couldn't find you anywhere."

"It's so good to see you." Heat rushed to Summer's face. Was she going to cry?

Posey took her in, then peeked over her shoulder as her smile faded. "Hello."

Summer turned to Yvonne. "This is Yvonne Smith."

Posey patted the woman's shoulder. "Are you well, my dear?"

"Not really." Yvonne drank from her cup, not knowing who Posey was or what her reported abilities were.

"No. I see that." She paused. "You're going to be fine."

Yvonne's eyebrows lifted. "How do you know that?"

"I just do." Posey almost twinkled at times. This was one of them. "Take care, dear. Now, Summer, can I talk to you privately?"

"Of course. Let's go into the office."

"That young woman is very sick," she said the minute the door was closed.

"Yes. It's her liver. She's searching for a donor."

"Hmm. Well, I think she'll find it. But it's not going to be easy."

Summer refrained from getting into the whole story. She wasn't certain if Yvonne would want her to. It wasn't her story to tell. "I'm sure. So, what's up?"

"Have the police gotten back to you about the bag of hair and teeth?"

"No. They're so busy trying to find Mimi."

She lifted an eyebrow. "I see you're selling the bookstore."

Summer looked away from her.

"I see. Be careful, Summer. I've been having dreams."

"Dreams?" Summer never wanted to be disrespectful to Posey and her way of thinking. But . . . dreams?

"Dreams about a castle."

"A castle . . ."

"It's cold and dark. Very musty. And I was very hungry. And frightened."

"What does this have to do with anything, Posey?"

"I think it has to do with you. Does any of it make sense to you?"

"Of course. The Bellamys have that castle. But it's office space now and not used very often. I was just there today and looking through the windows. That view . . ."

"You were there?"

"Yes, just briefly."

"I don't think that's a good idea." Posey shook her head.

"But the Bellamys are my family."

She grimaced.

"What do you know, Posey?" Had Hildy ever mentioned the Bellamys to Posey?

She paused and looked into Summer's eyes. "On one level, I only know as much as you. Hildy never told anybody anything. But on another level—the spiritual one, if you will—I sense a family filled with dark secrets and strife."

"Name one family that doesn't have those," Summer said.

"This is different. I think you'll find out. It will be like peeling a big, stinky onion. Each layer will get worse."

"Good god, Posey."

She laughed. "Okay, I do have a flare for the dramatic. But please be careful."

"Do you think they're violent?"

"I meant to be careful with your heart."

Summer swallowed hard. She probably didn't need Posey to tell her that, but hearing it from her mouth gave it heft. She nodded. "I will be. So . . . no visions of Mimi?"

"I've tried. The only message I'm getting is about a blue castle."

"Could she be in the castle?" Summer said, more to herself than to Posey. The castle was more gray than blue, but in a certain light, it might be considered blue. "Could someone be holding her there?"

"Perhaps . . . but you were just there. Did you see anything?"

"No. As I said, it was empty. I didn't walk around the building and investigate. I was there to see the family, and when they weren't home, I took a walk to the castle."

Posey shivered. "Something or someone is at that castle. But you shouldn't go poking around there."

Summer wondered if she should tell Ben about this. Then she shrugged it off. What would she say? Posey's having dreams about the castle and thinks Mimi might be there, hidden in its depths somewhere?

"Summer, promise me you won't go over there."

"How can I do that? They're my family. Of course I'll be going over there."

"That's not what I mean. I mean, don't go poking your nose in at the castle searching for Mimi or anything else."

"Fine." But even as she said it, she knew it was a lie. Posey probably knew it too.

Chapter Fifty-Six

Good-byes and Merry Christmases said, Posey and Summer parted. It was almost time to close the bookstore.

"If you can stick around, we can go over to the Bellamy house together," Summer said to Yvonne.

"Sounds good to me," she said. "I'm going to find a chair. I need to get some work done."

Summer nodded. "Poppy, I'll take over the register. Why don't you clean up a bit?"

"Sure thing, boss," she said.

Poppy's palpable disappointment hung in the air. Summer wished she could tell her it was all fake. That she'd never sell the bookstore, that she'd be here until the day she died.

But, of course, she couldn't.

"I adore your new Shakespeare section." A woman placed her books on the counter. "Not sure what Hildy would think of it, but I love it."

"You knew my mom?" Summer scanned the books in.

"Yes, of course. Everybody knew your mom. And nobody had a bad word to say about her. I miss her. She was quite a presence." She slid another book onto the counter.

The words warmed Summer even as she scanned the books in. She missed her mom with an almost inescapable rawness. But when someone said pleasant things about Hildy, it made Summer feel better. Her mom had made a difference. Had she? Had any of her students been so moved by her teaching? Summer didn't think so.

She lifted her chin. "That she did." She placed the books in a bag.

"Have a Merry Christmas." The customer took the bag and walked away.

"Same to you."

Summer straightened the counter. They had two mermaid Santa pins left. The pins had done so well. She'd have to remember that for next year.

As they approached closing time, things slowed down. People had finished their last-minute Christmas shopping. Tomorrow was Christmas Eve, and they'd be open half the day. Hildy used to say it was worth it to open the shop on Christmas Eve for a few hours even though they barely sold anything, as most people were already doing Christmas at home. Mostly it was good to keep the store open for those who didn't have much of a family—the lonely people who came into the shop to be among other people, even if they didn't talk or buy one book.

After the crew closed up the shop, Summer and Yvonne made their way toward Summer's car. A part of Summer couldn't believe she was taking Yvonne to the Bellamy house. But the reporter was sick. Surely she hadn't made that up, and Posey had kind of confirmed it.

Summer texted Sam once they were in her car. *Are you home? I'm coming to see you and I have a surprise.*

No response.

She searched through her message trail. He hadn't responded all day. And he wasn't home. Maybe they'd been out all day. Perhaps he wasn't the sort to always check his phone.

"Thank you for doing this," Yvonne said. "I know you're not fond of me and what I do for a living."

"We went to school together years ago, but I don't know you. It's not that I don't like you." Shards of shame traveled through Summer. "But it's true that I have no respect for journalists anymore."

"I'm just doing my job."

"But that article about Mimi . . ."

"Her publicist set that up. Wasn't my idea."

"Do you always run articles publicists set up?" Summer stepped on the brake to stop at a light.

"I only do it when my boss tells me to."

"You have no choice?"

"Not usually."

They drove along in companionable silence.

"Where do you think Mimi is?" Yvonne said.

"I have no clue. I wish I did. How about you?"

"I admit I wondered if the Bellamys had something to do with her disappearance."

"Why's that?" Summer made a left onto the road where her new family lived.

"It makes sense. She brought the story up again. About the murder. They have to be upset about it."

"I'm sure it upset them. But to kidnap the writer? I'm not sure that's their style." Summer pulled up into their driveway. "But I understand why people might come to that conclusion."

The house was still dark, and there were no cars in the driveway.

"I don't think they're home," Yvonne said.

Summer checked her phone. Still no word from Sam. How strange.

They exited the car onto the paved driveway. Summer pulled her coat closer around her as the wind picked up. They walked up the sidewalk, and she pressed the doorbell. Yvonne hung back.

No answer.

She pushed the bell again.

No answer.

"This is so strange," Summer said. "They must still be out."

Yvonne harrumphed. "Or maybe they skipped town."

"I doubt that. Why would they do that? This is their home."

"That's just my paranoid reporter's mind." She shuffled her feet. "Let's just go. It's not happening today."

"I guess you're right," Summer said, but a knot was forming in her stomach. Where could they be? "Let's look around back."

"Why?"

"This is a huge house. Maybe they didn't hear the doorbell."

Yvonne shrugged. "Okay."

They walked around the back, past the well-placed shrubs and rock garden. The house was dark in back too.

"Let's walk down here a minute." Summer headed for the path to the castle.

Yvonne stopped in her tracks. "Why?"

"I love the view from there, and I want to check it out."

"It's trespassing."

Summer eyed her. "That's rich, coming from you. You can stay here or go back to the car."

Yvonne drew in air. "Okay. I'm coming with you."

Chapter Fifty-Seven

Yvonne on her heels, Summer made her way down the narrow steps to the castle. Both stood and took in the view. The sun hung low in the sky, and muted grays and pinks splashed across it. The shimmering sea reflected the colors.

Summer walked to the same spot she'd been to earlier, feeling like she was doing something wrong, and peered into a window. It was the same scene as before. Nothing was different.

"What are you doing?" Yvonne whispered.

"I'm just looking." Summer turned to her. "Why are you whispering?"

Yvonne shrugged and gazed off.

Summer walked around to the front of the castle.

"Where are you going?" Yvonne followed her. "This is creepy."

"I'm looking around." Summer kept walking. "I told you that."

"But they aren't home. Nobody is here. Why are you doing this?"

"I'm just curious."

They walked around the next corner of the castle, and Summer peered into the window.

Gulls flew over, cawing. One swooped and landed at Summer's feet.

Another sound—another unfamiliar cawing—erupted. "What was that?" She turned to Yvonne.

"A bird?" Yvonne said, but her eyes were wide as the moon.

Summer tried the door. Locked. Of course. "Is someone inside?"

"I don't think so."

Prickles traveled up and down Summer's spine. What was that noise?

More birds came and landed at their feet. Summer loved the gulls. Always had, but she wished they'd be quiet. "I'm certain I heard something else."

"What does that bird have?" Yvonne pointed.

Summer squinted. One of the birds had something shiny in its beak. She drew closer to it, scaring it, and the bird dropped what it held onto the ground before flying away.

Summer reached for the object and held it up. "It's an earring."

"Well, that could've been here for quite some time," Yvonne said.

Summer studied it. It looked familiar. Had she seen someone wearing it? Or something like it?

No. It bore the same design as a few pieces of her own jewelry. The jewelry her mom had given her, with the Bellamy crest on it. She shivered. Cold crept through her. Something was going on here. *Danger!* her mother's voice said in her head.

"We need to go." She reached for Yvonne's elbow and pulled her along.

"Okay," she said. "What's wrong? You've gone pale."

Summer surveyed the area, saw nothing, nobody. But she tucked her head into her arm, as she had the distinct impression that someone was watching them. "Let's talk when we get in the car."

They hurried up the stairs and down the driveway.

Summer finally breathed when she got into the car. Breathed in and out. *In—one, two, three; out—one, two, three.* Just like Dr. Gildea had taught her.

"I don't know what's going on here," Yvonne said as she buckled herself in. "What's got you so freaked out?"

"The earring must belong to a Bellamy."

"Why do you say that, and so what if it is?"

"I say that because of the design. I recently learned about it. It's the Bellamy crest, if you will."

"Well, they live on the same property as the castle. It's not unusual that someone would lose an earring and it'd turn up down the hillside."

Summer let out another breath. What Yvonne said was true. Why was she so scared? "I don't know. It's weird that they've been gone all day and then I find an earring. Just weird." She dug her key out of her pocket and slipped it into the ignition. Then she pulled her phone out of her other pocket to check her messages. Nothing from Sam. "I'm not hearing from them either, which is really strange."

"Maybe there was a family emergency. Let's check the hospital."

Summer started up the car. "I will. But first I'm going to the police with this earring."

"The police?"

Summer couldn't tell Yvonne that Ben had asked her to check in on the Bellamys earlier. He hadn't said not to tell anybody, but it didn't feel as if she should. "I'll drop you off at your car first."

Yvonne yawned. "It's getting late. I do need to get home." She paused. "I remember when I could stay up until nine or ten. But these days . . ." She drifted off into quiet.

Summer flipped on the radio. Strands of "Jingle Bells" filled the car as the two of them headed for Beach Reads and Yvonne's car.

Summer's heart went out to Yvonne, a person she'd disliked only yesterday. Maybe she was getting kinder with her old age. She hoped so.

After a few minutes of silence, Yvonne took up the conversation again. "I don't understand why you're so freaked out," she repeated.

"I'm not," Summer lied.

"Why are you going to the police? It's just an earring. Something's telling me you're not telling me the whole story."

"You're right. I'm not. But believe me, it's nothing for you to worry about."

"Why don't you let me decide that and just tell me?"

"I don't think so." Summer pulled her car into the parking lot where Yvonne's car was. "Good night, Yvonne."

"Oh, all right." She unbuckled her seat belt. "I hope that whatever it is, you're not in over your head." She glanced at the FOR SALE sign.

The woman's instincts were sharp. Summer could see why she was a successful reporter. But Summer wasn't budging.

"Seriously," Yvonne said. "Mimi is still missing. Whoever has her isn't playing games."

Summer shivered. "Good night, Yvonne."

She exited the car. "Good night Summer."

Summer watched as Yvonne walked to her car and started the engine. Then she readied herself for a visit with Ben Singer.

Chapter Fifty-Eight

Summer hadn't been at the station since her mom died. Today, the parking lot was full. She guessed that a missing-person case did that to a small-town police force.

She parked, exited the car, and fingered the earring still in her pocket. She still had it.

When she walked into the office, it was buzzing with people, movement, and energy.

Ben Singer just happened to be within eyesight. Summer moved toward him.

"Can I help you?" a woman behind the desk said. Summer didn't recognize her.

"I need to see the chief."

"What's your name?"

Ben walked up to them then. "How can I help you?"

"Can we talk somewhere private?"

"Sure. Follow me."

Summer had been down this hallway. Emotions welled within her. Fear. Sadness. Frustration. It churned inside her as she walked. They ducked into his office.

"The Bellamys haven't been home all day, and Sam hasn't answered his text messages."

One of Ben's wiry gray eyebrows went up.

"And when I was over there, I walked around a bit. The castle is so . . . interesting, and the view is stunning." She paused. "I found this on the ground." She handed him the earring.

"Is this Mimi's?"

"No. It belongs to a Bellamy."

"Which one?"

"I don't know."

The eyebrow went up again.

"I'm sorry. See the design on it? It's the Bellamy crest, so to speak. I have a few pieces of jewelry like that. My mom gave them to me over the years."

He held up the earring, eyeballing it as it dangled. "Interesting."

Silence permeated the room.

"What do you think, Ben?"

"I'm concerned about the Bellamys, but we'll track them down. No need for you to worry."

"Hank will be back tomorrow, so I can send him over there." He smiled at Summer. "The Bellamys don't care for me. I'm sure you understand. I don't like upsetting Rima if it's not necessary. The murder almost broke her."

What an odd thing to say about her. "She seems okay now. In fact, she seems very strong."

"Oh yeah, the broken ones can seem stronger than most. It's all a ruse."

That was the most ridiculous thing Summer had ever heard. "Hmph. Okay. Well, I need to get going. My babysitter awaits."

"Babysitter?"

"Yes, everybody's insisting on taking turns staying with me until the Mimi thing is over."

"Good idea." He led her out of the office and through the hallway.

Summer hadn't noticed the blue aluminum Christmas tree on her way in. It struck her as a hopeful but pitiful decoration.

"Nice tree," she said flatly.

Ben laughed. "Take care, Summer."

"You too."

She opened the door and stepped out into the evening air. So cold for December. It was usually mild.

She'd longed for snow as a child. *Just one white Christmas, please.* Her first white Christmas ever had been in Staunton. February was the month they'd get snow on Brigid's Island, if they got snow. Winters would slip away without one flake. Of course, snow always looked like more fun than it was.

She checked her phone again. Still no word from Sam. Perhaps it was a brush-off. Maybe he and the rest of them were fine and he'd just decided to not have anything to do with her. Perhaps she wasn't worth the effort. Wouldn't be the first time she'd been—what did they call it now? ghosted? Yes. That was it.

Or maybe he was in trouble. But how? Why? What exactly was going on?

She gripped the steering wheel as she drove home. Mimi had been kidnapped by someone who wanted the bookstore. Taken right out of Summer's house. Someone had broken into Summer's place several times. Now the Bellamys seemed to be missing.

Surely not. A whole family just missing?

Summer's stomach growled. She'd not eaten in a while. She parked her car and made her way to her front door, where a box sat with a note on it.

Summer, I believe this might be yours. We found it in the backyard a few days ago and finally figured out who was in these photos. Your mom! No idea where it came from!
—Harold, owner of Missy

She cracked a smile. Missy was the cat who stopped by to stare at Mr. Darcy. And every time Summer ran into Harold, he introduced himself that way.

She unlocked the door and wrapped her arms around the box, lifting it. *I'm not waiting another minute. I waited too long. Almost lost these photos for good.* She set it on the kitchen table just as a knock came at her door.

"Yoo-hoo. It's us." The door opened, and in walked Aunt Agatha, Mia, and Piper. "You get all of us tonight!"

"And we brought food!"

Summer's stomach growled again. "Fabulous!"

"Is that what I think it is?" Piper said, eyeing the box on Summer's kitchen table.

"Yes, evidently whoever took it realized it was the wrong box and left in it in the neighbor's backyard."

"Let's look at pictures after we eat!" Mia said.

"Summer may not be ready," Agatha said.

"You know what, Aunt Agatha? I think I'm as ready as I'm ever going to be." After the strangeness of the past few days, Summer wanted to enjoy every minute she had. And, after getting to know the Bellamys a bit, she was more curious than ever about her mom's relationship with her dad—and his family.

Yes. Opening the box of photos and sharing it with her mom's family seemed like exactly the right thing to do.

Chapter Fifty-Nine

After dinner, the group gathered in the living room, with Mr. Darcy out of his cage and in the midst of it all. He hopped onto Summer's lap. She stroked his feathers, and he purred. Then he hopped off her and walked around the room as she opened the box.

She pulled out a photo to see a very young Hildy wrapped in the arms of a man who resembled Sam. Her father.

Piper was sitting next to Summer on the couch. "They look very happy."

"They do." Summer passed the photo to Aunt Agatha.

Her aunt smiled. Reverence came over her face. "Look at them. Young and in love."

"Let me see," Mia said, reaching for the photo. "Wow, she was so gorgeous."

Summer dipped her hand back into the box and pulled out another photo. She gasped. Her father was holding a very tiny baby. Was that her? It must be.

"What is it?" Aunt Agatha said.

Summer couldn't speak.

"It's Omar holding her when she was a baby," Piper said. "He was around, even though he married someone else."

"It was complicated," Summer said.

Piper grunted and handed the photo over to Agatha and Mia.

"Who are all these people?" Summer said, studying another picture.

Piper pointed. "There's Hildy, Omar . . . is that Rima?"

"Yes, it must be. And Hassam. This must be Arwa and Jamila."

"Which is which?" Piper asked.

"I'm not sure." Summer rose from the couch in search of her bag with the research in it. The article had photos of Jamila. She found it on the kitchen table and brought it into the clutch of Merriweathers studying photos. She pulled out the article with the photo. "This is Jamila."

"Okay." Piper pointed to one of the women in the photo. "So this must be Sam and Fatima's mom."

"They sort of look alike," Mia said. "Like they're related."

"Maybe they are. Who knows?" Agatha said with a flat note in her voice.

"Well, they are from the same town in Egypt. So it's a distinct possibility," Summer said, reaching into the box for more photos and pulling out another one of her mom and Omar, walking along the beach, the castle in the background.

Next was a snapshot of Rima, Omar, Arwa, Hassam, and Bashir.

"Lovely family photo," Piper said.

"I can't get over the resemblance. Look." Summer held up the newspaper article.

"That's not Arwa," Piper said, scrutinizing the family photo again. "That's Jamila, their maid. Why would she be in a family photo?"

Mia reached over. "Wait. There's something written on the back."

Their names.

Summer read it over and turned the photo back around. "Well, according to the label, this is not the maid; it's Arwa."

She placed the photo down on the table, and then she placed the article next to it. It was the same person. She was certain.

Mr. Darcy walked through the middle of the group, whistling, prompting Mia to reach out and stroke him, then Piper as well. Summer watched, then went back to studying the photos.

It hit her with a stone-cold thud. She took in the room around her. Was she dreaming?

Aunt Agatha smiled as her eyebrows lifted. Summer was indeed here in the flesh. Mia's head tilted. Piper's arm went around Summer.

It was the same person.

"But—"

"It seems crazy," Piper said.

"Can it be?" Agatha said.

"I don't get it," Mia said.

Summer pointed to the newspaper. "If this is Arwa, then who was murdered?"

"And what happened to the real Jamila?" Piper said.

Summer dumped the box of photos on the table. "Let's sort this out. Photos of my mom and dad in one pile. Family photos in another."

This was not the time for sentiment. There was no time to dwell on her mom and dad and what could have been. Summer didn't know what this was, but it felt momentous.

"Okay, now what?" Mia said, her eyes alight with excitement.

"Let's place the photos of Mom and Omar back into the box and study the other photos."

Agatha scooped the photos of the loving couple back into the box, and they were left with about fifteen pictures to study.

"Let's take out any photos where Arwa or Jamila are not in them," Piper said.

"Yes," Summer said. She slid three photos out of the pile.

"They do look very much alike," Agatha said. "They could be sisters."

"Secret sisters?" Mia said.

"Or it could just be happenstance. Look at Penny in your school, Mia. You resemble her, and yet you're not related at all," Piper said.

"I agree. It could be happenstance that they look so much alike. But what's not happenstance is that one of them was killed." Summer paused and regarded each of the Merriweather women. "The paper said it was this one . . . and yet."

"Why? Why would they switch them out?" Agatha said.

Piper placed a photo back on the table. "Imagine how difficult that would be. It means that . . . let me think . . . it means that Sam and Fatima's mother is the maid. That the heiress is the murdered one."

"It seems impossible to pull off," Summer said, picking the photo back up.

"Not if you have enough money," Mia said. "Rich people can do whatever they want."

"That's not exactly true," Piper said.

"This was the 1980s. Not exactly the Dark Ages," Agatha said. "But still, the technology wasn't what it is today, of course."

"And I guess the most important question in all this is what it has to do with Mimi. She's still missing. Did she find out about this and threaten to tell someone?" Piper said.

"Her book doesn't go into the possibility of switched identities at all. She missed the mark on that one," Agatha said.

Summer's brain clicked into gear. If Mimi's book didn't dredge up the possibility of switched identities, what reason could someone have had to take her? Maybe Piper had been right a few days ago when she suggested that Mimi's kidnapping had nothing to do with her book. And everything to do with the bookstore.

Summer's head swirled with ideas. "Mom had to know about this."

Agatha nodded. "I was thinking the same thing."

Piper slammed her hand on the table. "She was aware, all right. And it scared her so bad she never had anything to do with them again."

Summer's heart raced, even as she traced her fingers over the photo of her with her father. Her mom must have had weak moments, allowing him to see her, but then completely cut him off at some point. "And she tried to make sure I never did."

Chapter Sixty

In one swift moment, Summer's hopes for a close family on her dad's side were dashed. Her chest hollowed and burned.

"Summer, are you okay?" Aunt Agatha reached across the coffee table for her hand.

Summer's hand rested in hers. She nodded.

"Sam and Fatima must not know a thing about this. Think about it. It's their mother who was the young medical student working for them. She's the one that bore them," Piper said.

The room silenced.

Sam and Fatima. Medical student. The words rolled around in Summer's brain, and Aunt Agatha's cool hand squeezed hers.

A loud, choppy sound broke them from their circle.

"What is that?" Mia's eyes widened.

The women rushed to the front window. Three helicopters flew over.

"Helicopters?" Piper said.

"Must be an emergency somewhere."

"But three?"

"Let's turn on the news, shall we?" Agatha said.

"Easier to just look at your phone, Gram," Mia said, pulling hers out.

"Whatever." Agatha rolled her eyes.

"There! There's a ship on fire," Mia reported. "It's been on fire for a day."

Summer's stomach sank. The Bellamys had been gone all day. They were in shipping.

" 'A spokesperson from Bellamy Shipping says the fire has yet to be contained,' " Mia read. " 'Rescue ships are in place. So far, no lives have been lost.' "

"That must be where they are." Piper elbowed Summer. "They must be out there helping the team. I know I'd be there if it was my company."

"Indeed," Agatha said.

"That's one mystery solved. Maybe," Summer said. "I can't see Rima out there, though. She must be home. But why isn't she answering the door?"

"Wouldn't it be funny if they found Mimi out there?" Mia said, walking back to the table of photos.

"Mia! I'm sure it would be more of a relief than funny," Piper said.

"I think we better get to bed. It's getting late, and you have a big day tomorrow." Agatha led them away from the window. Just as she did, a pop sounded, and the front window cracked.

"Get down!" Summer said, heart racing, crouching on the floor.

Mia gasped. Agatha pulled her in and wrapped her arms around her.

"What was that?" Mia said, trembling, crouched on the floor.

Summer's breath shortened, and it was hard for her to get the words out. "I think someone just took a pot shot at the window."

Piper reached for Mia's phone and dialed 911. "We have an emergency . . ." She reported what was happening to the dispatcher.

Heart pounding, Summer made her way to the front door, placed her body against the wall, and tried to peek out the window.

"Summer! What are you doing?"

"Get back here!"

Summer's chest expanded, and she imagined herself as a bear. Her mind crackled with the need to know who had shot at them. She was so tired of being jerked around. She drew in a breath. Time to take matters into her own hands.

Another shot popped through the window. Summer ducked and ran upstairs, where she remembered that Mimi had a gun.

What would she, Summer Merriweather, do with a gun? She had no idea how to use one. But she could at least scare someone with it.

Her hand holding the pistol looked foreign to her, as if it belonged to someone else. Its cool metal on her skin was foreign to her skin. Her person. She raced downstairs with it, where her family sat on the floor.

"What are you doing?" Agatha said, holding a very shaken Mr. Darcy.

"I'm going out there to see what I can see."

"A gun? Where did you get that?" Piper asked.

"It's Mimi's."

"You have no idea how to use that thing."

Summer smirked. "How hard can it be?"

Piper gave off an exasperated sigh.

"Don't you dare go out that door!" Agatha said, standing, coming after her.

"I love you, Aunt Agatha, but I'm going." She rushed for the door. She was tired of being afraid, tired of being a victim. "I've got to put a stop to this nonsense. Once and for all."

"Summer, please—"

With that, Summer was out the door.

Outside, a group of neighbors stood off in a cluster.

"Did any of you see anything?"

A woman shook her head. "A man. He went that way. Over the dunes."

Anger tore at Summer. Over the dunes? The dunes were her place. Sacred. If land held memory, this beach held hers. Another invasion of her space.

"I called the cops," she said.

Summer moved forward, gun in hand.

"I'm coming with you," said Harold, owner of Missy the cat.

"Suit yourself."

Close on her heels, Harold whispered, "Do you know how to use one of those?"

She was focused on the sight in front of her. The grassy hillsides, then the dunes. He could be lying low anywhere.

"Do you?" Harold asked again.

She shook her head.

A shadow moved across the sand. Was it the grass blowing in the wind?

She and Harold stopped in their tracks, regarded one another. Summer's blood rushed, pulsed in her ears.

They stood a moment until it felt safe to move forward. They creeped along the path.

A soft footfall thumped. Summer stopped. Her heart might burst from her chest at any minute.

"Put your hands up," a male voice said. "And drop the gun."

A buzz of adrenaline tore through Summer. He was behind them. She glanced at Harold, whose hands were already up, eyes wide, head nodding for her to put her hands up.

Instead she turned, lifted the gun, and faced her stalker.

"You first," she said as she spun around to face her cousin. Bashir, shocked, stepped backward and tripped, dropping his gun. Harold rushed in and grabbed it.

"Drop it!" Another voice came from the sand.

Suddenly, three uniformed officers surrounded the trio.

Bashir continued to sit on the ground but placed his hands over his head. Harold dropped his gun, and Summer couldn't move.

"Drop the gun. Step away."

Her arm was still extended. Gun still pointed at Bashir.

"Summer." She heard a voice. Ben's voice. No, it was Cash. What was he doing here?

"Cash?" she said, her voice deep and trembling.

He stood next to her. "I know you don't want to shoot that man."

"I want . . . I want answers!"

He put his arm around her. "You won't get them by shooting him." He took the gun. "Especially with an unloaded gun."

Chapter Sixty-One

"You'll get your answers." Ben Singer cuffed Bashir. "But I'll get mine first."

"Why me? Why my house?" Summer glanced at her window with two bullet holes through the glass.

Bashir didn't even glance at her.

"Where's Mimi?"

Then he looked at her. "I have no idea where she is."

"I don't believe you," Summer said.

"Okay, Summer. I'm taking him down to the station," Ben said. "Do you want to come with us tonight or come in the morning? I assume you'll want to press charges."

Summer's jaw tightened. "You assume right."

Aunt Agatha came up beside her. "Let's go to the station tomorrow. You need some rest."

Cash stepped forward. "For what it's worth, I agree."

"How am I supposed to sleep?" Summer trembled. Her legs weakened, felt rubbery. Images moved through her brain. Her family crouched on the floor. The window cracking. Her chasing him through the dunes. What had she been thinking?

"You still have those sleeping pills." Piper wrapped her arm around her and led her back into the house, where someone had taped thick plastic over the two holes in the window, Mr. Darcy, back in his cage, stood silent and still.

Summer downed the sleeping pill and went to Mr. Darcy. "I love you, Darcy."

He didn't move.

"He'll be okay," Piper said. "Good thing he didn't get shot. He's just in shock. By tomorrow he'll be sounding off, like usual."

Summer wasn't so sure about that, but she hoped Piper was right.

She gathered up the remaining photos on the table. Some had fallen to the floor. There were pieces of paper there too. She picked them up. One was a canceled check. It was written out to her mother.

"What's that?" Piper said.

"A canceled check for twenty thousand dollars."

"What?"

"Made out to my mom in 1987."

"Your mom never had a nickel to rub together," Agatha said.

"I know. But this is canceled. She had the money somewhere in the late 1980s."

"That's when she started the bookstore," Agatha said. "We always wondered how she started it."

Summer could hardly look away from the amount. But her eyes drifted to the name of the company that had given her mom the check: *Sealife Incorporated.* She blinked. Blurry eyed, as the sleeping pills were taking over. "Piper, do you see that?"

"I do."

"What does it mean?"

"We can't know what it means. Not yet."

"But it's the same company!"

"Shhh. I know." Piper led her upstairs by the arm. "We need to be careful. We don't want anything to get out. Not yet."

"I'm sure Bashir is behind the kidnapping. Do you really think someone will show up tomorrow for the sale?" Summer sat on the edge of her bed.

"If Bashir has something to do with the kidnapping, he likely has a partner. He certainly has a lawyer and corporation behind him for the sale. So yes, we're going to proceed as planned tomorrow."

"With what?" Agatha stood in the doorway.

"Going to the station for her to press charges." Piper said quickly. Agatha didn't know about the pretend sale, and they needed to keep it that way. In order for this ruse to work, everybody needed to think the store was truly for sale.

Agatha squinted at her. "You two are up to something. Haven't we had enough? Can't you just leave well enough alone?"

"I'd love to. If only I could." Summer sank into the bed.

Agatha seemed to wilt. "I know. Listen, you get some rest. Tomorrow I'll make us a big breakfast and we'll get everything done we need to."

"It's Christmas Eve. Don't you have plans tomorrow?"

"Let's not worry about that," Agatha said.

"Is Cash still here?"

Piper nodded. Summer's eyes bored into her with the hope that her cousin would read her mind, and she nodded again. "We need to let him know."

"Know what?" Agatha said.

"Never mind, Ma." Piper took her by the shoulders and pointed her out of the room, flipped off the light. "Good night, Summer."

"Good night." Summer pulled the covers in close over her shoulders and neck. She reached for her nylon anti-spider mask and slipped it on.

Her long-lost cousin had tried to shoot her tonight. Not just her, but possibly the whole family. She shivered and pulled another blanket over her quilt, fashioned a warm cocoon. Tomorrow she'd meet with the lawyer for resolution. Mimi would be returned, and if all went well, Summer would still own the bookstore.

She closed her eyes and prayed for Mimi's safety. Prayed for the Bellamys, still out of touch. And prayed for the bookstore.

She drifted off, her thoughts melting into one another and slipping away.

She dreamed of Mimi walking the beach out by Mermaid Point. She wore a long white dress. Very Gothic looking. Mists fell around her, and she laughed and walked. She was fine. Mimi was fine.

Then Mimi turned into Hildy, who reached for Summer's hand and gestured to the sky. The fog fell away, and the Bellamy castle appeared. Hildy wrapped her arms around Summer.

Her mom's arms, her hug, filled Summer with a beam of warmth. She never wanted to leave. Her breathing deepened. She relaxed into her mom, the sound of Hildy's breath soothing her.

Oh Mom, I miss you. Oh Mom, what have you done?

What happened all those years ago?

Those years when you were young and so in love you weren't thinking straight?

How could you have known I'd be here grappling with those wispy tentacles you planted in 1987?

Chapter Sixty-Two

Summer awakened to Christmas Eve, hopeful. Whatever happened today, they'd be a step closer to resolution. She'd sign the documents. The buyer wouldn't find the problems with them for two or three days, and by then, maybe Mimi would have been found. After all, that was the deal—the bookstore in exchange for Mimi's safe return.

And today she'd go to the station to press charges against Bashir. Perhaps this would be the final nail in his criminal coffin. Ben had said he was already on probation. Attempted murder should get him off the streets for a while.

And maybe she'd finally hear from Sam or Fatima.

The scent of frying eggs welcomed her into the kitchen. Aunt Agatha stood at the stove. Mia had a plate in front of her already but glanced up as Summer entered. "Good morning."

"How are you, Mia?" Summer had slept the night away, and now she wondered how her niece was after all the excitement. "Did you sleep well?"

"No. I had to take something to help me sleep," she said. "Something my doctor gave me, in case I had trouble."

Piper tapped her fingers on the table. "I told her not to do it. And now she's having a hard time waking up."

"I have to be at the shop, to work. I needed some sleep."

"You can be a little late today. I think last night took it out of all of us." Summer reached for a coffee cup and poured herself a cup.

She sat at the table.

"I just can't get that check out of my head." Agatha slipped the spatula into the pan.

"I can't get Mimi out of mine," Piper said.

"Right? Who cares about the check, Gram? It was such a long time ago."

"You're right, Mia. I don't know why I care so much about it." Agatha scooped scrambled eggs onto a plate and set it in front of Summer.

Piper lifted her chin. "I've been thinking. You said Mimi was dropped off here by her husband."

Summer nodded and scooped eggs into her mouth. They needed more pepper. She reached for it. "That's what she said. At least I'm ninety-nine percent sure that's what she said. But then we found out she's no longer married."

"Could she have said boyfriend?" Piper asked.

Summer tried to recall. "I think the exact words were, 'My husband dropped me off and is going antiquing in Raleigh. Staying at Bluebeard's Roost.' "

The room quieted.

"Did you tell Ben that?" Piper asked.

"No. I just remembered it."

"Bluebeard's Roost? That's no franchise. There's probably only one of those."

Agatha sat down at the table. "What's your point, Piper?"

"I have no point. I'm just going over things in my mind, trying to make sense of them. Bashir said he had no idea where Mimi was."

"He's not going to tell you if he does," Mia said, rolling her eyes.

"Don't roll your eyes at your mother," Agatha said.

Mia crossed her arms.

"I think the police want to question him, in any case. They've been looking for him. He may know something he doesn't even know he knows," Summer said.

"Would whoever this 'husband' is still be in Raleigh?" Agatha said.

"Who knows? I'll mention it to Ben when I see him this morning. It won't take long for them to find him if he's at a place called Bluebeard's Roost."

The room filled with the sound of forks on plates and coffee cups landing on the table.

"Speaking of not being able to get things out of your mind," Mia said, "I'll never forget Aunt Summer running out of here with a gun in her hand." She shoved a bite of toast in her mouth.

Summer groaned. "What was I thinking?"

"You weren't!" Aunt Agatha said.

"It was badass," Mia said.

"Language, Mia," Piper said.

Mia looked at Summer and grinned.

Sumer's face heated. Of all the things it would be lovely for Mia to admire her for, brandishing an unloaded pistol and running after a crazed man who'd just shot holes through her front window was not one of them. She sighed.

"No, I wasn't thinking. It was as if . . . I don't know . . . something took over me. Adrenaline? I'm just so tired of being frightened and waiting for the next thing to happen. I think I wanted a bit of control. And guns don't give you that. I know better."

"When you know better, you do better," Agatha said. "What are you going to do now?"

"I'm going to the station this morning, then the bookstore." She glanced at Piper. The bookstore was where the meeting would go down with the "buyer." Summer's stomach tightened. She hoped Cash knew what he was doing.

Of course he did. Of course. A warm sensation filled her as she remembered him being beside her last night.

Why had she left that man standing at the altar? Whatever weird psychological thing had been at play for her, it had nothing to do with him. He was a fine man. Handsome. Smart. Good. She, and her bookstore, were in his hands.

Her life was turning into a multilayered *Alice in Wonderland* adventure instead of a well-planned trip. She'd worked hard for her degree and her life in Staunton. It was quiet, filled with rules—most of which she loved—and orderly. Now she was in a swamp of chaos. She's been in the muck for months.

Mia turned to Summer. "Why do you look like that?"

"Why are you watching me?"

"She's thinking about Cash," Piper said. "That's the only time she has that look on her face."

Summer stood from the table, face heating once more, picked up her plate, and headed for the sink. "Don't be ridiculous."

Chapter Sixty-Three

After filling out the report about last night's incident, Summer sat in Ben's office, waiting for him to return. She stood and walked around the room, pacing between the desk and the door. A shelf holding police books and family photos sat beneath the widows. She picked up an old family photo. Cash was about twelve in it.

"What are you doing?" Ben said as he walked in.

She held up the photo. "Cute."

"Yeah, that's one of my favorites." He walked around and sat in his chair. "Now what can I help you with? You said you had some information for me?"

She was still behind him. She placed the photo back down and stood next to him. "Yes, I remembered something." She eyed his desk. "Your desk is so neat that it's disgusting."

"Thanks?" His hand went to a group of papers. Summer's eyes followed.

"Is that what I think it is?"

"It's the missing pages from the crime report. They just found it in records." He slapped his hand on the desk. "How does that happen?"

"Seems deliberate. Can I read it?"

He held it in his hand. "After you tell me your news."

"I remembered that Mimi's husband, or whoever he was, was staying at Bluebeard's Roost in Raleigh. She said he was antiquing. So he wasn't going back to Pittsburgh."

"Well, that's interesting. Bluebeard's Roost? I've not thought of that place in years. I'll get Raleigh on it. I'll be right back."

He handed her the pages from the old report. Paper. There was something comforting about it. Her statement had been taken on the computer this morning by a young, fresh-faced administrative assistant to be stored on the computer for future generations instead of in musty, dusty old file cabinets.

As he left the room, Summer sat down to read Rima's words from more than thirty years ago. She bit her lip.

I was walking along the beach, early. I love to see the sunrise, and I saw the boat, on a sandy part of Mermaid Point. I thought it was strange. Boats don't usually come in there. I walked over and looked inside and there she was. I reached in and shook her. I thought she must be asleep. I knew she'd been out the night before. They all were out. Hassam, Jamila, Arwa, Bashir . . . They'd built a bonfire the night before . . . I watched from the house. But she wasn't asleep. She was dead. Gone.

The text continued describing the incident.

Summer's eye for language stopped her a few times. The words *I was all alone* were repeated, almost overdone. Or, as she'd say to her class, overwritten.

Then I blacked out. I don't remember anything until Hassam and Omar were sprinkling water on my face. But I was alone until then. I don't know when or how they found me. I didn't see anyone else on the beach before that.

Ben walked back into the room. "We've got someone going to check on the hotel. Probably not until tomorrow."

"Tomorrow? That's too late, Ben."

"It's Christmas. We're too short staffed to check on a notion."

"It's more than a notion. I mean, it might be nothing. But if he's there, he might know something that could help us find Mimi."

He nodded. "They will get to it, Summer. I promise."

Summer swallowed. *Damn, Ben.* He didn't understand that her time was limited. He didn't know she was going to the bookstore to meet a stranger waiting to buy it and return Mimi. She couldn't tell him. She held up the papers. "About this. She repeats over and over again that she was alone on the beach that morning. I found that strange and maybe revealing."

"She'd just found a dead person. She wasn't thinking clearly. Don't read too much into that."

"It's hard for me, Ben, because reading, writing, criticism . . . it's my thing."

His head tilted. "True."

"I think someone else was there."

"Go on."

"Someone she was trying to protect."

"Well, I'd thought about that. The sand . . . there were footprints, but they weren't conclusive. Not good enough for us to use. And they could have been hers or one of her sons'."

Summer blinked. Her sons. "One of them must have killed her."

He shook his head. "There's no evidence of that. You're being illogical."

"Can you just bear with me? Can you just make a leap of faith here?"

He lowered his head. "Summer, I'm too busy for this. We've got a missing person and an arsonist on the loose. I don't have time for this. But I will say . . . I had an inkling that she knew more then. But she was a mess. She was broken. I could only push so far."

His eyes met hers. Summer perceived the pain, regret, and maybe humiliation in them. This case had meant a lot to him. Mimi's kidnapping had opened the wounds. "I understand." It was the only thing to say to a cop who'd tried his best. A cop getting ready to retire, full of pride and regrets swirling around inside him.

The itch to know more poked at her. There was something here that could lead to the truth. "Do you mind if I take this?"

"You can have it. It's a copy." He opened his drawer. "I have two more inside here. Not taking any more chances with the clerks."

Summer clutched the papers, shoved them in her bag, and headed for Beach Reads.

Chapter Sixty-Four

Christmas Eve at Beach Reads was always a mix of lonely souls and last-minute gift buyers. And this year was no exception. One difference this year was that Cash, Piper, and an unknown lawyer sat in Summer's office waiting for her. She hoped this would work.

Her stomach waved and dipped as the lawyer stood and offered his hand. She shook it with hesitation. Lawyer or not, he was aware of Mimi's whereabouts and was a part of the plot to buy Beach Reads. Slimeball.

"Let's get right to it, shall we?" he said, with an accent Summer couldn't place. Texas? Oklahoma?

"Certainly," she said.

Then came the signing of the sales documents. Fake sales documents they'd never get through the banks or through the lawyer's corporate headquarters. "Plenty of illegal Easter eggs," Cash had said.

The lawyer stood and shoved his papers into his briefcase. "You'll have thirty days to vacate the premises once the contracts go through."

Summer stood, looked him in the eye. "When can I expect to see Mimi?"

His expression turned to stone. Cold stone. Pure evil came over his face. "I'm sorry. I have no idea what you're talking about."

Summer glanced at Cash, who was pale, nodding, as if to say, *Don't say another word*. As if she could. Fear tore through her. Mimi!

The lawyer grabbed his coat and placed his hat on his head.

Was the kidnapper going to kill Mimi? Was she already dead?

Summer should have gone to the police. Dread traveled up and down her spine. "I'm sorry. My mistake."

The lawyer nodded. "Merry Christmas." And then he left the room.

Summer, Cash, and Piper stood quietly for a minute.

"They're not going to let her go," Piper said.

"We've been searching for days . . . I just don't know where else the woman could be," Cash said.

"I mentioned this to your dad earlier, but there is one place that came up on my radar last night. Bluebeard's Roost in Raleigh." Summer explained it to Cash.

She knew what she had to do. She had to take a trip to Raleigh. She reached for her purse and coat.

"Summer—" Piper said.

"Wait," Cash said. "It could be dangerous."

"I'll be careful. I'm sure they aren't expecting me. I'll have the element of surprise on my side."

"Hold on. I'm coming with you," Piper said. She stopped. "I can't believe I just said that."

"Me too," Cash said. "I'm coming too."

Summer didn't have time to argue with them. If they wanted to join her, so be it. The more she considered it, the more her certainty grew. Mimi could be at the hotel. She had to try. Had to do something. And it had to be today.

"Where are you going?" Poppy yelled after them.

"Oh, sorry." Summer turned to her. "Something's come up. I need to go to Raleigh. Close up the shop, and I'll see you at the party."

"Is everything okay? You three all look like hell."

Summer nodded. "We're fine."

And they left the creature comforts of Beach Reads and Brigid's Island behind. The trip would take about an hour, longer if there was traffic.

* * *

Cash sat in the back seat, quiet for most of the ride.

"According to Google, we're two blocks away," Piper said.

"Pull over," Cash said.

"What?" Summer said.

"Pull over. I have a plan."

Summer drove until she found a spot. She twisted around to eye him. "Spill it."

"The police already know about this, correct?"

"I told your dad. He said he'd let Raleigh know but that because of the holidays, they were short staffed and had other priorities with the arson of that ship."

"Okay, we ask at the desk."

"Ask at the desk?" Piper said. "What do we ask? 'Is someone being held here against their will?' "

"No, Piper. We ask if they rent long-term and if they do, do they have any long-term residents now. Because we have a wealthy client interested in renting several rooms for an extended period of time."

"Okay, then what?"

"Then we ask if we might talk to any long-termers as a reference."

"Would they allow that?" Summer asked.

He shrugged. "They should." He paused. "But here's the thing. Even if they don't, if someone is holding Mimi in this place, they will be alerted by our presence. They will scatter. There will be movement. So, while one of us is talking with management, the other two should be watching the entrance and exits. You see what I'm saying? Anything suspicious, dial 911. Then the cops have to come and investigate."

"I hope she's here. After all this," Piper said.

Summer turned on her signal and looked in her mirrors. No traffic today. "It's a good plan. I'm in."

"Piper?" Cash said.

"Sure."

Summer drove toward the hotel. Lit palm trees lined the street. Storefronts were filled with fake snow, lights, and sparkles. But gravity permeated the car as they moved forward to Bluebeard's Roost, sitting higher than the surrounding motels and hotels. It almost looked like it was perched above the rest. It was a sky-blue three-story building, decorated with blue lights for Christmas.

"Taking the blue very seriously," Piper said.

"Bluebeard was a pirate, right?" Summer said.

"Yes, but he was also a chicken named after the pirate. This place is named after the beloved rooster," Cash said from the back seat. Summer and Piper turned to look at him. "What? I researched it on the way."

Piper rolled her eyes. "Of course you did."

Chapter Sixty-Five

"This hotel has way too many exits and entrances," Summer said as they stepped out of the car.

"Right, but there's a back to the building, so someone should go around there," Cash said.

"And someone should stay here. It's a great view of the front of the building," Summer said.

"I'm happy to do that," Piper said. "So, which one of you is going around back?"

"I'll do it," Summer said.

"No, I'll do it," Cash said. "I think you should go inside and ask questions."

"Are you kidding?" Piper said. "She's the last person to be able to think and talk right now."

"But going back there could be dangerous. It's the most likely way they will try to get out."

"I'll do it," Summer said. "I just have to wait and watch and then call 911 if I see anything, right?"

Cash drew in a deep breath. "Right."

"Is your phone charged?" Piper said.

Summer nodded. "Is yours?"

"Yes."

"Are we ready?" Cash said.

They nodded. Piper, Summer, and Cash regarded one another. For Summer, it was almost as if they had slipped back to twenty years ago. She swallowed the lump creeping in her throat. *Now is not the time to get sentimental. Now is the time to stay sharp.*

"I hope this works," Piper said. "I hope she's here and she's fine."

Summer swallowed again. If Mimi was here, she would probably not be okay. She would probably be hurt, even if she was still alive. God knew how she'd been treated.

"Okay," Cash said. "Let's go."

Summer and Cash walked toward the front office. He walked inside, and Summer slipped around to the back of the place. Cell phone in hand. Heart racing.

Even on Christmas Eve, this place had a full parking lot. Didn't people stay home for Christmas anymore? Maybe they were here visiting family. Maybe it was home and they didn't want to stay—or couldn't stay—with their families.

She walked down to the end of the blue building, aiming for inconspicuous. Nonchalant but watchful. Nobody had come out of any of the doors. The parking lot was quiet. Summer was beginning to wonder if this was a good idea. It had sounded like a good idea. But she hadn't had time to think it through.

She walked back toward the office. A woman came out of the back with two children and headed for a minivan. Nothing out of the ordinary about that.

She scooted to the edge of the building and looked around the corner. Piper was leaning on the back of the car, arms crossed. Head up. Summer shivered. If anything happened to Piper, she'd never forgive herself for dragging her into this.

She turned back around to her post.

A car pulled into the parking lot. A young woman emerged with a bag of groceries. The closer she got, the more recognizable she became.

Yvonne Smith.

It all fell into place as Summer stood there, planted, unable to move. *Fool. Summer, you are a fool.* Hot tears ran down her face in a rush of emotion. Her fists balled. Was any of Yvonne's story true? That she was sick? That she needed a transplant?

Summer wiped her face with her sleeve and sniffed as her heart raced so fast that she felt certain anybody within ten feet could hear it. She ducked behind a car, her cell phone in her trembling hand. If she called the police now, what would she say? Yvonne was doing nothing suspicious at the moment. She had a bag of groceries and was heading inside.

Maybe she should make something up. That's what she'd do. She'd tell the police a young woman was in trouble. And she was. Oh boy. She was.

First, she texted Piper and Cash. *Yvonne Smith is here.* Send.

She stood on wobbly pins and fell forward.

No, she hadn't fallen. She'd been pushed, hard. What the—?

And then the throbbing started.

* * *

Summer's head throbbed. She tried to open her eyes, but they felt as if sandbags sat on them. Where was she? She was no longer in the parking lot. No. She was on something soft. A bed?

"I told you not to get involved with her," a male voice said. "She's a Bellamy."

I'm not, Summer wanted to say. *I'm a Merriweather. Through and through.* A burst of pride popped in her chest.

"Okay. I thought she could help."

"Help what? Did you think they were going to welcome you with open arms because of her? They don't care about her. They don't care about anything." His voice was full of spite.

"You're a Bellamy too," Yvonne said.

Bellamy? Who could this person be? It certainly wasn't Bashir, who was being held by the authorities.

"And so am I," she said.

Well, at least that part wasn't a lie. Summer struggled to open her eyes and finally surmised why she couldn't. There was a blindfold over them. Her hands were tied in front of her. She was on a bed. She stopped herself from screaming. Best to lie here and pretend she was still conked out.

"What is she doing here?" the male voice asked.

"I don't know. You know as much as I do. She was here when we pulled in."

They don't know about Piper and Cash!

"I think we're going to have to pack up. If she's here because she knows we have Mimi . . . we can't risk it."

"What will we do with them?" Yvonne asked.

"We have no choice. We'll have to get rid of them."

"Wait—"

"Listen, Yvonne, I know you like Summer. She tried to help you. But now she knows too much. If word gets out about the murder, we lose everything. I'm sorry."

"I never wanted this!"

"I know."

"It's gotten out of hand!"

"I know."

"I just wanted a chance to be healthy. You said you'd get the test and help if we matched."

"And the bookstore, don't forget."

"Well, yes . . . but only because they never gave my mom a thing. She was forced to give me up for adoption. Hildy got money. My mom got nothing. I got nothing."

Summer's ears were burning. How dare she. Her mom's name coming from Yvonne's lips was a dagger to Summer's heart. If she could rise from this bed and wrap her hands around the woman's throat . . .

She vibrated with anger and for the first time understood crimes of passion. Hildy Merriweather might have been given money, but she'd worked every day of her life to build Beach Reads into what it was.

What it is.

"I think we should leave them here. I'll get a new ID and we'll go overseas. London? They will never find us," Yvonne said. "I don't want to kill anybody. Please. That's how this started. Years ago, with our dad killing Arwa because she threatened to tell about my mom's pregnancy."

Dad? A Bellamy had killed Arwa? Because of an unplanned pregnancy? Summer's foggy brain tried to sort this out. This person in the room with them must be a brother of Bashir's. Summer had heard he was visiting. What was his name . . . Zouhir?

"My father was never the same after that. But he had no choice. She was threatening him. It would've taken the family down." His voice cracked. "Our father is dying. When he confessed to Bashir and me, it almost killed him. He made us promise to keep his secret. To work to keep his legacy protected. But this secret almost broke him."

"I think it would break us too. I'm sorry. We're not killers."

"But they know who we are!"

"Please! Don't!" Yvonne said.

Summer gasped for air. Sweat poured from her. Her father's brother, Bashir, had killed Arwa. She'd been threatening him to tell his family about the woman he had gotten pregnant—Yvonne's mother, whose name Summer had never learned.

"Okay! We need time. Let's give them the drugs. By the time they wake up, a maid will have found them."

They? So Mimi must be in the room. Still alive. Where were Piper and Cash? She longed to sink into the relief of knowing they weren't going to kill her and Mimi, but she couldn't quite do that. Not until she saw Piper and Cash were safe. Surely by now they'd called the police. Surely by now they were here, somewhere on this property.

She tried not to flinch as a needle poked her arm. God only knew what they had just injected her with. Where was Mimi? Where were Cash and Piper?

Yvonne Smith and Zouhir Bellamy had engineered this. They were half brother and half sister. What Summer didn't know was how they'd found out about each other. She didn't know if Yvonne or Zouhir was the person who'd been breaking into her home, or who had conked her on the head.

But what she did know was that their father had killed Arwa. Then the family had switched the identities of the women. But why and how?

Summer sank into a thick pool of questions, words, and images, which melted together into black.

Chapter Sixty-Six

Black gave way to images and sounds. Disjointed. Nonsensical. Pounding. Words. "Police!"

Scuffling.

Shaking. "Summer! Summer! Wake up!"

"Mimi!" Another voice. Piper.

Big, warm arms encircling her. "What did they do to you?"

Summer concentrated hard, lifted her arm, but it took all she had, and everything went back to black.

* * *

When Summer awakened again, she was on a gurney in the parking lot. The cold whipped across her body. She shivered so badly that she imagined falling off the gurney. They lifted her into an ambulance, and she lifted her head. The scene in front of her included Cash, Piper, and several police officers.

"Where are you taking me?" Summer managed to say when the door shut.

"Taking you to General. We're just going to make sure you're okay."

But she was in Raleigh. She needed to be in Brigid's Island. It was Christmas Eve. Aunt Agatha was expecting her. "But my car," was the only thing her mouth said, but her mind was reeling with words like *Piper*, *Cash*, *Mia*, *Christmas*, *home*.

The paramedic laughed. "Your friends will take care of everything. Don't worry. We're just going to make sure you're okay. They shot you up with heroin."

Holy smokes. Heroin! Summer had never taken anything like that in her life. No wonder she was so out of it. Students had been caught with it and expelled. What would they think of her now? She laughed.

"What's so funny, lady?" the paramedic said, smiling.

The disconnect between Summer's brain and her mouth held firmly in place. She couldn't express why she found her predicament so funny. She laughed until she slept.

When she finally awakened a third time, she was in a soft blue hospital room, with the TV playing an old cartoon—*Frosty the Snowman*. Her eyes focused, and she cleared her throat. She blinked as Cash came into view, sitting on a chair at bottom on the bed.

"Cash?"

He looked up at her, smiled. "There you are."

"What happened? Why am I here?"

He stood and walked around to the side of the bed. "They drugged you. Yvonne and Zouhir tried to escape, but the police got them. They're in custody. They also got this Bashir guy. He admitted to breaking into your house, leaving the bag of teeth and hair, and hitting you over the head. Crazy. "

"Why? Why harass me?"

"Because you were getting close to solving the murder. He and his brother were trying to protect their dying father. When Yvonne contacted them about her liver disease, she also mentioned Mimi's book. Evidently, they tried to stop the publisher from publishing it, and when they couldn't, they figured they'd buy all the books they could. Illusions of grandeur, anyone?" He shook his head. "Evidently, Yvonne used everything she knew about you to freak you out and put you on edge. She planted the spider and the note."

This didn't surprise Summer, "What about Mimi?"

He shook his head. "She's in bad shape, but she's alive."

"What does that mean?"

"She's been held captive for five days, drugged most of that time, so it's going to take a while for her systems to return to normal," he replied. "She'll be here a while."

"Her husband?"

"There is no husband. The man who dropped her off on Brigid's Island was Yvonne's partner, who seduced Mimi when she was here doing research." He paused. "Mimi thought he was her boyfriend. They really toyed with her."

Summer's brain hurt. Mimi was dating Bashir's brother? No, she *thought* she was dating him . . . He'd been setting her up, knowing she'd be back to the island. "But why?"

Cash shrugged. "I'm not sure."

"It makes no sense."

"Hey, I recognize that crease." He leaned over and touched her between the eyes. "Stop worrying and get some rest. It will all come out eventually. No point in stressing over it."

She gazed into Cash's eyes and found nothing but warmth there. No judgment. No expectations. She reached for his hand and squeezed it. It felt the same way it had all those years ago. A little rough with time, but the sinews and bones were in the same places and fit against hers in exactly the same, comforting way. "Thank you."

He blinked quickly and looked away. "Of course."

Piper walked into the room. "You're awake. Good. Because we need to get you out of here."

"Okay, let's go," Summer said. She tried to sit up, fell backward.

Piper laughed. "Not like that. We have a wheelchair ready for you."

"Okay, well, I'm ready to leave, but—"

"You want to see Mimi."

Summer nodded.

A nurse walked in the room with a wheelchair. She tilted her head toward Piper. "This one says she will take good care of you, so we're letting you go."

Cash helped her from the bed and into the chair. His eye caught hers, and her face heated. The man whose heart she'd broken all those years ago was helping her into a wheelchair. Humiliation swam through her. "I'd like to see Mimi."

"She's unresponsive," the nurse said. "But I can take you in, if you want."

Summer nodded. "I'd like to lay eyes on her."

The nurse wheeled her out of the room as Piper held the door open. Cash and Piper filed behind her as she was being wheeled down the shiny, busy hall.

The nurse used her hip to open the door of a patient room and wheel her in. On the bed lay Mimi, who'd lost weight and appeared to be a shell of her former self. No color in her skin. Barely breathing. Hooked up to a saline drip. Hand bandaged where her finger had once been.

"She's very dehydrated," the nurse said. "In shock."

"Mimi?" Summer said.

No response.

"Mimi, I just wanted to let you know it's all over. We solved the murder. And we're all going to be okay," Summer said. "And as soon as you're out of this bed, we'll have a party for you, invite your publisher, agent, all the media you could handle." Summer smiled. If that wasn't a strong enough seed to plant, she didn't know what was. She glanced up at the nurse. "Thank you." She sighed. "I want to go home."

The word *home* spun out of her mouth and landed in her chest. Brigid's Island. Home.

The nurse wheeled her out of the room, where Piper and Cash waited.

Chapter Sixty-Seven

Aunt Agatha's Christmas Eve dinner transformed into a Christmas Day brunch. Cash was settled in with his family for the day. Mimi was still unconscious. And Yvonne and Bashir's brother Zouhir were still being held without bail. Summer couldn't think of a better Christmas gift than knowing those two would be put away for a long time.

Except knowing that Mimi was awake and would be okay.

"How are you feeling?" Aunt Agatha asked, passing the mashed potatoes as the candles flickered.

"Slightly hungover." Summer took the potatoes and sent them down to Mia. Just the scent of them turned her stomach.

"You're not eating much."

"I can't. Not much of an appetite." Summer stared at the Christmas tree on her gold-rimmed plate. Her aunt used these dishes every year. A few slices of turkey were probably all she could eat.

"Just eat what you can," Aunt Agatha said. "Then I want to know everything."

"You and me both," Josh, Piper's husband, said. "I can't believe you two are off acting like you're teenagers again."

"Don't give teens such a bad rep, Dad," Mia said and laughed.

Summer cracked a smile and glanced at Piper. "Right?" she said in her best impression of a teenager.

Piper laughed.

Summer had sat at this table perhaps hundreds of times and wasn't certain she'd ever noticed the beauty of the red lace tablecloth, the crystal candle holders, the loving arrangement of photos on the wall. She'd been here but not present. Maybe just living in her own head. Maybe not as observant as she'd assumed. She sipped her wine, and warmth spread through her as she took in the scene of her family gathered together at the table. A place set for Hildy.

Gratitude welled inside her. It had taken her years and losing her mother to cherish this. Not everybody had this warmth surrounding them.

"Are you okay?" Piper reached over and touched her hand.

She nodded. "Better than ever."

* * *

The day after Christmas, the Mermaid Pie Book Club gathered for a party. Summer felt better than she had the day before. She'd gone home after brunch and the exchange of gifts at Aunt Agatha's and slept the rest of the day and all night.

She walked into Beach Reads with an armful of gifts and cookies she'd baked this morning—her mom's vegan chocolate chip cookies. The group had expected them from her mom every year, but they probably weren't expecting them this year.

Glads, champagne glass in hand, walked over to help Summer with her packages. "Wow. Woman, you've got a lot of stuff here." She took the plate of cookies. "Are these what I think they are?"

Summer smiled. "Yes."

"Hey, everybody! Summer brought Hildy's chocolate chip cookies!"

Marilyn and Poppy squealed.

Cookies and cakes had been stacked round the bookstore. A champagne punch in a huge punch bowl sat on the register counter. Harp music played softly in the background.

"It's been quite a season. I think we broke records this year," Poppy said. "I hope the new owner appreciates that."

New owner! Summer could now tell everybody that the sale of the bookstore was a sham. She poured herself some champagne punch and clinked her glass with a fork. The party quieted, and heads turned to Summer.

"I have an announcement to make," Summer said. The Mermaid Pie Book Club gathered close. "The bookstore has not been sold."

"What?" Marilyn said.

"Shh!" Glads poked her with her elbow.

"When Mimi was missing, Beach Reads was what the kidnapper wanted. They wanted the store in return for Mimi." Summer flashed back to the room and heard Yvonne's voice. "It's a very long story. And someday I'll tell you in detail what went down. But for now, just now, the bookstore is still mine, and I plan to keep it that way."

Poppy's face crumpled with sobs. "Thank goodness!"

They all gathered around Summer in a group hug.

"And thank goddess you're okay," Marilyn said. "Kidnapped? Mimi was kidnapped?"

"Speaking of Mimi," Piper said, holding up her phone. "She's awake!"

Summer's heart burst. Mimi was awake!

"I have her nurse on the phone on FaceTime." She held up her phone, and the crowd gathered closer. "Put her on, please."

Mimi's face came on the screen. She grinned from ear to ear when she spotted the crowd gathered at Beach Reads. "Merry Christmas, everyone!"

"We're so glad you're okay!" Poppy said.

"I'm too ornery to die," she said.

"You and me both!" Summer said.

"Now, Summer, I remember you saying something to me about a party . . . and the media! Let's wait until I can get my hair done," Mimi said, smiling.

She'd heard Summer even when she was unconscious.

"You're on," Summer said.

Mimi stopped smiling. "Seriously, thank you for not giving up. Thank you for saving me."

A heavy hush fell over the room.

"I feel so ridiculous, allowing myself to be duped by Zouhir. I trusted him, and all he really wanted was to save his father's reputation and legacy, at any expense, including hatching a lame plan to get his hands on Beach Reads with his long-lost sister. Didn't work for them, did it? It's good to know that side of the Bellamy family will likely lose it all. I'm sorry I brought this trouble to your island, to your bookstore, and to your family."

"Nonsense," Piper said. Summer, speechless, leaned into her cousin and nodded. She held up her glass.

"To Mimi," she said.

"To Mimi," the crowd of women parroted.

Mimi smiled, tears sparkling in her eyes.

"Okay," the nurse's voice said, and her face came over the phone. "She needs some rest. Merry Christmas!" She clicked off.

"Well, this holiday season has certainly been filled with surprises," Glads said. "Who knew that our little event would set all this off?"

"Crazy, right?" Poppy said.

"You better think twice before inviting cozy mystery authors to the island again," Marilyn said and laughed.

"Who knew?" Piper said.

Summer shrugged. "I'm eager to put it behind me. Do we have a few romance authors lined up for Valentine's day?"

"Yes, a lively group of BDSM writers," Marilyn said.

Summer's face heated. "What?"

Marilyn laughed. "Just kidding."

Summer playfully swatted at her. "Can we make a rule? No BDSM authors, please?"

"Actually," Marilyn said, after the giggles died down, "we have a special guest coming on Valentine's day. Hannah Jacobs."

Summer's heart skipped a beat. She'd read everything the woman had ever written, including *Nights at Bellamy Harbor*, which was a loose retelling of her parents' love story. Hannah Jacobs, a writer friend of Hildy's, was the only person Summer's mom had let in on their story.

"That's lovely."

"We had to pull strings, of course. She's a very busy lady. But she has a new book coming out, and she thought so highly of Hildy," Marilyn said. "So she agreed to come to Beach Reads."

Summer sipped her punch. Things were looking up. Mimi was going to be fine. She was keeping Beach Reads. And Hannah Jacobs was going to visit.

She delivered her cookies and gifts to her mom's—and now her own—good friends in the bookstore that had meant everything to

Hildy Merriweather. Summer didn't know much, but she did know she'd protect her legacy for as long as she could.

She had one more stop to make today—and it was one she dreaded.

* * *

As Summer drove to the Bellamy home, her hands gripped the steering wheel. Yvonne was still being held in jail, as were Summer's cousins—both Bashir and Zouhir, his youngest brother. Her half brother and half sister had been distracted by their ship catching fire and all the resulting chaos. But Summer had finally pinned them down on a time to visit.

Her stomach waved as she wondered about Sam and Fatima. Did they know the identity of their mom? That she wasn't the heiress of an oil fortune? That that woman had been killed and the employee had taken her place for the entire marriage?

Summer's father hadn't married the heiress. He'd married the employee pretending to be the heiress. What little family Jamila had were in Egypt and elderly, except for her brother. She'd taken on Arwa's identity just to save the Bellamy family from ruin. And people thought Shakespeare had created unbelievable melodrama . . . this was real life. Family. Fortunes. Deception.

And Hildy Merriweather, all sparkles and free love, had known about it and done her best to protect Summer from it. No, she hadn't kept her father a secret because of heartbreak. She'd kept her father a secret because of treachery.

Chapter Sixty-Eight

Sam answered the door with a smile. "So good to see you."

Summer followed him in. "I've been worried. Are you okay?"

"Yes, we're all fine, but we were at sea for a few days because of the accident. No cell phone coverage," he said.

They walked into the great room where she'd sat with them all once before. Rima and Fatima were both there and welcomed her.

"Is everything okay?" Fatima said. "You don't look well."

Summer looked her straight in the face. "I'm not okay." Her voice quivered. "I'm here to give you some bad news."

"What is it?" Sam said.

Summer sat down. The others followed suit. "Rima, should you tell them, or should I?"

Rima's face fell. "I have no idea what you're talking about."

"Your cousins, as you probably know, are in jail. Zouhir and Bashir kidnapped Mimi, and then Zouhir and Yvonne Smith grabbed me out of the parking lot of Bluebeard's Roost."

"Yes, we knew he was in trouble, but we didn't know he harmed you," Sam said. "Our lawyers have been trying to help him."

"You may want to reconsider," Summer said.

Sam's mouth fell open.

Summer recapped what she'd learned. The most difficult news she delivered was that their mother was not who they believed. Then she dropped the bomb in an already quiet room.

"Your Uncle Bashir killed Arwa." Summer's voice quivered. "I heard the confession from Zouhir when I was tied up in the hotel room."

"It was an accident!" Rima spat, red-faced.

"That may have been what he told you, but shooting a woman in the heart is no accident," Summer said, as gently as she could. But there it was.

Sam's face fell. "Why didn't you tell the police the truth?"

Rima's black eyes filled with water. "A Middle Eastern man accidentally kills someone in 1987? Do you have an idea how much most Americans hated us then?" She glanced around the room. "How many still do? Nobody would have bought it then. He'd have gone to prison."

The room stilled, and Summer's eyes stung. She blinked hard. Rima still believed it was an accident.

"You don't know that," Fatima said. "Whether it was an accident or not, you were cowards. Every one of you."

"Fatima!" Sam said.

But Summer agreed with her sister. The Bellamys hadn't done the right thing because they were afraid. Their fears might have been well-founded. But still.

"Look what's happened. One cover-up. The killing of a woman who was supposed to marry. We grew up with a mother with a fake past, a made-up everything. She wanted to be a doctor. Instead, she became a housewife and mother."

"She was very happy with your dad!" Rima said. "It was different then! Marrying your father was a step up for her."

Fatima and Sam exchanged glances, leading Summer to believe they weren't happy.

"Look," she said. "I have no idea how you two must be feeling. But whoever your mom was, she loved you. So, she was not the heiress she pretended to be. Instead, she gave up her dreams to protect a man she believed was innocent. A man she loved. She sacrificed her future. Sounds pretty remarkable to me."

Rima sobbed. "She was an amazing woman."

"She wasn't the only one to sacrifice," Fatima said, reaching over and wrapping her arm around Summer.

The gravity of Hildy's decision to walk away from this family struck Summer. Her mother had loved Omar and they probably would've married, regardless of what his family said. But she must've known what had happened. She must have been scared. She must have seen the lies spinning out of control. She'd turned her back on it all. And never looked back.

Their lives would've been very different if she'd made another choice. In some ways, easier—they'd have had money and everything they wanted.

Summer stiffened. Money had never been the key to Hildy's happiness. But she had taken money to buy the bookstore. Was it hush money or guilt money? Whatever it was, it was Hildy's business acumen that had grown her business into what it was today. The seed money had given her a start, for which Summer was grateful.

"It was her decision," Rima said. "We didn't force her. She knew what dire straits we were in. She knew the marriage had been planned from birth. She knew what these contracts meant. And she thought she could help. And she did . . . for many years."

It was hard for Summer to imagine how embedded these contracts were in the family's culture. Having grown up in the United States, she found the idea of a marriage contract implausible. But she tried not to impose her values and beliefs on other people. And obviously this family had changed, even though old families all over the world still practiced arranged marriage.

It was still hard for her to imagine how they'd pulled off this ruse. Summer had no idea how they had managed to keep Arwa's family from figuring out that Jamila was not their daughter. The fact that Jamila wore the burka in public and that her own family never came to visit must have helped. But the Bellamys must have had moments of sheer panic and terror that they would be found out. Summer knew Jamila's brother had come to collect what he thought was his sister's body, but she didn't know if he'd actually seen her. Or if he had, if he'd recognized her. She'd been shot and left in the water for hours before being dragged into the boat. A lot could happen to a body to make it hard to distinguish. Summer shivered.

"How long did you plan to keep this secret?" Sam asked.

Rima lifted her chin. "Your father never wanted you to know."

The room silenced again.

"He didn't see the point in upsetting you. He felt this talk of lineage was ridiculous. He loved your mother eventually. She was a good wife and mother, and that's all that mattered to him."

"Not all, obviously," Fatima said.

Summer loved her sister. Fatima didn't hesitate to show how she felt or give her opinion. Summer was beginning to see how difficult that might have been for her growing up. Or maybe the fact that she was so outspoken was something her mother and father had fostered in her. Summer liked to think so. But if there was one thing she'd learned during this whole thing, it was that families were hard to see into when most things happened in private, behind closed doors.

"He agreed to marry her under false pretense to please his father. In the meantime, keeping this huge secret that the real Arwa was dead and lying to her family all these years about it. Lying to both families." Fatima wiped her hands together. "As if it never mattered."

There it was.

"It wasn't easy for him," Rima said in a bitter, hoarse voice.

"I should think not," Fatima said.

"In any case, it's over," Sam said.

"Indeed. Your Uncle Bashir is being arrested as we speak," Summer said. "There's no statute of limitations for murder, even if it was an accident." Summer knew it hadn't been. She hoped Sam and Fatima knew it too. Rima had spun the darkness into a web of hope as a way to save her sanity.

Rima lowered her head and sobbed. Sam wrapped his arm around her.

"Finally, justice for Arwa," Fatima said. "For both of them."

When Summer left the Bellamy house, she felt as if she were shedding layers of herself. She moved freer than she had in years. She knew the story now. Owned the story. And was moving beyond it.

Prologue

August 1987

The sound of gunshots woke them.

"What was that?" Hildy sat up, clutching Omar.

He stood, blankets falling away onto the sand, pulled on his T-shirt. "Stay here, Hildy."

"I will not!"

"I mean it. That was a gunshot."

"Then stay here. With me!"

"I can't. Someone might be hurt. But I don't want you involved."

Hildy stood, unable to follow him, knowing his wishes, but her chest was on fire. The indignity of being left behind. She wasn't going to wait here forever. She'd give him time, but she had to get home before her mom and sister figured out she was gone. She and Omar had been meeting here every morning before sunrise so they could watch it together, talk about the future and their baby.

It was even more complicated than it had been last week. Because now his intended was here. The woman who was supposed to save his family by marrying him. He didn't want to. He'd come up with another plan to help them out of their financial problems. He didn't need to marry a wealthy heiress to do it.

Hildy and Omar would marry and raise their baby together, in the shadow of the Bellamy castle. She'd not go back to college this fall. She'd stay here and raise their children on the island where she'd grown up. She'd get her degree later. She envisioned a little house on the beach, brimming with children, books, and good homemade vegan food.

But an hour later, a bloody, beleaguered Omar returned to their cove.

"Omar!" She rushed to him.

"You need to leave," he said, stone-faced.

"What happened?"

"There was an accident," he said with no emotion.

"Omar? What kind of an accident?" Her voice quivered.

His face crumpled. "The less you know, the better. We need to get you home, away from this place."

She searched his face for answers. "Why? I don't understand. I—"

"Hildy, please. This time, don't question me." He picked up her bag, and a book fell out. He reached over and tucked it back inside. "I love you."

Why did it hurt when he said that? Why did it feel as if there had been a shift in him? Why did it feel like more was happening than an accident?

"Omar!" she cried. "What is going on?"

He shoved her bag at her. "Please leave. Now."

She searched his face for answers, but none were forthcoming. She took her bag. "Fine."

She started to walk away, then turned to him, anger flaring in her. "But I'm going to want answers at some point."

* * *

Later, Hildy would remember the way the wind whipped her gauze skirt around her as she walked away, the way her heart felt as if it would pound out of her chest and break through her beaded shirt. She remembered the exact location of the sun as it rose and the pink and purple hues spreading across the sky.

She remembered the look on her love's face. It hadn't made sense then. But later she found out that he figured he was watching his love walk away from him forever. His brother's stupid act would affect their family from that day forward. He must have felt utterly sick.

* * *

Later that day, she read about it in the paper. Somehow, an accident had turned into murder and the police were searching for a killer. Hildy pieced it all together right then and there. The family were gathering forces to protect Bashir, their wayward son. But she couldn't figure out the rest of it—the why, the when, the who.

She showed up the next day at the cove. And the next. And the next. Omar did not. Hildy Merriweather would not be jilted without an answer. No. She marched up to the house, knocked on the front door, and waited. And waited. She knocked on the door again. "I know you're in there! Open the door!"

Sickness shot through her. They were not going to open it. The door was shut for a reason. They were ignoring her for a reason. What kind of twisted thing was happening? Omar was her love. The father of her baby. She grew dizzy and threw up in their front yard, suddenly aware of her unborn child's health.

She focused on good things. Her love for Omar. The home they'd make for this baby and all the rest. Her sister Agatha, her mom and dad. The beauty of the beach.

She drew in air and walked on wobbly pins back to the beach. This stress was not good for her baby. She found their cove and sat on the sand, wrapped her arms around her middle. She didn't know exactly what was going on with the Bellamys, but she knew she suddenly felt very protective of the baby she carried. She tried to talk herself out of the danger she felt. Omar was a fine man. He'd not let anything happen to them. But the tendrils of premonition and danger circled within her.

Later that day, she received a phone call from Omar, asking her to meet him at the coffee shop.

"I don't think so," she said. "You've ignored me for days. You think you can snap your fingers and I'm just going to have a coffee with you?"

"I'm trying to protect you."

She hung up on him. Who did he think he was? Who did he think she was?

The phone rang. She picked up and hung up. Protection? She didn't need protection. She needed the truth.

Later, she called Omar. "I want the truth. I want to know what's going on."

"I've been trying to tell you, but you keep hanging up. And you won't see me." He paused. "It would be best if we spoke in person."

Hildy's stomach turned. She sat down on her bed. "I'm not feeling up to it."

"The baby," he said, his voice softening. "How about later? Can we meet at the cove at, say, four?"

The cove? Now he wanted to meet at the cove? "Why there?"

"What I have to say can't be heard by anyone but you."

* * *

He was there when she arrived. Stepped forward as if to embrace her. She stiffened.

"Hildy, first you must believe I love you and that baby you have growing inside of you," Omar said, his voice cracking.

Her heart sank hard. He was letting her go. Letting the baby go. Her brain swirled with confusion. What was going on?

"Bashir shot Arwa, by mistake, and my family . . . they switched her identity with Jamila." His chest rose and fell. His voice grew raspy. "I tried to tell them to tell the police the truth. The police here are not like the police they know back home."

"But then you must tell the police. It's up to you. You've got to step forward."

His face crumpled. "If only it were that simple." He breathed in and out several times, holding back tears. Hildy's heart raced as she shook with anger. "I have to marry her," he said. "My father insists. I must do it for my family."

"Wait a minute. Are you saying that you're marrying Jamila who's pretending to be Arwa just so that—"

"To save my family!"

She wanted to say it was the most ridiculous thing she'd ever heard. But his face stopped her. His black eyes were pools of grief and pain. He was torn between her and his family. She drew in a breath. She couldn't cause him more agony.

"I will be there for you and the baby as much as I can," he said. "I love you. I always will."

She searched his face for another answer. An answer she wanted. But all she found was the truth, and the truth was so full of treachery and lies that all she wanted to do was leave the cove and all the memories that filled it. A calmness came over her, one that emanated from her center. It was the baby. The baby filled her with magic, knowing, and pure love. She'd not have this child brought up anywhere near these people. Not even Omar, standing before her, keeping his family's dirty secrets.

There'd be no beach house full of children. There's be no more children. Not with him. Not with anybody.

"I've got to go." She started to walk away, and he pulled her arm.

"Please," he said.

She lifted her chin. "You've made your choice. You may think you're doing the right thing. But not in my book. I get to say who I want in my life. The kind of people I want in my baby's life. Let me go." She broke away from him.

As she walked out of the cove, she felt as if her insides might burst with anger. But she was resolved. This baby was already making her a better person.

* * *

When she returned home, there was an envelope waiting for her with a check for twenty thousand dollars. No note. No explanation. But she knew where it had come from. Her first inclination was to tear it up into hundreds of pieces, or to burn it. Instead, she placed it under her pillow, sobbing, hoping she'd awaken with answers.

How could she take this money? How dare they even offer it to her! She tossed and turned most of the night and had no answers in the morning. All she had was more tears and no ambition to even get out of bed.

A knock came at her door. "Hildy, are you okay?" It was Agatha, newly married, with a continual glow. Hildy pulled the covers over her head. Agatha cracked the door and finally shut it. Hildy couldn't muster the will to see anybody right now, not even her sister and best friend in the world. She was pregnant, alone, and the baby's father was a devasting disappointment.

She lay in her bed as a different sort of reality set in. How would she provide for this baby? Could she rely on her hardworking but mostly broke parents? Would that be fair to them? Hildy didn't know how to do anything valuable. She had no skills. She was majoring in business but had a long way to go to understanding it. She'd gone to school with the idea of starting her own business someday. Now there would be no degree, let alone a business.

Hildy flopped over on her stomach, sliding her hands on the pillow, feeling the rough edges of the check. She slipped it out and studied it, sniffling. Plenty of people started businesses with no degree.

She recalled reading about the Brigid Island's new boardwalk and how there were funds for starting new community-minded business. Maybe she could get one of those grants. She eyed the check. This would help too.

A door opened in her mind, and she saw a way forward. She'd read and learn all about running a small business herself. She'd create a community of people for her child. People she wanted in her life, her child's life. She couldn't think of any better start to a community than opening a bookstore. Readers were the best people she knew.

Hildy swallowed the rest of her creeping sobs and clutched the check. She placed her hand on her stomach and whispered to her baby, "This is for you."

Recipes

Hildy's Vegan Chocolate Chip Cookies

Yield: 11–14 cookies

Ingredients

Dry ingredients:

1 cup all-purpose, oat, or spelt flour
½ teaspoon baking soda
¼ teaspoon salt
¼ cup sugar, unrefined if desired
¼ cup brown sugar or coconut sugar
⅓ cup chocolate chips

Wet ingredients:

2 tablespoons milk of choice, plus more if needed
2 tablespoons oil
¼ teaspoon pure vanilla extract

Instructions

1. Combine all dry ingredients in a bowl, then stir in wet ingredients to form a dough. It will be dry at first, so keep stirring

until a cookie-dough texture is achieved. If needed, add 1 to 2 tablespoons extra milk.

2. Form into one big ball, then either refrigerate for at least 2 hours or freeze until the dough is cold.

3. Once the dough is chilled, preheat oven to 325 degrees F. Form dough balls and place on a greased baking tray, leaving enough room between cookies for them to spread. (You can also make extra cookie-dough balls and freeze them to bake at a later date.)

4. Bake 11 minutes on the center rack. They'll look underdone when you take them out.

5. Let cookies cool on the baking tray 10 minutes before touching, during which time they will firm up. If for whatever reason they don't spread enough (climate can play a huge role), just press down with a spoon after baking.

Vegan Chocolate Peppermint Cupcakes

Yield: 12 servings

Ingredients

Chocolate Cupcakes

Wet ingredients:

1 cup soy milk
1 tablespoon apple cider vinegar or lemon juice
⅓ cup grapeseed oil or any neutral-flavored oil
¼ cup applesauce
1 cup granulated sugar
1 tablespoon vanilla extract

Dry ingredients:

1½ cups all-purpose flour
½ cup Dutch-processed cocoa powder or any unsweetened cocoa powder
1 teaspoon baking soda
¾ teaspoon salt

Peppermint Buttercream Frosting

1 cup vegan stick butter, slightly softened at room temperature
½ teaspoon vanilla extract

½ teaspoon peppermint extract (more if desired)
3 cups powdered sugar
2 candy canes, crushed

Instructions

Chocolate Cupcakes

1. Preheat oven to 350 degrees F. Fill a 12-slot cupcake pan with your favorite cupcake liners.

2. In a **medium** mixing bowl, add the soy milk and apple cider vinegar. Combine and let sit for 10 minutes to create a vegan buttermilk. It will thicken and curdle slightly. **Set aside.**

3. In a **large** mixing bowl with a mesh strainer on top (or use a flour sifter), sift together the flour, cocoa powder, baking soda, and salt. Now whisk to combine well. **Set aside.**

4. In the **medium bowl with the buttermilk**, add the oil, applesauce, sugar, and vanilla. Whisk to combine well.

5. Slowly pour the wet ingredients into the larger bowl of dry ingredients. Whisk together until just combined. Small lumps are fine.

6. Divide batter evenly among the cupcake slots until each is about ⅔ full. Bake in the oven for 20 to 24 minutes. To check for doneness, **lightly** press the surface—it should spring back. (You can also use a toothpick and push it through the center—it should come out clean.)

7. Let the cupcakes cool in the pan for 10 minutes before removing. Then let them cool on a rack for at least 30 minutes before frosting.

Peppermint Buttercream Frosting

1. Add the softened vegan butter to the bowl of a stand mixer (or use a medium/large stainless-steel bowl with a hand mixer). Beat until fluffy, about 30 to 60 seconds.

2. Add the peppermint and vanilla extract and mix until incorporated, about 30 to 60 seconds.

3. Add the powdered sugar, 1 cup at a time, over low speed until fully incorporated. Scrape down the sides as needed. Turn speed up to medium-high and mix until smooth and fluffy. Taste and add more sugar if needed.

4. Fill a piping bag and decorate cooled cupcakes, then top with crushed candy canes.

Vegan Pumpkin Bread

Yield: 8–10 slices

Ingredients

2 cups (280 g) flour (spelt, all-purpose, whole wheat, or 1-to-1 gluten-free flour blend)
1 teaspoon baking powder
1 teaspoon baking soda
1 tablespoon pumpkin pie spice (or 1 teaspoon each cinnamon and ginger, ½ teaspoon each nutmeg and allspice, and a pinch of cloves)
pinch of mineral salt
⅓ cup (75 ml) neutral-flavored oil (or coconut oil in liquid state) or applesauce
½ to ¾ cup (150 g) sugar (coconut, turbinado, or organic pure cane)
⅓ cup (75 ml) water or unsweetened almond milk, at room temperature
1 to 2 teaspoons vanilla extract
1 can (15 oz) 100% pumpkin puree or 1½ cups (338 g) fresh pumpkin puree
small handful pepitas (pumpkin seeds) for topping (optional)

Instructions

1. Preheat oven to 350 degrees F. Lightly grease loaf pan.

2. In a medium bowl, combine flour, baking powder, baking soda, spices, and salt.

3. In a 2-cup measuring cup, combine oil, sugar, water/milk, and vanilla.

4. Add the wet mixture to the dry mixture along with the pumpkin puree and mix well.

5. Pour batter into prepared loaf pan, place in oven on center rack, and bake for 55 to 60 minutes.

6. Once done, remove from oven and let cool 5 to 10 minutes. Remove loaf from pan and transfer bread to a wire rack to cool slightly before serving.

7. Let cool completely before storing. Keep covered on the counter for two to three days. Sliced pumpkin bread is delicious warmed in a toaster oven, smeared with vegan butter, and sprinkled with pepitas.

Acknowledgments

I totally agree with Hildy—readers are the best people. I'm honored to be a part of your community. Thank you for reading my book.

A very special thanks to my editor Terri Bischoff and my agent Jill Marsal. I'm thrilled to have you both in my corner. Thank you to Rachel Keith, copy editor extraordinaire. Special thanks to Kathleen Chrisman for beta reading.

Thanks to my daughters, who egg me on, listen to my stories and ideas, and make me proud every day.

In gratitude,

"Maggie"